BLUEPRINTS

Focusing on novels with contemporary concerns, Bantam New Fiction introduces some of the most exciting voices at work today. Look for these titles wherever Bantam New Fiction is sold:

BANTAM NEW FICTION

BLUEPRINTS

SARA VOGAN

BANTAM BOOKS

NEW YORK • TORONTO • LONDON • SYDNEY • AUCKLAND

This novel is a work of fiction. Names, characters, places and incidents are either the product of the author's imagination or are used fictitiously. Any resemblance to actual persons, living or dead, events or locales is entirely coincidental.

I would like to thank the National Endowment for the Arts for their generous support while I worked on this book.

BLUEPRINTS
A Bantam Book / September 1990

PRINTING HISTORY
This edition was published simultaneously in hardcover and trade paperback.

Library of Congress Cataloging-in-Publication Data

Vogan, Sara.
   Blueprints / by Sara Vogan.
     p. cm.
   ISBN 0-553-07032-0.—ISBN 0-553-34959-7 (pbk.)
   I. Title.
PS3572.029B55   1990
813'.54—dc20   90–124
                                     CIP

Published simultaneously in the United States and Canada

PRINTED IN THE UNITED STATES OF AMERICA

FFG   0 9 8 7 6 5 4 3 2 1

To Adrianne and Gerry,
true friends

and

In memory of Michael,
who knew all along

*Special thanks to Gail Hochman and Deb Futter
who gave so much support and help*

The world breaks everyone, then some become strong at the broken places.

Ernest Hemingway
Farewell to Arms

My mother always kept plastic plants because they were easier to move and my father always watered them after each senseless fight. On the Tuesday afternoon before the fire, when I'd returned home after more than a decade, I took those poor plastic plants into the laundry basin in the basement and tried to refurbish them. Standing by the sink, a pot scrubber in my hand, I saw how faded the fake green leaves had become after thirty-some years sitting forlornly in windows. Mold from my father's useless watering caked the fake soil. The plastic was so old and brittle it shredded under the pot scrubber. After half an hour with the first pot of plastic ivy I pitched the whole collection in the garbage, got in my father's car and drove down to a florist. There I bought ferns, ivies, philodendrons, cacti, dracaena. I explained to the florist I only wanted the hardiest plants, survivor plants. "Make sure you talk to them," the florist told me. "Plants need attention, just like people."

When I returned my mother was curled on the couch, just in the same way she'd occupied that couch for as long as

I could remember. On her left was a pile of newspapers, even with the armrest. These were the papers and magazines she was planning to read. On her right was a slightly smaller stack: the articles she was saving. As I walked past her toward the dining room I could see the way she looked twenty-five, thirty years ago. Her hair was the same white blonde, her nails painted the same garish red. But twenty-five or thirty years ago she was thinner, and her face didn't sag beneath her dramatic eyes.

"What's all that?" my mother called to me.

"A spider plant and a dracaena." I placed the spider plant on the buffet and set the dracaena near the window. "The florist told me spider plants are good for purifying the air. He said every hospital room should have one. Smokers should fill their homes with them."

"We have plants." I could tell by her tone she knew what had happened to her plastic plants and had been waiting for my return so we could fight about it.

I walked back to the car for another armload.

"Just a minute. Stop right there, Maura. I want to know what happened to those plants."

"I threw them away."

Her voice was mockingly calm. "You threw them away. You haven't been in this house two days, you haven't seen either your father or me for years, and you decide to throw away my plants."

I set two ferns down on the coffee table, one for the bathroom and one for the kitchen. "That's right," I said. "Those things are so old they're falling apart. So I bought you some real plants."

"And who do you expect is going to take care of them?"

"Father will water them, just like he did the other ones."

"My mother gave me those pots before you were even born. You have a lot of nerve to throw them out." Her voice was a sneer.

2

"I'll retrieve your pots. But I think you should try real plants. Give you something to do." Hoisting one of the ferns I went into the kitchen where I knew she wouldn't follow me. Our various kitchens have always been a no-man's-land, abandoned as a desert. Every once in a while you'd run into my younger brother or sister, my father or mother, scouting through the refrigerator for something to eat. The refrigerator is always filled with half-empty packages. Pizza boxes, little white cartons that once contained Chinese food, foil-lined doggie bags. The only other food is usually self-contained. Pre-sliced cheese, individual servings of yogurt and tapioca, packaged lunch meat. My mother has never learned to cook. My father believes cooking is a woman's job. They compromise with take-out food and Howard Johnson-style restaurants. It wasn't until I was in college, living with Paris, a man who loves to cook, that I realized there were more spices than salt and pepper.

I decided to hang the fern in the window above the sink. But I'd forgotten to buy anything to hang the plant from. No problem. Like the magazines and newspapers, my mother has never thrown anything away. Whole drawers in our various houses are always filled with hardware. She's been known to save burnt-out lightbulbs. Once, when I was about eight, I watched one of the moving men open a bank of drawers in the kitchen. The first drawer was stuffed with empty paper bags. The second drawer held broken children's toys. The third and fourth drawers contained nuts and bolts, odds and ends of wire and string, broken hinges, cracked coffee cups, bent forks, knives without handles, clocks that didn't work, seashells. The moving man shook his head in wonder. And then he saw me standing in the doorway watching him. He put his finger to his lips, the sign for silence, and dumped all four of those drawers into a trashbag. I smiled and gave him the okay sign.

Since the last time I'd seen them, my parents had moved

3

several times, but I knew somewhere I'd find my mother's precious collection of junk. In the basement, next to where I'd left the plastic plants in their simple red clay pots, I found an entire cabinet devoted to the broken things my mother saves. And, just as I'd hoped, there were enough wires and nails, hooks and eyes, to fashion two plant hangers. Like any other unselective collector, my mother sometimes saves things that are intact, or even have a bit of value. The value today was the fact I wouldn't have to go back into town before I could hang up the ferns.

"Are you getting my pots back?" My mother was standing at the top of the stairs. "If you're going to go to the trouble to rescue those pots you might as well keep the plants in them."

"The plants go," I said. "I told the florist I wanted survivor plants. These aren't African violets. They're about the easiest plants in the world to take care of. Give them a try. If they die you can get more plastic ones." I heard her huff off back to the couch.

My mother has been retired from life for at least the forty-some years I've known her. As a child she acquired a romantic streak and a vivid imagination which crops up in conversations with Mrs. White. When I started dating I'd come home to find her lounging on the couch in a nightgown as if waiting for a lover. She thought I was Mrs. White. She told me all her secrets then. I can never predict what she will do. All through the years since I left home the phone would ring in the dead of night and my mother would confide to Mrs. White some disaster, like the loss of her plastic plants. So far, in the day and a half I've been here she hasn't called me Mrs. White once.

I returned from the basement with the jerry-rigged plant holders. I was standing on the stepladder, trying to screw a hook into the ceiling to attach the hanger, when my mother

4

came into the kitchen. "I called Drew," she said. "He wants to talk to you."

Screwing hooks straight up is awkward work. "I'll call him back."

"Now," my mother said. "Get down this moment and talk to your brother. He's the only sensible one in this family." She sounded like she was talking to a ten year old.

With one more blow of the hammer I unfortunately smashed the hook. I looped the wire around it anyhow. I pulled on it, testing it. I could see my reflection in the window over the sink. Only a little after six and getting dark. Getting to be winter, an Eastern winter with snow and hail and sleet, not the sunny California winter days I prize. I noticed the scallops under my eyes, huge sockets only properly seen when the face is a skull. My face in the darkening window like a photographic negative, my blonde hair silver, my green eyes black pits. I am no longer young, and bright, and full of promise. I'm a middle-aged woman with a spotty track record that can be read in my face. I got down from the stepladder and retrieved the fern.

"Now," my mother said again. "Your brother's a very busy man."

I remounted the stepladder and hung the fern from the makeshift loop. To my surprise it held. Most of my home carpentry jobs are never really successful. In the morning the fern might be smashed into the sink. "Okay," I said once the job was finished. "I'm coming."

"She wants me to come over," Drew said when I got to the phone. "She says you're tearing the house apart."

"The first casualty in any conflict is always the truth," I told him. "I threw out the plastic plants and bought some real ones. Nina seems to think that's a major crime."

"Nina's good at coming up with major crimes. But this is sadistic, Emery. Those plants will die once you go back to the West Coast."

"You can take care of them. Or let them die. I just couldn't stand the sight of those moldy old things."

"She wants me to come over for dinner," Drew said.

"Oh terrific," I said. "What are we going to do?"

"We've got the same three choices we always have. I can cook. You can cook. Or we can go out."

"I'll cook," I said. "I get so embarrassed when we fight in restaurants. Besides, the fight will be about me, so I'll just keep busy in the kitchen."

"Can I bring anything?"

"Yeah, something for me to cook."

"Go to the store. I don't know what you can cook. If I bring the food I'll end up cooking it. See you, Emery."

Drew hung up and I took the other fern and hanger into the bathroom. I could tell from Nina's silence she was pulling one of her favorite tricks, the first of her tricks we learned as children. Wait Until Your Father Gets Home. She sits on the couch, reading from the stack of newspapers and magazines, and pretends she's gone deaf. As children we used to try all kinds of ploys to get her attention, feigning broken arms, fires, fierce fights. Once, when I was ten, I sat on the coffee table and told her a story about a magical raven for over two hours. She never looked up, seemed to pay no attention to me as she leafed through the pages of a magazine until she heard my father's car pull in the driveway. With my father home, her eyes lit up. I remember thinking then that if I'd been invisible before my father's arrival, I was nonexistent in the shine of his light. "Go on now, Maura," my mother said, the first words she'd spoken in over two hours. "Your father's home."

Anyone who cares anything about me calls me Emery. My full name is Maureen Emery Lannier. When I was growing up all the girls were named Sally, Debbie, Susan, Bobbie, Carol, Toni. Maura made me feel like an immigrant from a poor country. In the various towns we lived in I tried on different names. Lani, abridging Lannier. Mo, short for Maureen the same as Maura. Roxie, taken from my favorite movie theater. But none of them ever stuck. My teachers called me Maura, the kids in school called me Maura. My parents called me Maura. Drew and my sister Julia called me Maura. By the time I went to college I hated my name so much I dropped it altogether. Emery, my grandmother's maiden name, felt right. I liked the idea of grinding and polishing, a hard abrasive substance. I grew to see myself like that: grinding and polishing myself to remove the traces of Frank and Nina from my life. I don't think I'm an abrasive person but I knew I needed some of that quality to keep the boys off me in high school. I would need it to find work once I left college. So by the end of my freshman year I'd developed a new concept of myself, scouring away Frank and Nina so I could grind up against the real world.

My mother was still sitting on the couch, reading a magazine, when I came down from the bathroom. "I'm going to the store," I said. "Drew's coming for dinner."

She didn't bother to look up.

"When's Father going to be home?"

She lit a cigarette.

I took the keys and went out to the car.

The reason I'd returned to my parents' house was that my father was dying, according to my mother, that is. Frank, although his health isn't good, has no notion of dying. The sun rose this morning because Frank said it was okay. Now that he's retired he's learned sign language and talks to the deaf. One day a week he visits the terminally ill or disabled, picking up newspapers and candy bars and mailing letters, the world's oldest candy striper. On Saturdays and Sundays he transports kittens and puppies from the SPCA to the local mall and tries to talk people into taking them home.

Of course, this was all before the fire.

Last week Nina called me in San Francisco and told me,

matter of factly, that Frank was dying and she was going to come visit me in the hopes of meeting a new man to take care of her. Since Nina married Frank at the age of eighteen she's surrendered any idea of taking care of herself. If Frank dies Nina will have to find someone to replace him, preferably younger since men die at an earlier age than women. Imagine, taking my mother to a singles bar. I called Drew, as I always do when something's at stake. Even though he's two years younger than I am, Drew's the only one of us to have acquired any common sense. Drew has confidence and courage, and most importantly, a sense of calm in crisis. When Julia died Drew was the one who took charge. This has always surprised me since I felt my father would be the stoic one, the one to talk to the government, the missionary outfit she worked for. Drew contacted the agencies, arranged the memorial service. My father sat in a chair on the patio watching birds flit over the backyard.

It was Drew who decided I should make this trip home, find out for myself what was happening with our parents. 'You're right there,' I said. 'Just tell me what's going on.'

'You haven't been home since the ceremony,' Drew said. 'Look at it this way. If Frank's dying don't you want to see him before he kicks off? I'm telling you, Emery, you'll regret it if you don't see him until he's boxed in a casket.'

So I've been here less than two days. Nina's angry because I bought plants, Frank's been too busy to talk to me, and Drew has his job to consider. I feel lost in their new house, reduced to a child once again. For dinner I decide on broiled lamb chops, Frank's favorite. I'll make potatoes au gratin, a salad, toast garlic bread to keep me busy in the kitchen while Frank and Nina get drunk before dinner. Odds are we won't eat a thing, or perhaps Drew and I will eat cold lamb chops and potatoes after Nina has locked herself in her bedroom and Frank has stormed out to a bar.

Frank was home when I returned from the store. Seeing

8

my father these days is always a shock. My memories are of a much younger man, a man about thirty-five with the strong shoulders of a swimmer and the lean legs of a runner; his hair is streaked sun-blonde and his nose and chin are the only sharp angles on his face. The man sitting across from my mother is the same man I remember. It's just that he looks like someone else.

His face could have been sculpted by Picasso. Deep Vs hang from corner to corner under his eyes. The lines running from his mouth to his nose form a sculpted M. His skin is so papery I believe I can see his teeth beneath his cheeks. My father, six feet tall, now weighs one hundred and sixty pounds.

"Maura," he said, as though he were glad to see me. "Your mother says you've decided to redecorate the house."

I shoved the bag of groceries at him. He would have taken it from me anyhow. Frank's frail body houses the mind of a much younger man, a man who would never let a woman carry a bag of groceries. "Does anything look different?"

"Looks the same to me." He headed toward the kitchen. "But your mother has a finer eye for that kind of thing than I do."

"We're having lamb chops for dinner," I said.

Nina was right behind us. "You didn't ask me if we could have lamb chops. Personally, I'm hungry for Chinese."

"Lamb chops will be fine," my father said. "I understand Drew's coming over. How about a drink, Maura?" He put the bag down and went to the cabinet. Since kitchenware has always been in short supply in our homes, the cabinets house electrical tools, tax records, broken appliances, unanswered mail, and alcohol.

"You're not supposed to drink," Nina said.

"I haven't seen Maura for years. A couple of drinks isn't going to kill me."

9

"Since when did you ever limit yourself to a couple of drinks." My mother took the bottle of scotch from him and went back to the living room.

My father simply opened another cabinet and produced a bottle of wine. "Lamb chops," he said. "How about some nice red wine, a good cabernet sauvignon?" He reached into another cabinet and produced two jelly glasses. I kept unloading the groceries, waiting to hear what story Nina had given him about the redecorating, the plastic plants. "Well," he said as he handed me a glass. "Cheers." He clinked glasses with me and took a sip. "Well," he said again. "I guess I better go see what's bothering your mother."

I poured the wine down the sink. I love to drink, it frees my mind from its obsessions and my body from its annoying aches and pains. But they say every cell in your body is replaced once every seven years and if that's true, my new cells have developed a bitter allergy to alcohol. I'll have a drink now and then, but only with someone I trust, who's close to me, like my friend Victor. Someone who accepts the macabre changes I sometimes go through when I drink. I had decided I wasn't going to drink around my mother. She has that game honed to an art and I was determined not to play.

My father left me alone in the kitchen, walking through the dining room with an old man's shuffle. His joints have grown stiff. Sometimes he has difficulty rising from a chair. He hasn't said a word to me about his illness, hasn't mentioned the possibility of death. But then, in the time I've been here, most of our conversations have been meaningless. Did I have a good flight? Did I sleep well in the guest room? Will I need the car while I'm here? When am I going to get married?

This last question is as meaningless as all the others. Frank believes I'm the only middle-aged woman in North America who hasn't even tried the institution of marriage. He's given up hope he can convince me to find a man to take care of me. He makes it sound like buying a new sweater. His favorite saying is: At least if you were divorced you'd have something.

He's been on this marriage kick for the last twenty-five years, to the point where that question, coming from my father, is as clichéd as 'Hi, how are you?' He doesn't expect an answer anymore. Only once did I hear him seriously reflect upon the fact that none of his three children had ever married. This was right after Julia died, fifteen years ago. Julia was seven months pregnant. Frank sat with me on the patio, drinking, and it was so late at night the crickets weren't even singing. 'That might have been my only grandchild,' he said. 'You and Drew, you're so much alike, I can't expect anything out of either of you.'

I began slicing potatoes, listening carefully to see if Frank and Nina were fighting yet. But there was just the murmur of voices from the other room, a comforting sound in any other house but this one. The murmur of voices in our home meant they were talking, and when Frank and Nina started to talk they eventually began to argue. Perhaps they thrive on argument, challenging each other's wills. I'd like to believe their happiest times are when they are silent with each other, sitting side by side watching TV, across from each other in a restaurant, on top of each other when making love.

Drew came into the kitchen carrying some packages. "Hey Emery," he said, "do you like escargot?"

I took a package from him. "You think they're going to eat escargot? We're fixing dinner for a man who won't eat anything but red meat and a woman who wants Chinese tonight."

"If you like escargot, this is just for you and me. If you don't like escargot, it's just for me." Drew understood food in our family long before I did. When we were kids Drew saved his allowance for candy bars, apples, strings of beef jerky, which he hid throughout the house. Nina never suspected until the day she scooped the wash out of the clothes chute and dumped a Hershey's chocolate bar, two oranges, and a box of Junior Mints into the washing machine. The oranges thumped around like live things trying to escape. Nina blamed the stashed food on me because I was the oldest. That was always her reason for punishing me, because I was the oldest. I should know better. But how? By intuition? For years it made as much sense as punishing me because I was the blonde, or the one in second grade.

"Let's save it for after the fight," I said. "There's no point putting it on the table for them."

"We could eat it now," Drew said. "That way at least we'll have something in our stomachs."

"You do it," I said, "I've got dinner to make."

We were standing by the stove and refrigerator, across the room from the sink. At that moment we heard a terrible crash. Whirling around, we discovered the fern cockeyed across the counter and the sink. The fronds trembled like palsy.

"Nina's right," Drew said. "You're making a mess of this redecorating job."

"What the hell's going on in here?" My father stood in the doorway and, like Alice in Wonderland, I shrank to twelve years old. I'm sorry, Daddy. I didn't mean to do it. It was an accident. It wasn't my fault.

"Emery's plant got thirsty," Drew said.

"Her name is Maura. I don't know why she can't use the name we gave her. Emery's a last name, for god sakes. And look at the damn mess in the sink."

"I'll clean it up," I said. "It won't take a minute."

Nina stood beside Frank, her hands fisted on her hips. "What did I tell you? She's been here less than two days and she thinks she owns the place."

"It's just a plant," Drew said. "Here, let me help you."

As Drew came over to the sink to see if we could salvage

the fern, Nina turned on Frank. "Look at the mess she's made. This is our house. We've worked long and hard for this place, a place for just the two of us, not a place overrun by children."

"Maura's just arrived," my father said. "Why don't you get off the kid's back."

"Why don't you two go back in the living room and let Emery and I handle things out here?" Drew suggested.

"Since when do you kids run this place?" my mother said.

"We've been running this place for as long as I can remember," Drew said. "Go on. Let us get to work." He went to the utility cabinet and produced the broom and a dustpan.

My father said, "Get away from there, Maura. You'll cut yourself." He came over by the sink to help us and I felt the backs of my ears tense.

"We'll have to go out," Nina said. "Your father has to eat at regular intervals and by the time you get this mess cleaned up there'll be no time to make dinner. I think we should go down to Hop Soy's. You see, Maura, this would have never happened if you'd left things as they were. Your father and I can get along perfectly well without your meddling."

"For Christ sake, Nina, just shut up," my father said. "Go get me my drink from the living room. This won't take long."

"I'm going to call Hop Soy's," Nina said. "There'll be dirt all over this kitchen for days. You can't cook clean food in a dirty kitchen."

"What do you care?" Drew said. "You can't cook."

"I'm going to call Hop Soy's," my mother said.

"Bring me my drink while you're up," my father said, as he removed shards of the pot and tossed them in the garbage.

'While you're up' has always been one of my father's favorite phrases, no matter if you're talking on the phone, watching TV, or doing homework. Even if you were having

13

sex. His favorite request for 'while you're up' was for half a grilled cheese sandwich. Not a whole one, only a half.

"The rootball looks intact," my brother said. "All we need is a new pot. But this baby might be too heavy to hang."

"I'll get one," I said. I would have walked to town for one, just to get out of that kitchen, but instead I went to the basement to get one of Nina's old red clay pots.

I left for college right after my sixteenth birthday and quit coming home out of self-defense and on the strong recommendation of my therapist. But Drew is right; I want to make some peace with them before they die. I always think of them as dying together. I can't imagine one without the other. Nina's plans to come live with me could be more of the fanciful ideas you have to expect from my mother. She's the one who bequeathed me my notions of escape. For example, when she watches a movie and a woman packs up to leave my mother is constantly amazed that this monumental task can be accomplished with only one suitcase that doesn't seem to weigh the heroine down. With all the moving we've done my mother has become an expert on packing. 'I wish I could do that,' she'll say. 'I wish life were as simple as they make it in movies. No loose ends. That's the death of every woman, you know. She strangles in all the loose ends.'

Things were almost back to normal in the kitchen. Drew had taken the soil and fern out to the back stoop and my father was washing down the counter with a dishrag. My mother was nowhere to be seen, but his drink was sitting on the counter. I handed the pot to Drew and went to help my father.

"I think Chinese is probably best for tonight. We'll have the lamb chops tomorrow," he said.

"Count me out," I said. "You guys go. I need a little peace and quiet tonight. Jet lag. Did you know your body needs twenty-four hours to decompress for every hour you're in the air?" Facts usually engage my father. Our conversations

14

are mostly along the how-to line. If your plane is delayed he can tell you how many hours a pilot must log to obtain a license, or the qualifications needed to be an air controller.

"Your mother will be disappointed." He didn't look at me as he continued wiping down the counter.

I wanted to say 'Screw her,' wanted to yell obscenities loud enough for the neighbors to hear. But I was still twelve years old, terrified of an old man, an old woman, and the violence that could suddenly erupt. In high school I wanted to be a geologist, a volcanologist to be specific. I've always felt a natural affinity for volcanos, earthquakes. "Some other time," I said. "I just don't feel up to it tonight."

My father took a last swipe at the counter. "Do what you want. You never listen to me." He picked up his drink and went back to the living room.

This passive resignation from my father surprised me. My father gives orders, the only kind of conversation he's capable of. I think my fascination with volcanos, tornados, earthquakes, is my reaction to being my father's daughter. Like Mount Saint Helens, my father is the sleeping, solid, giant most of the time. Then, without warning, he erupts with plans or violence. 'You'll do as I say.' My mother, on the other hand, is never to be trusted. She'll lie about the weather. She'll tell you the sky is green.

"Here." Drew set the repotted fern near the window. "It will do just fine here until it dies."

"You better go check the bathroom," I said. "I hung another one up there."

Drew shook his head. "You shouldn't shortchange Nina," he said. "You really are making a mess of this redecorating business."

"Fuck you," I said. "I bought some plants. Take them to your place on your way home."

"I might," Drew said. "You've forgotten who you're dealing with here. They can make a major issue out of how to use a toothpick."

"They're going to Hop Soy's," I said. "I'm going to eat your escargot."

"Like hell. You'll get your half and no more. We'll do it like school kids. One for me, and one for you . . ."

"Then we'll really have a fight on our hands. You babysit them tonight and I'll take over tomorrow night. And I promise to leave your escargot alone."

"Listen, Emery. I haven't really talked to you since San Francisco, and that was, what, two, three years ago. Let them go to Hop Soy's and we'll pig out on lamb chops and escargot." He held his hand out in a slap-five.

"Done." I smacked my palm against his. "But you break the news to them."

I began recleaning the counter my father had wiped down. His vision's going and he probably didn't see the swirls of dirt he'd mopped across the counter. I wondered if I'd remained close to my family if these changes in Nina and Frank would be less shocking, if somehow I would have been able to outgrow the age of twelve whenever I was around them.

Nina entered the kitchen. I could hear the tap of her heels on the linoleum. "Why are you doing this, Maura? You have no idea how much this hurts your father."

I threw the towel down on the counter. "Doing what?"

"I don't mean the plants, all this." She swept her hand over the counter to indicate the fern, the mess. "Your father hasn't seen you in years and you won't even go out to dinner with him."

"You're the one who wants to go out. I thought we were going to eat at home. You invited Drew over for dinner, remember?"

"I invited Drew for dinner. There's no law that says when

you invite someone for dinner you have to eat at home. The lamb chops were your idea."

"Father likes lamb chops. It's one of the two foods he'll eat. I don't know what you expect him to eat at Hop Soy's."

"Your father likes Chinese. We go out for Chinese quite often. But that's not the point, Maura." She took a long drag from her cigarette. "You have no idea how ill he is. And even if you don't care about that, the least you could do would be to be civil while you're here. It wasn't my idea for you to come out here. You invited yourself."

"And you invited yourself to come live with me if Frank dies."

"When Frank dies. What else do you expect me to do?"

"Mother, look. You and Frank go have dinner, if that's what you want. I'll clean up the kitchen and make something for Drew and myself."

"That's not the point. You were always his favorite, Maura. He wants to visit with you now that you're here. Why don't you come to dinner with us."

I closed my eyes so tightly oil-slick-colored spots appeared. This was a mistake, another mistake. I should have stayed in San Francisco. "If he wants to visit with me so badly, why is he never around? I've been here just over a day and this is the first meal we've even attempted to have together. If I catch him on the fly I might get to say hello. He flits in and out of here with the speed of a laser beam."

"Don't give me that. You call up and say you're coming to visit, give us no warning whatsoever. You expect us to drop everything just because you blow into town?" She arched her brows, widened her eyes which stretched out the crow's feet. She was still a good-looking woman, a little on the heavy side but not bad for a woman nearing seventy.

"He doesn't want to know what I'm doing. If he's glad to see me it's only because he likes to have me around. Not because he wants to know what I'm doing."

"He has to keep busy," my mother said. "That's what's keeping him alive. He's not the type of man who can just sit back and let the world go by. As long as he eats regularly, takes his medicine, and doesn't get too excited, he'll be fine. Then you come along with your emotional circus and throw a monkey wrench into our lives and wonder what we're upset about."

There's no arguing with a woman like this, whether she's your mother or a perfect stranger. It is like arguing with a wooden merry-go-round horse. How do you talk to the wind? "What time did you make your reservations? Hadn't you better get going?"

"Listen to me, Maura. I have no idea why you're here. But I'm going to be damn sure you don't hurt your father. You were always a hateful and malicious child. You bit your piano teacher on the hand, remember? You'd strip the shadow from a stranger's back. I don't expect that's something a person outgrows." She whirled on her heel and made one of her dramatic exits from the kitchen. Her perfume hung in the air.

The backs of my ears continued to ache as I listened to them getting ready to go. My father asked me twice if I wouldn't change my mind. I heard him ask Drew if he could talk me into it. But finally they left. Only then did I realize I'd chopped an entire garlic, fifteen or twenty cloves, my hands keeping time while I held my breath.

Drew had taken the lamb chops out to the grill after Frank and Nina left. The escargot was warming in the oven. I was tearing lettuce leaves for salad when Drew brought the chops in. "Forget the rabbit food," he said. "Let's just pig out. Let's OD on cholesterol, sodium. Let's pour all the alcohol in a soup kettle and drink it with ladles, Kamakazi style. I know a guy who has coke and crack. Let's do it all."

"Baby brother," I said, "you're letting them get to you."

"Listen Emery. You aren't around. You don't go through this shit two or three times a week."

"You had your chance," I said. "You were the one who decided to move to San Francisco, and then bagged out."

"You sound like Nina, you know that?" He began putting the food on the table. "Maybe her personality is contagious. You never sounded like this in San Francisco. Give it a rest, okay? For me."

"Coming back here is the height of masochism. I don't know why I let myself in for this shit."

Drew put an Art Tatum tape on and cut into his chop. "You don't understand. You miss a lot with your Escape Artist act. Your Houdini imitation. This last year, since they moved here, has been like living through a car wreck, a car wreck going on in slow motion all year long." He looked at me sternly, gesturing with his fork. "First there's the signs of danger, the nervousness, the attempt to keep from hitting the retaining wall. The skid, trying to get the car under control. Then each motion of the car as it hits the wall takes days. The front end squishes up as slowly as the moon changes phases. The car starts to fly up into the air, flipping over and over, beginning to fall."

"That's what I like about you, Drew. You always come so quickly to the point." We talk in riddles, or perhaps we each have a foreign language we fall into when we're around each other. But I was sorry he'd had such a bad year and wondered what else was going on besides our parents.

"Let's eat and get the hell out of here before they get back," my brother said. "Want to scout out the neighborhood? Go to a club? What do you want to do, Emery? Now that you've come home."

I tried one of the escargot, quite good for inland food, none of the stale, frozen taste I expected. Drew only bought the best. "I want to go back to San Francisco. But if I hop on a plane tonight I'll never even know why I came out here."

"To see me." Drew smiled. Smiling makes his face look most natural, light comes into his hazel eyes and all the lines in his face fall into perfect harmony. When he's angry he looks as if he's wearing makeup, all his features accentuated.

Drew is always in motion as if he were constantly emitting light or radiation, a force field around him that makes him seem a size larger than he actually is. When he's angry or happy his six foot four seems to stretch to seven feet. He looks loose, double jointed, fluid, expandable. Although he's my younger brother I look to him for protection. He seems big enough, sensible enough, to take on the world. This constant quaking of nervous energy is like blood to him. When he is calm, while driving or asleep, he looks slightly ill, his features pasted on as if a pallor had drained him of his soul. And in Drew I can see the mental makeup of my family. We're all adrenaline addicts except, of course, Julia. The motion and energy around us gives us something to focus on, as if energy were tangible and could be contained. Calm, quiet, serenity, peace are hostile threats to us. The calm before the storm. The quiet in the eye of a hurricane. The serenity of prayer is really time for calculation. Peace is a lull between wars.

"What is there to do in this town, anyway?" I asked.

"The usual life-avoidance routines." He plucked an escargot from its shell. "Get drunk, smoke dope, make money, fuck around. I believe I've scoped out most of the action."

"You should have given San Francisco a try," I said.

Two years ago Drew quit his job as a banker and decided to move to the West Coast. His trip dovetailed nicely with the first stirrings of my parents' decision to move to this inland city, this place Drew calls home. He showed up on my doorstep driving a blood-red classic Corvette Stingray. His idea of moving to San Francisco was to bring a bunch of business suits, his answering machine, his color TV, and VCR. He stayed with me for a couple of weeks and it was only then he began to call me Emery. None of my friends or

lovers even knew my first name was Maura. Maura, the An-
glicized version of Moira. I'd discovered Moira was one
of the Fates, the one who controlled Nemesis. I was told
Moira means 'bitter water' in Hebrew. I hadn't used it in over
twenty years. When Frank and Nina call me Maura I look
around to see who else is in the room.

"Why did you really leave San Francisco?" I asked.

He cut another piece of lamb chop. "In some ways
we're the exact opposite, Emery. In my address book you take
up two pages, front and back. You've lived all over the country, just like we did as kids, with all of Frank's transfers. It
doesn't seem to bother you to pack up and move to a new
place. But me," he took a bite of the meat. "Me, when I found
a place to settle, I didn't ever want to move again. I thought
all that trauma was over. I could meet my neighbors, get to
know the people I work with, hell, maybe even buy a house.
Then Frank and Nina started talking about moving here and
that probably had a lot to do with my dissatisfaction at the
bank. But I never could feel I had my feet on the ground in
San Francisco. I couldn't get used to all the people, I mean
business-suit types, partying in the middle of a work day. It
just seemed like one big party town to me. I like to party as
much as anyone, but I need to work to make the partying
seem real, to mean something. When the bank offered to
take me back, promote me even, it just seemed like that's
what I was supposed to do."

"Then don't bitch about babysitting Nina and Frank.
There are banks all over the country."

When I came home for Julia's memorial service over fifteen years ago Drew got out his bamboo flyfishing rod and
went out to the backyard. I watched him methodically cast
into the grass over and over again. The only other movement
was the moon inching across the sky.

Sometimes it happens like this: One day with nowhere to go I end up at the Steinhart Aquarium, following the albacore, manta rays, and tarpons as they lazily circled the roundabout. These fish look eternally drugged to me, so placid, fins barely moving, as they drift with the current. I always marvel at the sharks, keeping to the far wall, mixed in among the herd. They open their mouths with the swift, neat precision of a cat's yawn. On this particular day I walked hypnotically beside the circular tank when suddenly, only a few feet in front of me, a silver flash. A vivid red stain appeared and the schools broke into flight. A thresher shark, tail snapping about like a pennant in a strong wind, mowed through the underbelly of a tuna. Silver scales sparkled through the variegated water, scarlet, blue, silver, green. The tuna's head drifted toward the floor of the tank. Other sharks pivoted in the water and sped toward the gore. The sharks tore through the remains of the tuna, each other, fish panicking toward safety. There was no place to go in the circular tank. Children shrieked, but most of us stood transfixed. The water became

23

violent and murky, but we continued to stand there until a guide hustled us away.

There are some things you just can't prepare for.

I'd been home three empty, endless days and was planning to return to San Francisco at the end of the week. It seemed I knew no more about what was happening to my parents, the state of my father's health, than when I stepped off the plane. Mistakes. I'd already chalked the whole visit off and contented myself with reading every book I wasn't familiar with scattered throughout the house. Harold Robbins. William Warner. Nadine Gordimer.

I suspect Nina fell asleep on the couch that night, a cigarette burning precariously in the ashtray, a fresh bottle of scotch sitting on the coffee table. Perhaps the smoke woke her, or the hiss and crackle of the bone-dry newspapers. Nina has never been one to stay calm in crisis. Both she and Frank believe, like American tourists in foreign countries, the louder you yell the quicker the service.

"Ah! Jesus! Frank! Frank? Where are you?"

As I startled awake I noticed a commonplace smell like burnt toast. Nina could have broken a tooth, locked herself out of the house. Anything was possible. I grabbed a sweatshirt and moved sleepily toward the stairs. I still had that sleepy floating feeling.

My mother was standing in the middle of the living room dancing from one foot to the other, her silky nightgown swirling around her legs, more like a woman afraid of a mouse scurrying across the floor than a person staring into a vortex of flame. She held the scotch bottle against her chest, protecting it. I watched the flames lick through the stack of newspapers, her ever-present collection that has taken root like mushrooms sprouting beside the couch in every house we'd ever lived in. At that point the couch wasn't even on fire. Imagine a magician who crumbles a rag and a moment later releases a dove. The burning stack of newspapers was as contained as a dove winging its way to freedom. Or think of trash fires in oil drums. Those were my first images of it: ice skating on a pond, the chill of the air, the crisp swooshing sounds of my skates across the ice, and the sight of those burning drums signifying warmth. The flames licking the air like startled birds. Perhaps I stared at the newspapers too long. Perhaps Nina didn't see me standing at the entrance to the living room. I kept hearing her, but the sounds didn't register any more than the screams of kids on a roller coaster. "Jesus! Jesus!" And then, just as I turned to say something to her, she poured the bottle of scotch on the flames.

"Don't!" But it was too late. The alcohol went up like some flaming dessert in a French restaurant. The flames kissed the ceiling and crested, caught the curtains on the way down.

The arc of the scotch washed the arm of the couch and the fire now curled around her in the shape of a C. My mother noticed me for the first time. "Where's Frank? Call the police."

She continued standing in the middle of the burning living room while I went to the kitchen for the phone. The smoke rolled through the room and seared my lungs the way a deep drag on strong marijuana would. My head felt as light as if I'd been smoking dope. I forgot the phone and searched under the sink for a pot or kettle. The fire still didn't look very serious to me. Douse it good with some water and it would go out.

But since neither Nina nor Frank cooked it took much longer to find any kind of pot or kettle than one would suspect. I was in my own home looking for an old soup kettle I keep right under the sink to catch the slow leak dripping from the drainpipe elbow. I found a pair of galoshes, a mirrored jewelry box, a hoard of seashells. In the adjoining cabinet I found liquor. The next one held a collection of framed pictures that had never been hung.

There was a popping sound, like the sound of glass Christmas ornaments hitting a hardwood floor, then Nina's shriek and a musical waterfall like wind chimes. Blown glass musical notes shattering once they were played.

Smoke was now roiling through the first floor as I made my way back to the living room. Flames danced independently in the air, ungrounded, weightless. Unmoored and free-floating as thoughts. Instinct is a funny thing. I remember an earthquake Paris and I experienced in the middle of a balmy spring morning. I was on the phone, Paris in the shower, and I watched as the hanging plants began to sway, heard the glasses rattling in the cupboards. Paris came dashing out of the bathroom, a towel trailing behind him, shouting, 'We've got to get out of here!' Politely, I told the man on the other end of the line I had to hang up, although it was a local call and he undoubtedly was experiencing the same earthquake. I put the phone down and followed Paris out the back door and down the stairs to the garden. We passed our cat, running up the stairs into the house. Animals are supposed to have stronger instincts than people. Paris and I wanted out of a house we believed might collapse on us. Our cat wanted in. We never knew who was right, ourselves or the cat. I thought the earthquake lasted several minutes, long enough to watch the plants sway, to politely get off the phone, grab my cigarettes, and run down the stairs after Paris. I stood in the garden and everything was extremely still. I expected the ground to buckle, the trees to whip around as the roots popped. But everything was as still as a photograph. We looked at each other. Paris fiddled nervously with his towel. And then we went back up the stairs into the kitchen. The cat was eating from his bowl of kitty chow. The plants hung serenely from the ceiling. In the cupboards I discovered some of the glasses tipped over, nothing broken. Later, on the news, we learned the earthquake registered 4.5 on the Richter scale and had lasted twenty-eight seconds. For twenty-eight seconds the earth had moved. It's funny, those twenty-eight seconds caused less damage than the big one in '89, the 7.1 that lasted only fifteen seconds.

We don't think when we panic, our atrophied senses colliding with our intellectual mind. The safest and most logical thing to have done that night would have been to run out the back door to safety. But I was curious as to what made that popping sound. In spite of the smoke, or maybe I wasn't even aware of the smoke, I made my way back to the living room. Color hung on the air like spots before your eyes. Nina still stood there, fire raging in a G clef all around her. The front window was gone, fingers of flame reaching out toward the trees in the yard.

Nina coughed and sputtered. "Where's Frank? Mrs. White, we've got to wake Frank."

My eyes burned and I could feel the heat as if the living room was a sauna. I picked a spot where the flames were a tiny red and yellow string racing across the floor and leapt into the circle with Nina. I grabbed her by the arm and pulled her with me toward the door.

"Where's Frank?" she kept shouting. I herded her across the licks of fire and out the front door.

We stood in the yard watching the flames devour the window frame, saw the glass sprayed across the grass. "Mrs. White," Nina asked, as casually as if she were noting the weather, "did you call the police?" My mother's emotions change as quickly as flipping a coin.

The wind was high and gusty, blowing great sheets of flame back into the house. "The police?" My thinking was about ten steps behind when I realized she meant the fire department. No. I'd forgotten about the fire department in my search for the pot. A pot of water wouldn't do any good now. It seemed less than a minute had passed, yet the fire was now totally out of control.

My parents' home was part of an apartment-like complex. The fire swept along the common wall to the next residence. But the front door stood as strong and still as if it was merely holding off the night.

Nina reached into the pocket of her scorched peignoir and pulled out a pack of cigarettes, lit one. She looked at me lazily, a bored expression on her face. "I'll go wake the neighbors. You go get Frank. While you're in the bedroom, there's a batch of papers in the third drawer of the dresser. The mortgage, insurance. Be sure to pick those up on your way out."

The dream-like feeling vanished and I began to shake all over when I realized exactly where we were, what was going on. Nina wanted me, or her imaginary Mrs. White, to open the front door, as if I were coming in out of the rain, go up the front stairs, gently wake my father, calmly search the bureau for some papers, and return as if we'd merely forgotten something as we prepared to take a trip.

If I opened that front door a wall of flame would engulf me. The stairs to the second floor would probably be on fire by now. Where was Frank?

I watched Nina cross the yard toward the neighbors when an explosion, the gas lines between the two condos, knocked her flat. I was on the ground too, the stubble of grass against my cheek. I thought my ears were ringing, until I realized I was hearing sirens coming from far away, soft and slow as music in an elevator. When I looked up and my vision cleared I could see the neighbors, all elderly like my parents, coming out into their yards in their bathrobes and slippers, tottering around as if the ground was a field of hot stones.

I sat up on the grass, watching all these people moving in slow motion. The whole front of the house was in flames now, and more glass spewed out of the second story windows, falling on us like a rainstorm. I watched Nina pawing around in the grass, looking for something she'd lost.

"Hey! God damn it! Somebody do something!" The voice was above me, screaming from the night sky. I looked up but at first couldn't see anything through the smoke. But then the voice sounded familiar, although I had a hard time placing it. "Hey! God damn it!"

Clinging to the top of the trunk of the tree in the front yard I saw a blue figure wavering in the fire's light. The branches of the tree nearest the house were burning, barely. And then I realized the figure in the tree was Frank.

"Get a ladder!" someone close to me yelled. The sirens were louder now. A waft of water sprayed over me as someone turned on a garden hose and pointed it toward the house. The water hit the tree, causing all the leaves to shudder. Frank was yelling again: "Not me, God damn it. Get me out of here!"

Later I marveled at a seventy-two-year-old man, a dying man according to Nina, crawling out of a second story window and leaping into the branches of a tree while his house burned around him. But at the moment it seemed quite natural, at least to me.

Nina was standing under the tree. "Get down from there right now!" She yelled at him as if scolding Drew when he was a child. "You'll hurt yourself." She seemed to have forgotten about the fire, although the sirens had become a continuous wail, earsplitting as the trucks pulled up in front of the building.

A man smelling of rubber pulled me to my feet, wrapped a blanket around me, and guided me away from the front yard. Another rubber-coated man, his yellow helmet a crest tapering down his neck, approached Nina, and she turned to him, her hands on her hips, commanding: "Get him down! He'll hurt himself up there!"

I noticed many of the old people held cats or small dogs,

clutched boxes to their chests, or fiddled nervously with the sashes on their robes. The fire crew swarmed around us, rearranging people like boxes or chairs, spewing water from hoses as round as anacondas. It took two firemen to get Nina away from the tree. A third brought a ladder, a polished wooden ladder, to help Frank down out of the branches, which were burning now. Imagine that wooden ladder catching fire, square after square after square. An ambulance arrived.

Sitting safely on the running board of a fire truck, I began to enjoy watching the lights of the fire play against the throb of the water directed toward the house. Blue is the hottest, most intense, area of a fire and I watched the front of the building bathed in flickering blue light. A crash as loud as a sonic boom brought the front eave of the house down into what was left of the second story. The night was as bright as dawn and the rolling smoke stung my eyes. I traced the gilt gold letters on a box next to me. LIFE NET.

Nina was beside me. "Where's Drew?" she whispered. "Did you wake Drew?"

I was thinking fairly clearly now and knew Drew was safely asleep in his apartment overlooking the city. Someone should call him, and I began to rise to ask one of the people standing around watching the fire if they would ring him up when Nina grabbed my arm. "Julia," she said, and there were tears in her eyes. "Julia and Drew. Now there's only you."

Water played over the front of the house and I remember thinking of this as if it were a battlefield, the translucence of the water pushing back the multi-colored flames. Nina kept repeating "now there's only you." A fireman placed Frank beside us and he slumped back against the truck and closed his eyes, his breathing choked and ragged. LIFE NET. I watched as white-coated paramedics hustled over to us and began running their hands over our bodies like policemen performing a strip search.

As I combed my hands through my hair I felt the singed ends. And then suddenly I realized I ached all over and my bare feet began to itch. Nina and Frank were both coughing and choking as the paramedics tried to herd us into the ambulance. "No," I said. "I want to call my brother." But what I really wanted to do was watch the fire consume my parents' home. I wanted to see every house we'd lived in go up in flame and smoke like this one. I wanted Drew to see it too.

Sparks shot into the night, windblown stars whirling away. I missed some of the interplay between the fire and the sheets of water because there was a long argument with the paramedics about going to the hospital, which Frank finally settled with an authoritative: "Let her do what she God damn wants." I was six years old again. The sun came up today because Frank said it was okay. Someone from across the court volunteered to call Drew. Even Nina realized we were all safe, but only after she demanded our reassurance that there was only the three of us. "Drew's on his way," I said.

"Julia's gone," Nina said, but she looked doubtful, as if expecting my sister to come walking out of the flaming ruins of her house. "Julia's been gone a long time, hasn't she?"

"Yes," my father said. "It's just a house. We'll get another."

My attention was on the shell of my parents' home as one of the ambulances pulled away. Wood, plaster, lathing. I once visited a house in Florida made entirely by hand of cut coral. Coral walls, stairs, garden chairs, tables. There was a tower composed of almost three hundred tons of coral rock. The stones were said to weigh more than those used in the Great Pyramid at Giza. There was an obelisk and renditions of Mars and Saturn. All made of coral. That house would never burn. Chunks of coral bigger than the pillars at Stonehenge. The Coral Castle of Homestead, Florida. A man's life work. Coral. Stone. It would last a thousand years.

The life of this fire was drowning under the heavy blasts

of water. Firemen scurried around the burning house, destroying walls with axes, blowing out windows with water. If this house had been out in the country, away from any other structures, I would have enjoyed watching it burn to the ground. But the walls and the roof of the row house next to my parent's was also on fire by now. A paramedic settled me into a police car to wait for Drew, with the promise Drew would take me to the hospital as soon as he arrived. Another ambulance sped off, Frank and Nina and an old woman who lived next door all locked up inside.

Safely in the police car, the fire now looked like a movie I was watching at a drive-in theater. Pulling the blanket around me, I got out and stood behind the hook and ladder truck. The air smelled like a dirty ashtray. The building popped and hissed as the fire crew worked to keep the blaze contained. I imagined chairs going up in a flower of flame, dresses in closets vanishing in whispers, pots and pans melting as slowly as pouring honey. What had we lost? I kept asking myself. Was there some piece of our history Frank and Nina had saved which was now vanished completely? I thought of Julia, as gone as if she'd existed only in my mind. But if Nina saved paper bags and broken screws, perhaps she'd saved something of Julia, a childhood toy, a favorite book. Gone.

Drew pulled up in his BMW and I watched as he stood for a moment looking at the flaming ruins. The fire now snaked up the charred walls, fingers reaching for the sky where the roof had been. I could see wafer-thin Giacometti faces in the burned struts. I felt like a child again as I walked over to my brother. Shark attacks at the Aquarium. The unpredictability of every single event.

Drew put his arm around me and pulled me close. "Nina's right," he said. "You're really making a mess of this redecorating job."

"Oh, it's redecorated, all right. A brand new start." I

watched the yellow and blue light of the fire. Primary colors. "Do you suppose ghosts are exterminated by fire? You know, like witches and vampires when they're burned at the stake?"

"Witches and vampires." Drew seemed to be truly considering this. "No. I think ghosts are different than witches and vampires. And I don't think we're watching any ghost souls wafting in the smoke. There's nothing but junk feeding that fire. It's a wonder this hasn't happened before."

We watched the firemen beat down the crest of the flames as the sun began to rise. "Nothing but junk," Drew repeated. He didn't ask about Nina or Frank, he didn't ask about me, merely held me in the wing of his arm as the firemen steadily doused the flames. Soon the fire was more smoke than anything else and the air around us hissed, snakes whispering in my ear.

Drew laughed. "I used to try to think of all the places we lived. Keep a list of them, every house in its proper order. Try to remember the different bedrooms I slept in, the different kitchens. Now they just run together. This could be any of those houses we once called home."

"It's all of them," I said. "Spontaneous combustion. Imagine it. As we stand here two dozen houses all across the country are going up in smoke and flame."

He looked sadly at the flaming ruins. "You're probably right. Maybe in that sense a lot of ghosts are going up in smoke tonight. Don't forget, all that junk we hauled around all those years was a kind of anchor. Remember when we'd open the boxes in a new place? Mom looked at everything as if she never expected to see it again. Her form of Christmas. She was always so delighted at rediscovering all of her junk."

A memory of my mother, her hair caught up in a paisley turban, an old blouse tied at the waist, a pair of my father's blue jeans held up by his big black belt. "Oh look, kids. The ginger jars Aunt Constance brought back from the Orient."

Drew asked only one question before we left for the hospital. "You do that?" he wanted to know.

"Nina. I think it started in her pile of papers to be read."

"Figures," Drew said. "Want some clothes before I take you to the hospital?"

The sun was beginning to rise, a bright orange disk behind the plumes of smoke.

As a child I believed the world was anything you could imagine and I was filled with a desire to own a revolving glass door. I'd seen one in a department store when I was five or six and wanted it the way some children pine for a puppy or a bike. I expected Santa to bring me one and set it up in our living room on Christmas morning, gleaming glass and shining brass. I would walk round and round in that door, swinging past all the furniture. I believed I would be able to go faster and faster inside the glass door, running, making myself dizzy the way you get when you push yourself higher and higher on a swing. That Christmas morning was my first great disappointment. How much we intuit as children, yet aren't experienced enough to really know. I've been in that revolving glass door all my life, sometimes going faster, sometimes slower. My life has whirled past me. It's a magic door, just the way I wished it to be when I was a child. I can step out of one of those pie-shaped wedges and into a brand new slice of life.

This was most obviously apparent when I was in high

school. Most girls are given curfews when they go out on dates, but I wasn't. Not because my parents trusted me but simply because they were too busy. My mother read. My father worked. Since I didn't have a curfew I was very popular; the boys thought they could keep me in the back seat of their cars until I gave them what they wanted.

But I didn't give them what they wanted and spent most of my dates wrestling with the boys until I wore them out. Discouraged at best, hating and cursing me at worst, the boys dropped me off, not even bothering to walk me to the door. That moment, opening the front door to our house, was worse than wrestling with the boys. Often I thought of sleeping on the front stoop until morning, so I could avoid my mother. But I would get cold and uncomfortable and eventually always went inside.

My mother would be on the couch, a bottle of scotch on the coffee table, two glasses, one usually about half full. "Oh, Mrs. White," she'd say. "I'm so glad you're here. I was hoping you'd drop by tonight."

"Hi Mom. It's me, Maura. I think I'll go on up to bed." Her blonde hair was carefully combed over her shoulders, her makeup emphasized her large, dramatic eyes and generous mouth. She arranged herself on the couch to reveal her long, shapely legs under the sheer nightgown and peignoir sets my father always bought her. Those sexy nightgowns intrigued me since, as far as I knew, she never wore them to bed, only to sit through the night on the couch. What ran through my father's mind as year after year, Christmas, anniversary, birthday, he purchased those silky gowns? She always left them strewn across the dresser, like her jewelry, when she finally climbed into bed after my father left for work in the mornings.

"Nina. Call me Nina. Sit down. Sit down. Here." She'd reach over and splash scotch into the empty glass. The timing was tricky. Nina, when sober, always appeared a bit false, as

36

if she were putting on an act to hide a secret flaw. Frankly, I enjoyed my mother most when we were drinking, not when she was sober or drunk, but those early stages about a quarter of the way down the bottle, when she was just loose enough to appear to be actually talking to you, revealing something about herself.

"You know, I was just thinking about a winter I spent with Constance and Leland. We went marlin fishing. I caught my first marlin that day. And the thing I really remember was seeing a giant sea turtle. It looked like the roof of a De Soto floating on the ocean. We were way out at sea, couldn't even get a glimpse of the land and it was like we'd been transported to another world. As I was fighting the marlin I truly believed if he pulled me overboard I'd be able to live in the water just as surely as I could live in the air. If I pulled that marlin out of the water I knew he would die. And he did, of course." She took a sip of her drink, savoring the scotch as she rolled it around in her mouth.

"I landed him, well, I was too little to actually land him. Uncle Leland helped me. But I fought him for an hour, watched him leap out of the sea, fought him all by myself until I tired him out. Constance kept telling me not to quit. Aunt Constance never let anyone quit." She gave a short laugh. "I'm surprised Constance even died. She would never quit anything. Never quit anything."

"Mom, I want to go to bed." But I learned very early that would be useless. The couple of times I did mount the stairs and try to retreat to my room, my mother would be right behind me, the bottle of scotch in hand, and she would sit on the end of my bed and continue talking to Mrs. White, whoever she thought that was. A therapist told me to think of those stories as grown-up lullabies, meant to help me fall away from troubles and into sweet dreams. Marlin fishing. Sea turtles. My sweet dreams are of sailing away in a yellow biplane. Flight. Freedom. I know other people dream of settling down. Or owning something as fabulous as a race-horse. Or being loved by someone who understands you perfectly. All very nice ideas, just not my notion of sweet dreams.

There was a lucidity in my mother's madness. The first time I went up to my room and locked the door I heard her slump down against the wall and continue talking, only it was just a murmur, like the sound of water flowing slowly in a brook. The next morning when I arose to go to school she was gone. But when I came home from school that day I found she'd removed all the locks from all the bedroom doors. When my father asked her about it she said it was a safety precaution. In case the house caught fire we could all get out that much more quickly.

"But I haven't told you about the turtle yet," my mother would continue. "It was as big as the roof of a car, and the same color as Leland's De Soto. Funny, but at first I thought it was our De Soto, floating there next to the boat in case we wanted to go for a ride. But then the turtle lifted its head and looked at us. Turtles have yellow eyes. That's when I thought if I fell overboard I'd be able to live in the water as easily as in the air. The turtle appeared when the marlin was making a deep dive, trying to get free. I just had to let him have his head or I'd snap the line. So there I am, a kid, strapped into the chair with the line whizzing out, watching this turtle watching us. And that's when I knew I could beat that marlin, when I knew he couldn't live in the air. Aunt Constance had the marlin stuffed and hung it over the sofa in the living room."

"What happened to it?"

"Oh, I think after Leland died, when Constance closed the house, she gave it away. She was always giving things away. As if anyone would need a stuffed marlin."

"But why didn't she give it to you? It was your marlin."

"Because I wasn't there, you see. Constance was like

that. I'm sure she would have given me my marlin if I'd been there. But when she cleaned out the Florida house I was somewhere else, I don't remember where, and so Constance forgot about me. Besides, Frank would never let me keep a stuffed marlin. He gets seasick, don't you know, every time he gets on a boat." She poured more scotch into our glasses. "I've been trying to talk Frank into taking me to Europe. Just the two of us. Maura's old enough to take care of Drew and Julia. Frank and I could take one of those cruise ships to Europe, have a real vacation, for god's sakes. But, of course," she lifted her eyebrows in her dramatic expression, "Frank would never think of taking a vacation. And on a ship? Don't be silly. Do you think Frank would go for the idea of being seasick for a week? We went to Cuba by boat once, years ago, just the two of us. It spoiled the whole trip. After that we didn't go anywhere we couldn't drive."

"Mom, I'm not old enough to take care of Drew and Julia. I don't want to take care of them. And if Daddy doesn't want to go on a vacation, why don't you just go by yourself?" That was my plan. Since the age of fourteen I'd become fanatic about saving my money. It seems so silly now. I counted the days until high school graduation like a prisoner. As if leaving home would automatically jettison all my problems and no new problems would ever plague me. They say youth is wasted on the young, but it's not youth so much as that innocent sense of the possibilities of the imagination. In that sense, my mother has never grown up.

Her eyes opened wide, the way she did when she flirted with my father. "You know Frank would never let me go alone." She leaned toward me. "Frank's afraid I'll meet someone else. And I would too." She swept her hand through her hair. "I'm still a very attractive woman. I could find another man. If I go on a vacation by myself it would be with the express intention of finding someone to really take care of me. Frank knows that. That's why he would never let me go off by

myself. But you know, Mrs. White, one of these days I'm
going to make up my mind and really leave him. You can't
imagine what it's like being married to a man like Frank.
Frank isn't a man. He's a machine." She shook her head sorrowfully, little halos of light catching her blonde hair. "My
mother was right. I should have never married Frank. I should
have married that Air Force lieutenant. I wanted to be a
dancer, did I tell you that? I can still tap dance. I was going to
marry an actor. I heard he's performed off-Broadway."

The synapses in my mother's brain are as jumbled as a
pile of pick-up sticks. Sometimes I imagine her mind as an
Eskimo skipping from ice floe to ice floe. The floes are all
different colors. Mauve, chartreuse, turquoise, amber, kelly
green.

When my mother dies I'm going to have her tombstone
inscribed 'She danced in her dreams.' Her dreams are more
real to me than the facts of her life. My memory has become
infected with the way she saw herself. Singing in a nightclub,
walking into a grand hotel, flying solo across the ocean. She
wanted to join the Rockettes. She thought of herself as the
type of woman Hemingway would have married.

Yet for some naive reason I believed my mother had a
perfect childhood. I used to envy the aunts and uncles, cous-
ins and grandparents, her sense of extended family, of relatives to take care of her. The people in my immediate family
have brief lives, a flash of color and then they're gone.
There's no way to check out the stories. But a perfect childhood doesn't translate into a perfect life. Nor will a wretched
childhood mean that you've paid your dues and insure future
happiness.

After Drew had checked me through the hospital, and
I'd been given some kind of sedative, I lay in his bed in his
apartment overlooking the city and thought about all this.
Who were these people, my parents? My mother and I had
been closest when I had been Mrs. White. And my father?

40

As a child I was always jealous of my parents' fights. All that focused energy and attention. It was thrilling, awesome as a volcano. I loved to hear Frank yelling at my mother, the power of his voice. To us kids, our father was a remote figure, as difficult to imagine and conjure up as an image of God. We didn't know where he went every day, what he did. What tides dictated where we would live from year to year, sometimes season to season. Our father passed through our lives with the same consistency and familiarity as your favorite checker at the grocery store.

Frank was always remote, as if he were handling a beautiful, poisonous snake, always cautious, as if he lived his life walking under perpetual ladders, waiting for bricks to drop upon his head.

I can count the memories of my father on one hand. No matter where we lived one memory serves for every evening Frank came home. My parents would share a bottle of scotch and talk about things only grown-ups could discuss. "Go on now," our mother would say. "This isn't talk for children." When Frank would turn on the TV to watch the news Drew and I would take off, on our bikes in the summer or merely bundled up in our heaviest clothes if it was winter. Drew and I loved to sit in trees during snowstorms, feeling the wind rocking through our bodies.

Weekends Frank always had some construction project going. He built a patio in Trenton, a dock on Lake Erie, a garage in Indiana. He painted a house in Ohio, refinished a basement in Virginia, tiled a bathroom in New York. Sometimes he enlisted Drew and Julia and me to help. He called these "family days" which meant Drew and Julia and I hung around to fetch beers, hammers, wrenches, whatever Frank needed to work on his projects. Our parents once bought a house facing Lake Erie and although giant boulders held the bank, Frank wanted to put in a dock. He secured dozens of railroad ties for the crib and then proceeded to fill the crib with rocks. At one point a giant crane was erected near the railroad ties to pry rocks out of the water, raise them, and drop them into the big square crib. Drew and I spent that whole summer scouting the beach for stones we could carry back to the crib. Julia, the baby, sat peacefully under a tree munching on dog biscuits.

When I was fourteen my father and I spent about three weeks together. After Drew was born Frank and Nina bought a dog, Ajax, and he became part of our family. I loved Ajax, told him all my secrets, and usually preferred being with Ajax than with any other member of my family, even Drew. I knew other kids had dogs, and some of their dogs died. But Ajax would never die. He'd always be my friend.

Ajax was twelve when his back legs began to give out. He was a golden labrador with beautifully feathered legs and ruff. Ajax had dignity. Ajax had integrity. It was embarrassing when Ajax began to totter. It was shocking when Ajax fell. It was frightening when I heard Ajax's claws scrabbling on the linoleum as he tried to rise.

Each night for about three weeks my father would come home from work and pick up Ajax and put him in the back seat of the car. I don't know why I was allowed to come along on these trips, but I was. My only responsibility was opening doors so my father could carry Ajax into the vet's office. Each night we visited a different vet. Each night the vet said the same thing: it would be best to put Ajax down.

For some reason I still don't understand, my father had no intention of putting Ajax down. Finally we found a vet who was willing to perform an operation. He would cut through the golden coat, into the hip socket, and scrape away the growth on the bones that was the reason Ajax kept falling down.

On a Wednesday night my father picked up Ajax and put him in the back seat. We drove to another veterinary office and I held the door as my father carried Ajax in. I couldn't really understand what my father and the vet were saying. In the previous few weeks I'd asked my father what the doctors had said, but Frank could never really explain anything more than the fact Ajax had a growth on his hip. This Wednesday night we left Ajax at the veterinarian's. We drove home in silence.

The next night my parents sat drinking silently. Drew and I were too depressed to break out our bikes and just walked aimlessly through the neighborhood until it grew quite dark. Friday night was the same. On Saturday morning my father told me to get in the car. I didn't ask where we were going but my hopes rose as I recognized we were headed for the vet's. There was Ajax, his beautiful coat shaved over his hips, ugly black stitches running along the sides of his spine. A big white plastic bell fanned out above his collar. The vet explained that was so he wouldn't chew out the stitches.

My father carried Ajax to the car and we brought him home. I spent hours next to the pallet I'd prepared for him, feeding Ajax tidbits of steak. His hips quivered and he squirreled around, trying to scratch the itchy stitches. The following Wednesday we took Ajax back to the vet to have the stitches removed. Ajax was as good as new.

In all that time, the closest I've ever spent with my father, Frank had nothing to say to me. He talked to Ajax. "It's going to be okay, old sport. You're a trooper." Ajax kept his bright eyes on us. I can see now why Frank enjoys his SPCA work on the weekends. The rapt attention of the kittens and puppies as they listen to the cadence of his voice.

The following year, at sixteen, I left home to go to college. I secretly believed Ajax died of a broken heart once I left. In March I got a call from my mother. It was the first time anyone from my family had called me at college. Nina was crying. "Oh, Mrs. White. Ajax is dead," she sobbed. "He was my only friend. He understood me. Now I'm all alone.

Could you come over? It seems I haven't seen you in such a long time."

I couldn't sympathize with my mother. She had my father. She had Drew and Julia. She could get another dog. I was eight hundred miles away at college where no dogs were allowed. Ajax had been the thread of my childhood, like beads on a string. No matter where we lived Ajax had been there. We'd kept him in hotels, trailer parks, rooming houses, foster homes, as well as the houses we lived in. With his passing it was as if all those places never happened. They became scattered in my mind. There was nothing solid and dependable to count on.

And so now I lay in my brother's bed. My parents were resting at the hospital. My brother was at work. I was sedated and not thinking clearly. All I could remember was my mother's loneliness, how she talked to me when she thought I was someone else. And my father's devotion to a dog.

Drew and I once found a dead duck in a field, miles from any water. It shimmered before our eyes, while everything in the tall grass around it lay perfectly still in the hot summer afternoon. We watched the feathers tremble, although the eyes were glazed and its feet were gone, mysteriously gone. I found a stick and lifted one wing. Underneath we saw a colony of wriggling maggots, feeding on the fleshy carcass of the duck. This is one of my earliest memories of transformation.

Memories can be transformed with the same certainty as a decaying duck. Although my parents' home held no memories for me I kept seeing the different houses we'd lived in as part of that fire. Flammable. Inflammable. Holocaust. Spontaneous combustion. Two dozen houses all across the country mysteriously bursting into flame on that one given night. The shimmering flames animating those houses, those memories, like the maggots in the duck Drew and I found.

I've always liked the idea that the words ravel and un-

ravel mean the same thing. Ravel: to separate or undo. Disentangle, entangle. Confuse. Unwoven, untwisted or unwound.
Unravel: to disengage or separate the threads. Disentangle.
To resolve, to clear up. Flammable: capable of being easily
ignited and burning with extreme rapidity. Inflammable:
flammable. Sometimes I get the feeling the whole world is
raveling, unraveling, or about to burst into flame, cause
unknown. Holocaust. Spontaneous combustion.

That first morning Drew lent me a baseball shirt and a
pair of jeans, much too large and too long, to take me down
to the hospital where they dressed my burns. They wanted to
keep me for observation. Smoke inhalation, delayed shock.
But I preferred to stay with Drew. We visited our parents, who
had decided to remain in the hospital, Nina for smoke inhalation, Frank for cuts and contusions from his leap into the
tree. We never spoke of it but we all realized they had nowhere else to go.

Drew and I drove back past the house and watched the
arson inspectors sifting through the ruins. The path of the fire
was easy to trace: the newspapers, the curtains, the wall
housing the gas lines. Had there been a funny smell associated with the house before the fire? they wanted to know.
Shoddy construction, they said. Mr. Bosson, the chief arson
inspector, was puzzled about the sudden spread of the fire.
You might have a lawsuit here, he told us. Yellow police
streamers cordoned off the charred ruins. I didn't tell him
about the scotch. What had Nina been thinking of? Had she
thrown that quart of scotch on the flames simply to see what
would happen? Or was it inevitable, because of the shoddy
construction of their new house, that their home would have
gone up anyway?

Perhaps we all dream of what it might be like to throw
ourselves from the top of a building or off a bridge. We don't
necessarily want to die, only to know what it's like to fly away
from your problems. A form of half suicide. Imagine throw-

ing yourself off a bridge and as you near the water you can say to yourself: This is what it's like to leave all your problems behind. Magically, once you know that, you can be returned to the bridge as complete and whole as you were when you jumped. But your problems have been dashed to pieces as they hit the water.

Nina might have been simply curious to see what would happen to the fire when she poured that scotch on the flames. Perhaps she wanted to watch the house burn, and having seen that, expected to return to the couch to mull it over.

That was Drew's theory, at any rate. He'd come to believe our mother was as irresponsible as a child. Perhaps she was suffering from the early stages of Alzheimer's disease, a disorientation that led her to believe the scotch was water. "Nina's never really been able to save anything," my brother said. "Look at us. About as useful as all her broken clocks and burnt-out light bulbs. We get everything wrong. Give her a dark night and Nina's liable to rave on about a clear view of the stars. And ignore the fact there's a major power outage."

"There's nothing you can do about a major power outage," I said.

"There you have it," Drew replied. "A perfect description of our family. You and I at least know it's a power outage. Dad will hunt around for candles we don't have. Mom will think they've turned up the volume on the stars."

I'd spent a day in Drew's bed, but that didn't accomplish much. Onward through the fog. There were clothes and toiletries to buy and I tried to organize the items as if I were awakening on a bright, clean day and could take nothing for granted. Priorities were reduced to whatever came to mind first. Toothbrush, toothpaste, mouthwash, deodorant. Underwear, sweater, jeans, shoes. The shoes hurt my blistered feet. Makeup, vitamins. Coat. Purse, although I had nothing to put in it. All to simply get out of bed and off into the world. The next day I shopped for myself and Nina, Drew shopped for Frank. I was a bit surprised to realize I'd spent over three hundred dollars on simply getting myself up and dressed for a day.

Drew took me back to his apartment and rubbed salve on my raw feet and listened to me cough while we looked out over the city. My chest felt as if it had been scrubbed with sandpaper and I didn't want to talk. What was there to say? Who should we notify? What about their insurance? Where would they go once they were released from the hospital? What did our parents need to start over again? Senior citizens. Golden Agers. They now had less at hand than teen-aged newlyweds.

Some of this we'd been practicing for all our lives. We'd shopped and cooked and cleaned since we were old enough to go to school. Frank had always been too busy. Nina never cared.

'My mother always had help,' our mother would say proudly, with a toss of her head, whenever we had to clean up for the real-estate people in preparation for another move. 'If I hadn't married your father I probably would have had help too. It's impossible to raise children without help. That's why I never became a dancer.' My mother has always altered history to suit her notions.

But she did have help, Drew and me. In the second grade I met a girl who told me a rhyme she'd memorized. 'Breakfast, lunch, and dinner I ate. / My bus number is 88.' That's how she knew which bus to get on to get home from school. Getting to school was easy, she said. Her mother walked her to the corner and waited with her until the big yellow school bus pulled up and opened its doors. Going home was more difficult since there was an entire field of big yellow school buses outside and only one of them, number 88, would take her home.

I told her the numbers I'd learned. Highland-3389 was the grocery store. Belmont-8972 was the department store. Madison-5164 was my father's office. I could control the world through the phone. Anything we needed was at the other end of the line. In the days before extensions we learned how to dial and how to shout. 'Call the grocer,' our mother would yell down the stairs, and she'd wait until I dialed. 'Is that the store?' She always checked to see if we connected with the right number. 'Tell them we need a quart of milk,' and she'd pause while I said 'A quart of milk,' 'a carton of Luckies,' again the pause while I transferred her request, 'a bottle of Old Smuggler, a can of split-pea soup, a loaf of Wonder bread, some Velveeta cheese.' About an hour later a car would pull up in front of our house and someone would ring the bell and hand me a bag of groceries.

I didn't realize phones could be used for simple conversations until I was in high school. But by then it was too late to break a habit. To this day I don't enjoy talking on the phone, except to talk to Drew. Phones are to convey information, not for entertainment.

To us, this was a normal part of growing up. It wasn't until I was in junior high and a Home Ec. class scheduled a section on grocery shopping that I discovered not everyone learned how to order groceries before they could read.

But late that afternoon Drew and I weren't sure how far we should go in ordering a new life for our parents. We'd never chosen the places they lived, the houses we'd occupied. We had no knowledge about their insurance, their health plans, their income. One night when I was in seventh grade my father called us kids into the living room and made us sit down in front of him. 'This is my paycheck,' he told us as he held a piece of paper out toward us. 'This is how much they take out for Social Security,' and he pointed to a number. He pointed to all the numbers, insurance, retirement, state tax, Federal tax, all his deductions. The whole time he kept his thumb over the amount he made. I was learning fractions that year and realized the numbers were meaningless unless we knew how much the total sum was. But when I asked my father about this he said, 'Your mother doesn't think it's a good idea for me to talk money with you kids.' And thus ended our first and only lesson about finance.

"They'll have to stay here," Drew said as he rubbed salve on my burns.

"Where are we going to put them here?" I looked around his apartment overlooking the city, the couch where I would sleep that night, the bedroom where Drew slept. The place had bachelor spelled all over it, lots of high-tech electronic gear, and a litter of plastic shrouds from the dry cleaner, unwashed dishes, half-read magazines and books.

"They can have my bed," Drew said. But as we looked at each other we knew that wouldn't work for long. Their new home was a three-bedroom affair, Frank's bedroom, Nina's bedroom, and a guest room where I'd been staying. Frank and Nina needed space the way fish need water.

"Come on," Drew said. "Let's go for a ride. I want to show you something."

We slid into Drew's BMW, a Bud Powell tape already in the deck. I was surprised when Drew took the turn away from town and out into the countryside. "Where are we going?"

"I probably would have shown you this anyhow. But I had this fantasy that one day I'd call you up in San Francisco, or wherever the hell you'd be living, and offer you a round-trip ticket to come see it. See it when it was done. But then, sometimes I don't even believe it will ever get finished."

"What are you talking about?" As a banker, or maybe because he's lived in one place during all the time I've drifted around the country, Drew and I have learned different lessons. He can talk about investments, capital gains. Words that make no pictures in my mind. Sometimes I listen to him as if he's speaking a foreign language, or imagine what he's saying isn't words, it's music.

"I bought a little place. A kind of retreat. A place to retire."

"Retire? Who can afford to retire?"

"Well, that's the whole point, you see. That's all men really do. All men want to get rich. Get rich, retire, and spend your days wasting your money." He shifted down a gear. "It's been rough since they moved here, Emery. I haven't told them about this place. I really wasn't even thinking about buying land. Sometimes things just happen. But it just felt right and now I'm all tied up in it."

Drew pulled off the highway onto a dirt road. I watched the sun slipping over the silvered fields. Stretches of open grassland were patterned by the immense shadow of the boxy BMW. The bright reds and oranges of the maples shimmered in the light breeze. Barbed wire ran along both sides of the dusty lane.

I wasn't familiar with this part of the country; we'd never lived near here when I was a kid and once I discovered how healing distance could be I'd never lived within five hundred miles of my parents. Last year when Drew told me they'd bought a condo across town from him I fully expected he'd pull up stakes and travel, like I had been doing for the last twenty-five years. But Drew and I aren't alike in that sense. Instead of moving away, my solution to any problem, Drew became even more settled. He now owned land.

The farmland looked Amish to me, the rolling hills and fields, the toasty-colored grass. I wanted to see solid, bright red barns instead of the broken, gray weathered buildings. Imagine plowing these fields with hearty draft horses, the men in soft hats and unruly beards, the skirts of the women dragging in the dust.

The wind waved the grasses like a gentle hand passing by, stroking them as you would a cat. The late afternoon sun warmed the car like sitting by a fire. Following the dirt road the fields became more golden and sparse. Stands of ancient trees flanked us. Drew made another turn and stopped the car.

"Get out and open the gate," he said.

"You open the damn gate." My body ached all over and it seemed as if the only comfortable position I'd been in since the fire the other night was slouched in the front seat of his car.

"Emery." His voice was very patient, as if he were talking to a small child. "I can get out of the car, open the gate, get back in the car, drive through, get out of the car, close the gate, get back in the car, and we can proceed. I've done it hundreds of times. It's a bit simpler if you open and close the gate while I do the driving."

"Oh. Right." Of course. But Drew had forgotten I was more familiar with flagging down taxis than the logistics of country gates. Wilderness survival has never been my strong suit.

There were two more gates and the surrounding countryside became hillier and more densely forested. Then, at the crest of a hill, Drew stopped and got out of the car. "There's a nice view from here. It'll give you the lay of the land."

Standing beside Drew I looked down into the shadows of the late afternoon light and saw a lake, and a couple of buildings separated by a mile or so across a rocky ridge.

"My kingdom," Drew said, waving his hand at the valley. "Or rather, the bank's kingdom. I'm only the king."

"You own all this?" Perhaps I studied too much Native American history, a passion of Paris' since he's part Cherokee. I can understand owning structures, houses, but I never could quite grasp owning land. Land, to me, is like a strong-willed horse. You might be able to ride him, but he'll go where he wants. Perhaps that's why I love earthquakes, knowing the earth moves.

"This whole side of the lake," Drew said. "It belonged to a hunting club in New Jersey. It came across my desk at the bank. This was right about the time I was looking for a house for Nina and Frank. I'd look at a couple of houses, and then drive out here and look at the lake. One day I just bought it."

We drove down the hill, rabbits and pheasants scuttling ahead of us. I remembered a story I'd heard about a car hitting a deer. The deer bounded away. The driver died, his head crushed into the windshield.

We stopped in front of an old building, its original purpose now impossible to determine. It was one story, with a steeply pitched roof like that of a church, hidden among the branches of the old trees. "There used to be a community of people up here about a hundred and fifty years ago," Drew said. "Over the crest of that ridge there's a lot of open plateau land. This was the church and town meeting hall. They had one paid employee, someone who could read, write, and ride. He was the preacher, the mayor, the teacher, the postal officer, and sometimes the doctor and dentist as well. He lived in that little building over there." He pointed to a shack under a collapsed roof. Rhododendron and rhubarb grew out of the windows and what must have been the door.

Inside, the far end was a huge fireplace, the fieldstone chimney lost above the rafters. Abandoned furniture littered the room. "This was the base camp for the hunting club," Drew said. "When they bought the place, back in the twenties, it was probably empty. A place to get in out of the rain." He walked over to a long bar built into the side, a partition. "I talked to one of the trustees and he said they paid some of the local people to fix this up. This is actually a very fine wood stove here and it still works."

The stove was enormous, with six burners and two ovens. A washtub up on blocks under a pump head must

SARA VOGAN

have served as a sink. Several narrow cabinets hung from the walls. The bar had a solid chopping-block top and served to divide the kitchen area from the rest of the room.

"This is what I love." Drew moved to a closet-like structure built into a corner near the fieldstone fireplace. He opened the door to a twenties-deco bathroom. Sink, toilet, shower, all done in pastel tile blocks. "Our great white hunters believed in sanitation. No shitting in the woods for these dudes. This must have cost them a fortune. There's a good well and the limepit's nicely situated away from the water. There's a holding tank up on the roof. Useless now. You have to flush out the basin with water from the pump. But I think it's a nice touch."

"You've stayed here?"

"I build a big fire and curl up in my sleeping bag. It's the sleep of angels, I tell you. I just use the kitchen for storage. I like the old cowboy-style cooking over the fire."

"I bet you've got a dozen flannel shirts."

Drew smiled. "You got it. Work boots. A whole different wardrobe from my banker's monkey suits."

I suddenly saw how much of my father my brother had internalized. The somber business suits, Monday through Friday nine to five. And the flannel shirts and jeans, work boots, for this project. So like what we called my father's Saturday clothes that he wore while he tiled bathrooms, built garages. The dock project.

He took my arm and steered me out of the cabin. "But this is only the last outpost of civilization. You haven't seen the castle yet."

We got back in the car and continued along the dirt road, over the ridge for a mile or so and then, suddenly, around a bend, I could see where Drew's dream took shape. Rising up beside the lake were the beginnings of a house.

As children Drew and I shared one burning passion: unfinished houses. The sight of all those pale boards reach-

54

ing up toward the sky like gigantic fingers always thrilled us. The crisp smell of sawdust stirred our imaginations. Long summer evenings gave us a chance to search out houses under construction. After dinner, or if we didn't have dinner, when our father turned on the TV news, we'd hop on our bikes and go in search of new houses. The 1950s were prime for that. Houses sprang up like spring wildflowers peeking through the crusty snow on the first truly warm day. To us, these sketches of dwellings were ships, planes, islands, caves.

And now Drew was building his own house and my first thought was whether he would ever want to see it finished, whether he really thought he would live here, retire here. So like our father, who never finished any of his projects. On a clearing facing the lake stood the foundation and the skeleton of the first floor, those fingers against the sky. A big-bellied cement mixer, stacks of lumber, rolls of tar paper, a portajohn, everything except workmen, crowded the layout of the house. I could tell, even from this bare outline, that Drew wasn't building one of those boxy dwellings we'd despised as children. This house would have many levels, maybe decks. I imagined it going up as a stack of various-sized building blocks. "Castle indeed," I said. The foundation appeared huge, looming in front of us in the late afternoon shadows.

"It's not as big as it looks. Come on, I'll show you."

We could have been ten and twelve again, only this time Drew played the part of the tour guide. As children, when we'd find a new house one of us, usually me, would tour guide the layout. 'An island,' I'd say. 'Here's the fresh-water spring, but over here,' and I'd walk a few steps away to a sketched-in bathroom or closet, 'is a poisonous volcano. This is the forbidden area, but you can't get to the freshwater spring without going around the poisonous volcano.'

Now Drew was doing the tour guiding. "A lot of this

is going to be decking. There's no basement. I don't have money to sink into the ground. So I had the architect design a series of rising decks. If I hit it big on the market I'd like to retire here full time."

"I had a lover once who took his retirement first," I said. "He didn't get a job until he was thirty-eight." Hell, they were all like that.

"Nice work if you can get it. You really know how to pick them, Emery. I've worked full-time for the last eighteen years. Do you know in the service or the post office you can retire after twenty years?"

"But not in banking, huh?" I couldn't think of any of my lovers who'd had a solid, establishment-type job. As if I was allergic to anyone who could commit to anything. Nothing like my brother the banker, my father the engineer. I'd dated musicians, landscape architects, perpetual students. Even Paris changed careers so that each time our paths crossed, he was in the process of becoming someone else.

"Only if you play the market," Drew was saying. "Come on up here. This is the first deck. I'm going to put a hot tub in, later, once everything's done. Even if California falls into the sea, it will have left the world the hot tub."

"California didn't influence you enough, baby brother. Even a novice Californian would put the hot tub in first. I think it's the greatest invention since the wheel."

He was lost in his own vision of the house. He climbed to the top platform, reached down to help me up. "This will be decking." He walked over and put his hand against the first strut of the house. "If you step through this door, Madam, I'll be glad to show you the inside."

I allowed him to open an imaginary door and walked across the plywood base for the flooring of his living room. "I'm going to take out the fireplace in the hunting lodge and rebuild it over there." He pointed to the far wall. "Standard stuff on this floor. Except I'm going to put in a solarium. Grow orchids."

"Orchids? What do you know about growing orchids?"

"Hydroponics. Same as raising dope. When I lived with Ginny, we used to grow dope in the bathroom. Back when all that was fashionable. No sense letting all that expertise go to waste. I could grow my own vanilla beans. Did you know vanilla is an orchid?"

"Cut the crap, Drew. Orchids and dope. That's like saying I should become a petty thief because I've been in jail." The analogy wasn't exactly right. I'd spent nights in jail as a protest against the war. Not for petty theft. Petty theft seems pointless to me. If you're going to steal, steal millions.

He draped his arm over my shoulder. "Emery, love, in some ways you are a petty thief. You snatch time. Keep it as your own."

"What the hell do you mean by that?" I never think of myself as stealing time.

"You're over forty, kiddo. And you're living the same as you did at twenty. Not many people can get away with that. You've got to have stolen it from somewhere because life just doesn't let you get away with that kind of behavior."

"A lot you know. The only difference for you is you've got more money than you did at twenty. You're even stuck in the same town."

"You see?" He smiled, lighting up his face in the dying purple sunset. "That's how I know. If you listen to the same song over and over you hear different things. You get deeper into the music. But you, you just touch down like a tornado on top of all kinds of music. You might know more music than I do but the music I know, I know better. I know it more intimately. I know what the composer was thinking while you go 'Gee, how'd he do that?'"

"Bullshit. I love this, Drew. Especially since you've got a deaf ear and can't carry a tune in a knapsack. What do you know about the way I know music?" I'd learned music from Paris. I doubted if Drew and I had a handful of songs in common.

He shrugged. "We all grow up in different ways."

As he walked me through the floor plan the house took on walls. I saw a spiral staircase when he pointed to the stairwell. "Old lighthouses," he said. "Beautiful places. If you stick around long enough I'll take you on one of my salvage trips."

"Stick around," I repeated. "I don't know what I'm doing here in the first place. I should go home."

"Guilt," he said. "The only surefire motivator in our family. Besides, you can't leave now. Things are more fucked up than when you arrived."

"Well, I don't know how staying around is going to help anything."

"It won't," Drew said. "It won't help anyone but you. You want to know what's going on with Flotsam and Jetsam? Now's your chance."

"Nina says he's dying."

"Maybe he is," Drew said. "I really can't tell. But this way, when he dies, we won't be strangers. It's not something I can really articulate. I just feel like I'm picking it up, like osmosis."

"You've had a year with them. I'm definitely not staying a year."

"Right," Drew said. "You're so busy."

Until two weeks ago there was no possibility I could just pack a bag and fly back to my parents, as if on call. Two weeks ago I had a job, a career. At some point I'll undoubtedly have another job, another career. But my mother's call came four days after my last day at work. The advertising firm I'd worked for was relocating to New York as part of a larger outfit. It's a small firm and although I do good work, I've never liked my boss, the president, owner, godhead of our little band of artists. When he asked me to go to New York I simply said no. I'd worked for Harold for three years and the idea of working for Harold for another three years was too much. I'd take my chances on the West Coast, I told him. I told myself it had nothing to do with the fact Paris now lived in Marin. But before Nina called all I'd done was clean my apartment and buy some new plants and clothes. I wonder what psychic sense my mother must possess to call at that particular time. If she'd called last month I could have begged off because of my job. If she would have called next month there would be another job I couldn't afford to leave. But she called two weeks ago when I had nothing but a past and no future. My mother's like that. She always seems to know exactly when to make her move.

Drew pointed to the sky. Upstairs study, bedrooms, bath. "There'll be solar panels on the roof."

"Who helped you put this all together? Ginny?" My brother and Ginny had lived together for almost ten years. A girl he met in college, and I always thought of them as growing up together, partners in life, the way Paris and I had grown up together, made our first adult decisions with the other person in mind. With Paris and me, those decisions had been mostly about leaving each other. But Ginny and Drew had elected to stay together until about eight years ago when she married.

"Ginny? Naw." His face took on a faraway look. "Although she would have liked this kind of thing. You know how other people enjoy reading or watching movies? Ginny redecorates in her spare time. She must have painted the apartment six times. It seems like every other month we had a garage sale."

"So what's with Ginny now?" Drew had been very vague when Ginny married. It was then that I realized how unequal our relationship was. I told Drew everything, as if he were my personal confessor. Drew listened, offered advice.

But he rarely asked my advice, rarely confided his problems to me. For years I assumed he didn't have any, and marveled how anyone in my family could adapt so easily to the rigors of everyday life.

"The guy she married beats her, not often, just occasionally. That's one thing I like about you, Emery. You're one of the few women I know who hasn't run her life according to her biological clock. Ginny had a kid in time for her first wedding anniversary. Said she thought it would save her marriage. I let them stay at my place when things get too bad. She thinks I'm the most wonderful guy in the world now. Says she never should have left me."

"Ginny has a kid, huh?" I met Ginny only once, at the ceremony after Julia died. She didn't look anything like I imagined her from listening to her voice when she answered Drew's phone. A small, tight, compact woman. A woman who married a man she knew less than six months, after living with my brother for over nine years. A woman run by her biological clock.

"He'll be lucky if he doesn't spend time in jail before he graduates from high school."

"Does Ginny know about this place?"

"This place is mine," Drew said firmly. "Only a select few know about it. I'm keeping it all to myself."

"Selfish bastard." He kept looking at the skeleton of the house and I could see how deeply he believed in his fantasy. His dream. Two things happen with dreams. Either you wake up and realize the dream is over, never really existed, or you abandon the dream for a different one so the dreaming never ends. He would never finish this house. He wouldn't want to complete the dream.

"When the architect gave me the overall height of the building I climbed that mountain back there," he pointed to the rocky slope behind us, "and took a rough approximation. From up there you can see clear across the lake." He pointed

60

at the land across the water. "That's an isthmus. From the second floor I think you'll be able to see over it."

"You're not listening, Drew. You think you're going to live your whole life out here? Alone?"

"I don't like flitting around like some kind of traveling salesman, the way you do. I need a base camp. Sure, I'd like to see the world. You might take off for Oslo or Tokyo. I'd come see you. But I'd have this to come back to."

"Ginny's not the only woman in the world." The sun was gone now and we stood in the twilight shadows of the struts of the house.

"Beautiful dreamer," he said. "People like us don't have many choices. Flotsam and Jetsam saw to that. Half my life is over. When I turned thirty-five I decided I'd made all the mistakes I needed to get on with my life, done all the research, so to speak. But I keep making mistakes, no matter how hard I try to avoid them. Never go to bed with someone who has more problems than you do. A couple like that sinks past pathology." He turned and guided me back toward the ladders, holding my hand in the dark. "All we ever learned how to do was to get by. If that's the only skill you've got, you don't have much to give."

"That's what I like about you, Drew. You're such an optimist."

He looked back at his unfinished house. A small fingernail moon was rising. "Yeah," he said. "I am an optimist. I'm building a house. I'm going to have a place to live, a place that's mine. I don't know about you, kid, but even if I don't finish it, I know I've got a place in the world. That makes a lot of difference to me."

As children Drew and I sometimes slept together. Usually only when we moved. The trucks would arrive, the moving men would pack up our belongings, and Nina would herd us onto a train, her favorite way to travel. Frank had long since been gone, off to his new job, in some new city. Frank always went ahead of us, 'getting things ready,' and we followed, slightly in advance of the furniture. But Frank never really had anything ready when we finally arrived in a strange new city. We'd camp in hotels, motels, once in a trailer park. On the train, in the various hotels and motels, Drew and I always slept together, to save space. We were only children, after all, smaller than a single bed. We could make do. Julia always slept with Frank and Nina. She was just a baby.

Like animals, we could sense a move long before Frank and Nina announced it. Frank would suddenly start showing up around dinnertime and that meant Drew and I had to become invisible, yet be constantly aware of the subtle timing of their inner thoughts. We learned early we wouldn't be missed until the sun went down, and sometimes not even then. But whether we'd be missed or not was hard to predict because the setup never varied.

We'd hear Frank's car pull into the driveway shortly after we returned from school. Nina would come downstairs, dressed and sometimes even wearing makeup, and they would sit at the dining room table, a bottle of scotch between them. That was our sign, that bottle of scotch in the dining room, since Frank and Nina never drank in the dining room except when discussing another move. Our dining rooms were usually more deserted than our kitchens.

We thought all families lived like we did, although when we talked to other kids it was rare to find one who'd even been to another state. Those kids talked of going on vacation, a word synonymous to us with not having to attend school while we moved. In Albany, when I was ten, Drew eight, Frank snagged us one night as we slipped out to the garage to get our bikes. 'We're going to have a family conference,' he said.

Our living rooms looked like most people's garages, repositories for boxes, broken furniture strewn around. Generally, by the time we moved again, Nina would have cleared a small place for herself around the couch for her collection of newspapers and magazines. Frank's chair, a big red wingback, would be somewhere near the couch. The rest of the room was used for storage. That night, the night of the family council, Frank herded us into the living room and we sat on the floor between the couch and the wingback. Julia, age four and still sucking her thumb, perched on the couch with Nina.

'Look at this,' our father said, gesturing to the rest of the room with his hand. 'This is no way for kids to grow up. And your mother and I can't live like this either.' This was news to me. We'd lived in some kind of gypsy camp all my life. I knew other houses didn't look like ours, but I didn't know why. Nor did I care. Now I realize I couldn't afford to.

As our father laid it out, Drew and I would be staying with 'friends'—his euphemism for a foster home. Julia would stay with Nina 'because she's just a baby.' I honestly didn't know where they would be going, nor did I care. That was the first time I remember standing up to my father. I don't recall intending to challenge him. I merely asked what would happen to Ajax.

'Well,' my father hesitated. 'We'll get another dog later, when we're all back together.'

At that time I had no full knowledge that Ajax was a dog, a pet. He was more like Drew, a brother, more real than Julia, my mother's baby, another pet to my way of thinking. Before long, I was screaming. My father yelled back, calling me a 'young lady' in a nasty voice. I punched my childish fists into his arms. Frank slapped hard enough to send me spinning across the room. I ran out of the house, Drew and Ajax right behind me, and into a secret thicket nearby, listening to Frank and Nina screaming at each other back in the living room.

That first night Nina found us, late when the stars were out and we were shivering with the cold. She coaxed us back to the house and I thought I'd made my point clear. I didn't mind if we were going to stay with 'friends,' whoever that might be. But I wasn't going to lose Ajax. Frank and Nina and Julia could go off to Crusoe's Island near Venezuela, my idea at that time of the most exotic place in the world, as long as I had Drew and Ajax. It seemed only right: Drew and Ajax and I, our mother with her baby, our father with his job.

But I knew I'd only won a skirmish, not the war. The next day Drew and I cut school, snuck back into the house, and began laying in supplies for a siege. The mind of a child isn't thorough. I remember we took five cans of Ajax's dog food, no can opener. We took the blankets and pillows from our beds, canned goods, and milk from the refrigerator. Nina slept through our raid in her big bed upstairs. Julia peered at us through the banisters, her eyes wide and solemn as an owl's.

We buried everything well back in the thicket, which led into the deep woods behind our house and eventually dropped down to a swift-flowing stream. We had our tooth-brushes, toothpaste, but no flashlight or bandages. Frank was home early again that night and ordered us to sit for another 'family council.'

'Your mother and I just aren't getting along,' he said. 'And this next job means I'll be traveling a lot. Your mother's not well. You kids are old enough to understand all this. And I promise, when we're all back together, we'll get another dog.'

With all the moving we'd done it seemed I had always been waiting for something better to happen, only to hear my father tell me the best of what I had was to be snatched from me. I could smell my fear on the air of the room like ozone after a lightning strike. I could feel a network of crazing going through me, like safety glass after an impact. This time Frank and I became more violent. I bit his hand, he hit me so hard he broke my nose. Drew sent up an ear-splitting shriek only an injured child can make and took the scotch bottle and smashed it against the window. Ajax sank his teeth into my father's leg, and that proved to be the moment of our escape. As I remember it now, Nina sat on the couch and continued to smoke her cigarette, Julia sucking her thumb beside her.

Once back in the thicket we realized we were still too close to the house. We made our way down the steep bank in the dusk, blood streaming from my nose. Every time I took a breath I felt the air sting my brain. Drew hiccuped in short bursts. We walked along the bank, upstream, all night. I'd read in some western a posse couldn't follow you if you went upstream.

The stream sounded like giddy music and the stars were

as bright as snowflakes suspended in the air. We came upon a refrigerator tipped nearly upright on the bank, gleaming ghostly white in the night, the door swinging in the wind. We heard animals startle and flutter around us, but we never saw them. Bats zipped back and forth over the stream. I wished we'd brought hats because bats could become entangled in your hair. Rabies.

That was the first sunrise I remember, opening as gracefully as a blood-red fan. We were deep in the woods along a cold boulder-strewn stream, our supplies left in our little fort back near the house. My nose must have hurt, but I don't remember it now. Pain is like that, you can remember it like an idea but never re-experience it the way heartbreak can sweep through you unawares. Drew kept sniffling, saying, 'I won't cry if you don't, Maura.'

Of course, we were found, but not until mid-afternoon the next day. I thought we were safe by then and Drew, Ajax, and I curled up in an old rusted-out Ford crashed down the bank. I remember thinking how romantic and exciting falling off a cliff to die would be. I saw our funeral as only a child can, Drew and Ajax and I sleeping peacefully in our coffins, while our real selves floated near the ceiling, watching how sorry our mother and father would be.

Ajax gave us away. They'd followed us with dogs and their barking excited him. Ajax barked back and although Drew and I tried to scramble to safety, we were no match for the state troopers. In the hospital Frank told them I must have broken my nose while walking up the creek in the dark. He would make up a similar story two years later when he broke Drew's arm.

But we'd won one important battle. A few weeks later when Frank and Nina dropped us off at the Potters we were allowed to keep Ajax. I very briefly entertained the notion that things might be better with the Potters, people I'd never seen before. But their house wasn't even as nice as our gypsy encampment. And their son, Owen, was retarded.

I never got to know the Potters well. Now I think they might have taken us from the Social Service people for the money, and as hostages to play with Owen. Drew and I had no intention of playing with Owen, whose head was a watermelon, loose-lipped mouth drooling, eyes slanted as a Chinaman's. Ajax curled his lip and showed his fangs whenever Owen came near him. Night after night Drew would crawl into my bed. 'I'm scared Maura. What if Daddy finds us?'

Daddy would always find us. Years later he would be a strident voice ringing in our ears as we lay awake, late at night like this, in distant cities. He and our mother would become as ever-present as the eye on a dollar bill.

I'd hold Drew, and he'd hold me. We'd tell each other stories about where we'd be by now if we were still following the creek bed. 'We'd be at the coast by now. I bet ships still need cabin boys. We'd sign on and desert in Spain.' Sometimes we would go down to the pantry where Ajax was penned and curl up with him. I don't remember how long we stayed with the Potters, thirty years ago now, but one day Frank and Nina and Julia showed up and we piled in the car and drove all the way to Detroit.

So it didn't make much of an impression on me when Drew took my hand that night while we looked out over the serried ranks of the city and led me to his bedroom. We curled up as we'd done as children, our arms around each other. But I was aware of the strength in his shoulders, the hair on his chest, the stale smell of vodka on his breath. Drew stroked the fine hair on my arms. "We're on a desert island," he said. "The SS *Frank and Nina* is smashed on the rocks. Wild animals call to each other in the darkness."

"Ajax will protect us," I said.

N ina called at six-thirty the next morning. I didn't recognize her voice. Nina—at six-thirty in the morning? "I need a suitcase," she said.

"A suitcase?" I rubbed sleep from my eyes and looked across the room at the packages for my mother containing a dress, underwear, shoes, that I was going to bring over later in the day.

"No one checks out of a hospital without a suitcase," she said.

My parents have lived on separate schedules all their married lives. My father gets up around five in the morning and I remember as a little girl I'd come down and watch him make his coffee. He'd give me a glass of juice and we'd go out to the yard and watch the birds as a new day began. My father used to know every bird in all the different neighborhoods where we lived. He'd point out the little crest that distinguished the brindled titmouse from the mountain chickadee. He could tell the difference between the parula warbler and the olive-backed warbler. Since we moved so often his goal seemed to be to identify all the birds in the area before we left.

My mother wouldn't consider waking before noon. That left summer mornings all to myself, a time I could imagine anything I wanted. Sometimes those fantasies were so strong I would be surprised and disoriented when Drew demanded I help him mow the lawn or do the laundry. My mother's life began at dusk. As the sun dropped her spirits rose, a light came into her eyes and her movements became more fluid and graceful. We would muddle through the dinner hour and then my father would fall asleep watching the news. Our mother drifted around the house ordering Julia and Drew and me as if she commanded an army.

The suitcase was only the first of a series of demands she made as the day progressed. She wanted to stop at the grocery store on the way to Drew's. "I'm going to make a cake," she told us.

"You've never made a cake in your life," Drew said, as he continued to pilot the BMW toward his apartment.

"That doesn't matter. I'm sure all the directions are on the box." Her voice was a hissy rasp, the effect of the smoke and fumes. Lauren Bacall is said to have gained her sexy, deep voice from screaming at a concrete wall for days until she ruined her vocal cords. I wondered if the musical pitch would ever return to my mother's speech.

Once settled in the apartment Drew and Frank took off to handle some insurance matters. Nina and I sat on the balcony, looking out over the city. "Do you remember when I took you kids on trips on a cloud," she asked in her new throaty whisper.

When we were young enough to take naps, Nina would bundle us into the big double bed for an hour or so in the early afternoon. Trips on a cloud, stories she told us until we fell asleep.

"Do you know where those places were?" she asked.

My favorite was Lapland, confusing that story with an actual lap. There was something magical about sitting in a grown-up's lap and I thought that the stories she told about Lapland must be actual pieces of the past. The stories she told when we went on trips on a cloud in the big double bed never happened. They were just stories, like fairy tales.

"When I'd take you kids on trips on a cloud I was going to all the places I never thought I'd see in the world. France, Hong Kong, Rio. Sometimes I would cry. I'd feel so lost lying in bed with you kids, knowing I'd never be any closer to Rio than I was at that minute."

I realized I was sipping a Bloody Mary. Talking to Nina, especially at this hour of the day, somehow I'd started drinking. I've never spent time with my mother without a drink in my hand. I'd automatically mixed two, forgetting my vow not to drink around Nina. And it soothed my sore throat, the sandpaper in my chest. "But you've been to Rio."

When Frank first retired, like so many men of his generation, he didn't know what to do with himself. All he'd known since his teenaged years during the Great Depression was work. He and Nina took a trip around the world for three months. And once they returned, when he still didn't know what to do with himself, they took another trip around the world, just in case they missed something.

"It wasn't the same. I was too old by then," my mother said. "There's a great difference between living your life and saving your life. I didn't know that then. I'm too old to live my life now. I have to spend all my time saving it. I should have lived it back when I had the chance. I'll never know what it feels like to make love on the back of a galloping horse. Did you ever see Rita Hayworth in *Gilda*? I always thought I should be the one in the slinky dress singing 'Put the Blame on Mame.' That's one thing I've always wondered about you. I've never known if you have any dreams."

"There's a difference between dreams and fantasies."

"Semantics," Nina said. "I knew Drew dreamed. I'd watch him on the swings, or playing with toy cars, and I'd know he was inventing something for himself, the way I invented myself as Gilda. And Julia dreamed. You could see it in her eyes, looking off to something none of the rest of us could see. But I could never look into your eyes. It was like trying to read the future while staring at a marble."

My dreams had mostly been about being cast away on a desert island, then rescued. I liked being rescued in a yellow biplane, or rafted back to the mainland by a school of porpoise. I became an expert on imaginary places. The Arabian City of Brass with floors of polished marble and pearls designed to look like running water. Alca, or Penguin Island, that drifted from the Arctic Ocean to France while the sole inhabitants, penguins, evolved into men. Makalolo in Africa, ruled by warrior queens who ride giraffes and feast on their predecessors to preserve the kingdom's spiritual heritage. Later I learned most girls dreamed about being mothers or brides or nurses, or at least that's what I've been told. My daydreams and my night dreams are opposite sides of a coin. In the daytime I dream I'm rescued from the island, becoming a Makalolo queen. At night I have anxiety dreams about the things I've lost or forgotten. Griffons, cocker spaniels, seahorses.

She held out her glass and I rose and mixed her another Bloody Mary, vodka being Drew's drug of choice. We couldn't sit there and get drunk all day. There were things to do, although exactly what I wasn't sure. Frank and Nina were homeless now. There must be something we should be doing.

As I handed her the fresh drink I said, "Mother, don't you think we should at least start making a list of the things you've lost. Insurance stuff. Things you'll need to get started again."

She dismissed the whole idea with an airy wave. "Frank will take care of that."

"I don't understand," I said. "You call me up in San Francisco to tell me you're going to start a brand new life with a brand new husband when Frank dies. Now, I know . . ."

She interrupted me. "I never said I would marry again."

"Whatever. I know losing a house isn't the same thing as losing a husband, but at least you might look at this as practice. What did you expect? That Frank would set you all up to go husband hunting before he died?"

"Not only do you not dream, you expect everything to be rational. There's nothing rational about losing everything in a fire. What do you want me to do? Go down to Macy's and start picking out china? If the fire hadn't happened at least I'd have had a base to operate from when Frank dies. Now we don't have anything. I might have to become a gypsy."

"Right. A gypsy." Nina's notion of a gypsy wouldn't include a caravan or even a backpack. She'd fly first class with Pierre Cardin luggage. Destination unknown.

"Why did you pour that scotch on the fire?"

"I did no such thing."

I wandered back into the kitchen, my third Bloody Mary that morning. Sudden Adult Brain Death. I hadn't even realized I was drinking until I found myself mixing the second one. There's nothing the mind isn't capable of when it turns against you.

Imagine my mother's mind as an Eskimo, skipping from different colored ice floe to ice floe. Cobalt blue, magenta, taupe. Her mind hops and skips across them, as light-footed as a ballet dancer.

I glanced at the morning paper strewn across the counter. FIRE RAVAGES RETIREMENT COMMUNITY. Always before headlines meant someone else's disaster, horrors happening to other people, usually someplace far away. What the hell were we going to do with them? I got out the phone book and looked up nursing homes. That would be the simplest thing: book them into a nursing home, catch a plane to San Francisco.

But I didn't pick up the phone. I didn't even call the airport for flights back home. Maybe I was drunk. My ticket had gone up in the fire, and somehow, that settled me right in the midst of their problems. I sat in the kitchen sipping my drink and paged through the phone book like a catalog, browsing the ads. Ambulatory and Non-Ambulatory. Home-like Atmosphere. Emphasis on diet, specialized care. Nutritionists. Certified Vitaminologist. Stress reduction via performing arts. Occult supplies. Crystals and wands.

I was looking through Off-road vehicles—equipment and parts, when Nina came into the kitchen to refill her drink. She placed a hand on my shoulder, and it trembled like a small, frightened animal. "Don't worry," she said. "I've got it all figured out. We'll buy a houseboat. They come fully equipped. I've always liked living on the water."

"Any lakes or rivers around here?" From Drew's apartment the view stretched over the city, out to the wheat fields beyond. Inland cities confuse me. I know there's a boundary where the city ends and the countryside begins but somehow that dividing line always seems arbitrary. A seaside city makes more sense to me: The city ends where it meets the ocean. But these flat inland cities seemed willed to sit on the plains. On the water the horizon is said to be twelve miles before the curve of the earth takes over. Perhaps it's the same on the plains. I wanted to see something spectacular rising from this city. Pyramids, the seashell opera house in Sydney, the Statue of Liberty, the Eiffel Tower. But I only saw glass and steel office buildings, low brick houses, and then the wheat fields stretching to the horizon. The only substantial body of water I'd seen was the lake in front of Drew's secret unfinished house. Secrets are as ordinary as air in our family.

"Besides," I said. "Father gets seasick."

"Or a Winnebago," she said. "Something mobile so we can get around. Houses are for people who like to stay home."

Get around. By the time I graduated from high school I'd been in sixteen different school systems. Geographics. If something doesn't work out in one place, try another. The allure of this idea is that the entire country was settled this way, restless people moving on to greener pastures. Yet all I've found is the same pasture over and over again. Only the boundaries are different.

Birds migrating along flyways. Salmon seeking the stream where they were spawned. Indians chasing the herds. Migrant workers following the rotation of the crops. I've often wondered if our family would have been happier if we'd lived in another time. Could we have accepted our life together more easily if it had been confined to the bed of a Conestoga wagon working its way along the Oregon Trail toward new land? With our luck we would have met the same fate as the Donner Party. Who would be the first to die? How do you cook your sister's thigh? Would it be like roasting a leg of lamb?

"There's an old proverb," Nina said. "If a fool throws a diamond in a well not even a hundred sages can get it back."

"What's that got to do with anything?"

"The house is gone. It's a sign we have to start over. You're never around. You have no idea what we've lost."

"How about all those clay pots your mother gave you?"

She waved her drink at me. "Exactly. There was a paring knife my grandmother, your great-grandmother, used. You might not know this, but I had baby books for each of you kids. I was going to open them and reread them on my seventieth birthday. I have the prom dress you wore, the one with the pink coat."

"I never went to a prom." Which was true. The closest I

came to going to a prom was during my senior year. We'd moved halfway through the year and since no one else wanted the job and I didn't want to sit in study hall, I volunteered to decorate the gym. I decided on a Greek motif, since most of my classmates were going off to college and those were the days when college didn't mean an education, it meant joining a fraternity or sorority. Party schools. The day before the prom I had the senior class out collecting greenery to hang in the cardboard planters we'd constructed. I spent the night of the prom at the movies, Marlon Brando and Trevor Howard in *Mutiny on the Bounty*. The next Monday I was excited to learn half of the senior class had contracted poison ivy. "You mean Julia."

"Whatever. It was a beautiful bright pink floor-length coat to go with all those gorgeous roses on the dress. I used to try that coat on every once in a while, waltzing myself around in front of the mirror." She sighed. "I wish Frank had learned to dance. I miss the flow and feeling of being on a dance floor." She took a few gliding steps across the kitchen, waltzing to an imaginary tune.

I stood up. "This is getting us nowhere. Father and Drew will be back soon and what are we going to tell them?"

"The doctor said I'm supposed to rest. Whatever needs to be done, Frank will see to it." She drifted off toward the deck again.

I watched her, my hands fisted. When I was a child Nina used to shake me by the shoulders until my head snapped back and forth, my teeth cutting into my tongue. I wanted to shake Nina, to throttle her, as she used to say. Shake some sense into her.

The phone rang. I answered it. Drew sounded tired. "Get Nina together," he said. "We're going for a ride."

"All Nina needs is a go-cup and a stretcher," I said. "Where are we going?"

"I'm going to show them the property."

"Don't. If they don't know about it they can't take it from you."

"I've got no choice at this point. I will definitely go bat-shit if I have to live with them for more than twenty-four hours. And you know it," Drew said. "We always do just fine until the twenty-fifth hour, then it's an emotional shoot-out."

"I'll call my bank." I felt my brother's desperation. "We'll put them up in a hotel and charge it to my credit cards."

"You don't even have a job. Besides, this could take months."

"I'll get a job and pay it off later. We can split it if you want." Of course the idea wouldn't fly, but maybe it would give Drew some options.

"No arguments, Emery. Be downstairs in twenty min-utes."

But Nina had no intention of going anywhere. She kept repeating that she was supposed to rest as I mixed up a pitcher of Bloody Marys. "I can't go gallivanting around, as if nothing's happened." I remembered the story of the drunk who told everyone he was going to commit suicide. His friends tried to talk him out of it, threatened to take away all his booze. That only seemed to make him more excitable. Finally, one guy went off to the store and brought back a half gallon of whiskey. 'You aren't going to give him that, are you?'

'Of course. He'll never do anything as long as he's got something to drink.'

Twenty minutes later, with most of the vodka in a plastic jug and the rest poured surreptitiously down the drain, I told Nina I was leaving. "Mix me a drink before you go," she said.

"Sorry. I used all the vodka for the go-cups." And I held out the jar of Bloody Marys toward her.

"Well, that's pretty dumb. You know Frank's not allowed to drink. And somebody has to drive."

"Then I'll drink it all myself. Bye. Drew's waiting."

Nina was suddenly curious as to where we were going and why. But she was still confused, or maybe drunk at this point. "A ride would be lovely," she said. "Where's my purse?"

I handed her the empty shoulder bag I'd bought for her yesterday. She tossed it away, as light as air as it landed on the couch. "We have to go shopping," she said. "There's so many things we need."

We were silent in the car, Frank and Nina mostly asleep while Drew and I, good children that we were, kept quiet so as not to wake them. But I kept catching Drew's eyes watching me through the rearview mirror. I felt sorry for Drew; I knew what he'd done. At some point during the morning with Frank, some moment when Frank began to sink under the new knowledge of what had happened to them, Drew offered him the lifeline of his property, a new beginning. I could imagine it all: Frank's defeat in trying to arrange a new place for them to live and Drew, just like when Julia died, taking over without Frank realizing.

I opened the gates when we came to them and watched as Frank and Nina roused themselves from sleep. "How lovely," Nina said. "We should have brought a picnic."

"We won't be long," Drew said. "I just wanted to show you something."

"Good," Nina said. "You have no idea how much there is to do."

We parked between the church and the caretaker's building with the rhododendron growing out of the doorway. Drew helped Frank out of the car and I realized how much that leap into the tree had cost him. He rose as if there were weights attached to his shoulders, steel rods driven through his knees. He favored his left leg, his right leg bound in a brace, and I could see bruises forming on the right side of his face. Nina held onto the plastic jug of Bloody Marys. "This must have been a lovely place at some point," she said.

Drew related the same history he gave me as he guided them through the building. He told them about the bank and the hunting club, and I noticed he was careful not to mention the construction of his new house further down the road. "Here's what I was thinking," he said. "My place is too small for the four of us. There's no need to spend money on a hotel until you decide on a new place. I've stayed out here before. You and Father can live in my apartment and I'll stay out here in the meantime."

"No way," Frank said. "You have to be at the bank every day. This place is much too far out in the country," as though he had any idea how far we'd traveled, "to try to commute to work. Your mother and I will camp here and you stay in town. We only need to be in town to handle the business with the insurance and the new house. How far are we from town?"

"About twenty-five miles. I only come out here when I want to get away from everything."

"If you'd marry you wouldn't need a place like this," my mother said.

"That's what I like about you, Mom. You make it sound easier than picking out a new car."

"It looks like a good project," Frank said. "A place like this will keep you out of the bars."

Drew settled himself on a stack of firewood, his long legs stretched out. "Well, I just thought this place would solve a lot of problems right now. You can always get in contact with me through the bank." I heard defeat in his voice.

Frank lit a cigarette and ran his eyes over the cavernous room. "You haven't thought this through properly. This might be a fine place to rough it for a weekend but the bank's not going to appreciate having you walk in every morning smelling of woodsmoke. You're a professional. We don't know how long it's going to take us to get things together."

"Actually," Nina said. "We're thinking of buying a boat."

"Oh for Christ sake." My father cast a disgusted look at my mother. "Can't you keep your mind on anything for more than a heartbeat? We'll talk about a boat later. Right now we need to get organized. We'll rent a car, get a couple of sleeping bags and Drew can get back to his life while we get on with ours."

"A boat really isn't a bad idea, you know Frank. Why not a boat?"

My mother wanted a boat, knowing my father gets seasick.

He ignored her, focusing on Drew. "Hell, I was raised in a cabin like this," my father said. "I probably know more than you do about how to get along out here. This might be a nice project, but you're a city kid. You can putz around out here, but don't expect to live here."

My mother leaned forward. "We once spent a week fishing, living in a cabin in the Adirondack Mountains, didn't we, Frank?"

Anger notched his forehead, then my father ran his hand through his hair, one of the first signs we learned. Explosion often followed that innocent gesture. "That's not the point, Nina. The point is Drew has a job. We've got the time. This place will do just fine until we get resettled." Frank can only give orders or explain how something works. Dialogue isn't a word in his vocabulary.

There was my father, thirty years ago, stripped to the waist, signaling the crane operator while he swung boulders into the crib for the dock. Frank, his clothes covered with splotches of paint, while he put the finishing touches on the bathroom in New York. Frank, a trowel in his hand as he mortered the bricks together for the patio. He'd set them out in a herringbone pattern and I remember walking duck-footed, in line with the bricks, all across that patio. I believed I would be grown up when my feet were as big as the bricks.

Imagine Nina cooking on the big wood stove. Imagine

Nina cooking. I wasn't even sure she knew how to boil water. But it was easy to picture Nina and Frank getting up in the dawn light, coaxing up the embers in the fireplace, setting on a pot of Drew's cowboy coffee. Frank would split wood while Nina collected eggs from the chickens, milked the cows. Frank and Nina thirty years ago. But then, I could also picture them fighting with the Resistance in France during the War, Nina tapping out Morse code signals while Frank guarded her with a Lugar. I don't know when I began having these fantasies about Frank and Nina but it seems they've always been associated in my mind with something more glamorous and dangerous than simply being my parents. Perhaps all children have these fantasies, never projections into the future, but images as real as dreams defining their parents before they took on the task of raising their children.

"No," Frank was saying. "There's no reason for you to take your vacation and waste all that time just to help your mother and me. Maura can stay with us for a few days, just until we're a bit settled out here. Then she'll fly back home and your mother and I will have some space and time to decide on what we want next."

"I really should go home," I said, the child once again, my voice too small for the statement I was making.

"Fine." Frank's tone was dismissive. "Do whatever you goddamn want. We have to get organized here."

As I listened to Frank and Drew batting ideas back and forth I quit noticing the brace on Frank's knee, the purple blotches beginning to surface across his face. I didn't hear Nina's wheeze and cough. Just because you've never seen a snowman decked out as a jogger or a trapeze artist doesn't mean it's not possible. I was six years old again and everything Frank said was possible for the future. Rent a car. Live in the hunting lodge. Why not?

But when Nina spoke, the scene dissolved. "We might travel," she said in her burned voice.

"Mother," I said, trying to sound diplomatic, "that might be a good idea later on. But I sure as hell wouldn't go to Podunk, Anywhere, much less someplace interesting, if I only had one dress."

"Give me a pen." Nina rummaged around the cabin looking for some paper. "There's so much we need. Just like Christmas shopping." I could see the light and excitement in her eyes.

"We'll divide up," Frank said with some spark and animation. "Your mother will take care of the clothes and bedding. Drew, you can drop me at a car dealership. You and Maura do the grocery shopping."

"Listen," Drew said, and I could see the panic rising in him. "You guys are going to stay at the apartment. You need to be in town more than I do. Let's not get out of hand here."

Frank looked at him patiently. "There will come a time when you will be responsible for what happens to me," my father said. "I'll be lying in a hospital, stuck full of tubes, and won't be able to take care of myself. Until then, I'm in charge of my own life. You're my son. You'll do what I say."

"It's my property," Drew said. "I only showed it to you so you'd know I'd be all right."

"Damn it! It's also your apartment. I'm not going to argue with you. We are not staying in your apartment. We don't have much cash right now. Until things are sorted out the cabin will be fine. Period. End of argument."

I tried to see behind their eyes. Making plans. I gave Drew a wink. Let them have this fantasy. One night out here would sober them up.

At the bank Frank and Nina picked up some temporary checks, they refused Drew's credit cards, and we dropped them off before going grocery shopping. Drew looked as if he had something sour on his tongue. "Come on," I said. "What else have we got to do for the afternoon?" A hangover headache was building, my forehead, the backs of my ears tightening. It felt like my eyebrows had gained weight. I was angry at myself for having those Bloody Marys. Or maybe the Bloody Marys were just an excuse for the tension I felt around my parents.

"Emery, love. You don't understand. They are in a world of trouble financially. It will take an eternity to process their claims and their mortgage payment will eat up just about all their insurance anyhow."

"That's your field. I don't understand anything about money. Don't tell me about money. The fact I can spend it doesn't mean I understand it. It's like I get bubbles in my brain whenever I try to think about it. Let them play around in the stores all afternoon. One night out there is all they need to realize how silly this whole thing is." I should go home. If I wanted to get drunk, get high, I'd do it with Victor.

Drew shook his head. "You've been gone. You don't know what they're like now. Car wrecks in slow motion."

I pulled a shopping cart out of the lineup. "Shopping carts were invented in Oklahoma City, you know that?" Facts again. A fact could be used as a tool in any emergency. The verbal equivalent of a Swiss Army knife. "They have a bronze statue of the guy who invented them, pushing a shopping cart, in the middle of the city square. What do you want for dinner?"

We settled on steaks and baked potatoes, one of the three meals Frank was guaranteed to eat, and headed back to Drew's apartment. He left me with the groceries and ducked into the bedroom. After I'd put all the groceries away I checked on him. He was on his knees, rolling blueprints into tubes. "Shoe boxes," I said.

As we moved around the country, in the wake of our father's jobs, Drew and I tried to keep track of where we lived by filling shoe boxes with treasure. We searched for Aztec gold in Connecticut. Dry, bleached twigs were really finger bones. We collected these precious items in special shoe boxes which we carefully buried in a secret place when our father announced we would be moving again. We put a note in the box, explaining what we thought the items were and signed our names. We were convinced someone would find one of our boxes and, like a careful detective, search us out. We would then reveal the location of the other boxes and would be famous. Now I can't even remember all the places where we lived.

"Damn straight." Drew tucked another blueprint into a mailing tube, ghostly white lines on the navy-blue paper as big as a sail. I didn't want to look at them. The blueprints confined Drew's house, boxed it up. I preferred the way I'd seen his house under the stars last night. The sweep and flow of it as Drew talked, not anchored, but floating in his imagination. "But at least this time I'll know where I'm hiding them."

"At the office?"

"For now. I'll take them out to the cabin once Flotsam and Jetsam get off their fantasy trip. I'll probably be able to get more done on the place if I'm actually out there." He looked around his cluttered bedroom. "I should pack up half this stuff," he said. "They could be here forever."

Nina came through the front door and collapsed in a chair. Wrapped around her, smothering her—the shawl collar winged to frame her face and brush the tips of her ears—was a fabulous champagne-colored fur coat. Sleek, as if it was still alive and had just groomed itself. She took a cigarette out, lit it, coughed as though her lungs were about to spring out of her chest. She continued holding the cigarette, the way she would admire a piece of crystal. "My," she said. "I haven't worked this hard in a long time."

I noticed there weren't any packages. "Did you buy anything?" I wanted to pet the fur, cuddle it into my face. A full-length, champagne-colored fur coat. Her idea of necessities for camping out.

She seemed to have already forgotten about the coat, absently throwing it back across the chair. "They'll deliver. Get Drew. I need to call some items in."

The pizza she ordered for dinner arrived first, around six o'clock in the afternoon, two hours before Frank returned, driving a new turquoise Buick sedan. Nina sat in a chair by the phone, waving her cigarette like a baton as she indicated to the delivery men where to put her purchases. Hudson Bay blankets, futon cushions. "No real need for a bed," she said. "A floor gives fine support for the back." Buckets, mops, and furniture oil. A case of scotch. A snakebite kit. An upright piano.

Drew, the plans for his new house rolled under his arm, left the apartment after the second delivery, a china cabinet, arrived. "You don't need that stuff here," he told Nina.

"It's not for here," she replied. "But I didn't know the address for your cabin. Tomorrow we'll rent a truck."

With Drew gone and Frank not yet back I watched the growing pile of stuff Nina thought would be useful for setting up housekeeping in the woods. Why would she need a cherrywood china cabinet?

"Where's Drew? How many plates does he have out there?"

I left her by the phone, calling in more orders, getting up only to answer the door for the delivery men.

I think about Paris and my heart crumbles in my chest, the way tall buildings fall away from the wrecker's ball. There's no reason for it, it just happens. Every man I've ever been serious about has a little of Paris in him. I've never had a brown-eyed lover since Paris, for example. Every lover possessed eyes with some of the depth or blueness of Paris' eyes. My lovers have always had nice hands and strong shoulders.

We met at the Steinhart Aquarium, although we didn't realize it at the time. It was when I watched the fish circling the roundabout, when the thresher shark attacked. The silver flash and then the vivid red stain in water. The chaos of fish fleeing, other sharks drawn toward the fresh kill. Instinctively, I backed away from the wall of the tank and into the body of someone behind me. He folded his arms around me protectively and we stood that way watching the frenzy. I recall thinking about how I'd once run my palm over the teeth of a shark's jaw on display in a shell shop, how those serrated teeth would feel slicing through my flesh, cutting through the marrow of my bones. The head of the tuna, separated from the body and drifting toward the floor of the tank, kept opening and closing its mouth, its eyes swinging from side to side as if looking for the rest of its body.

A guide started moving us away from the tank. I never turned around to look at the man who held me in his arms, my eyes still on the sharks tearing through the fleshy remains, snapping into each other. At some point the man released me and I realized later I should have thanked him, or at least said something. But what did I remember about the man who held me? Only that the hair on his arms was silky black and he had a solid, earthy smell like someone who worked around gardens or horses.

I'd been living in a pantry on Page Street at the time, if camping on the floor of a pantry, my stuff piled up on the shelves all around me, could be called living. Even the order of my things, like everything else, was reversed. Things I rarely used, boxes of winter clothes brought out from Boston, were on the lower shelves. I'd filled the easiest shelves first so the most essential items, toothbrush, underwear, ended up toward the ceiling. But I didn't bother to rearrange that pantry. After all, I was only camping there until I found my own place. A few days at best.

Most of the six weeks I occupied that pantry were spent sleeping with an artist who had a flat in North Beach. I went back to the pantry to change clothes, pick up résumés, or to check on my stash of drugs. Then the artist decided to move down to Half Moon Bay and asked me to sublet his apartment. I wanted him to invite me to move to Half Moon Bay with him, but took the apartment since that was all he offered.

I borrowed a van but had to park it over a block away. I asked all my friends to help, but somehow no one showed up. I began taking armfuls of my stuff off the shelves in the pantry and walking them down the block to the van. Two hours and several dozen armloads later I had almost filled the van when a guy stepped off his porch and asked if I needed any help.

"Looks like you're moving," he said, walking along beside me but not offering to take the stereo receiver out of my arms.

Jerk, I thought. He'd been sitting on his porch for the last hour as I trudged back and forth from the pantry to the van.

I fished the keys out of the pocket of my jeans and he took them, not the receiver, from me and opened the van. "We've met," he said.

I shot him a look I hoped would incinerate his balls. "Here," I said, handing him the receiver.

"Shark," he said.

"What?" I was sweating, my arms and back strained from trucking boxes of books, dishes, records, all that stuff that is worthless to anyone else but what I considered would cost a fortune to replace. I was living on unemployment at the time.

"Shark," he said again. "Where you moving to?"

"North Beach." I noticed his curly black hair, softly shining like an animal I wanted to stroke, and blue eyes sharp as slivers of deeply frozen ice. "Want to help me unload this?"

He jumped in the passenger side and we took off to North Beach. "You don't remember me," he said.

"Should I?"

"Ever see a shark attack a yellowfin?"

What were the odds of this happening? Two months previously, before I had to crash in the pantry, I'd been at the Aquarium when the thresher shark attacked the silver yellowfin tuna. I backed into the arms of a man with silky dark hair and a deep earthy smell. I looked at him.

"You could have thanked me," he said.

"For a cheap feel?"

"You seemed to appreciate it at the time."

And I had appreciated it, felt warm and secure watching a tank full of carnage. It wasn't until the guide tried to shoo us away from the tank that I realized not everyone would be fascinated by all that gore. I dimly recalled shrieks and screams, people running away. But I stood rooted in the arms of a man. This man? How could he recognize me if I didn't recognize him?

He reached his hand across the gearshift and flipped one of my abalone shell earrings, my baby loneies I called them. They were my favorites at the time and I wore them like a talisman every day. I still have them.

"Where'd you get these?"

"I found them. At the beach." I touched my right earring. "I picked this one up because I thought it was cute, so small. About a year later, in just about the same place on the beach I found another one and took it home too. I'd forgotten about the first. They're not exactly the same size, but close enough. I put the jump rings through them."

"They're nice," he said. "They're unique."

Parking in North Beach was worse than in the Haight. We finally found a spot on a hill so steep that if it snowed in San Francisco this would have been an ice chute. My apartment was three blocks away and we took armloads of my stuff down the hill and up another hill, up four flights of stairs to the top floor where my artist friend had lived. It's hard to make small talk while straining against twenty pounds of books, armloads of jeans and shirts, all the regalia a first-class hippie needed to live more permanently than those who camped in the parks and on the streets.

I didn't even know his name when we brought the last load up the final flight of stairs. We collapsed on the bed my artist friend had left me, a bed where I'd spent most of my recent nights listening to my artist friend grind his teeth in his sleep. Sex was different in those days, a courtesy between people. The dark-haired man rolled over to me, held me once again in his arms. "You really should have asked some-one to help you with all this," he said. He began to pull off my sweatshirt.

It's too late now for me to know how many lovers I've had. I only remember the exceptionally good ones, and the exceptionally bad ones. Paris topped the former category. Until that afternoon in the sunlit apartment in North Beach, boxes of my belongings scattered all across the floor around us, I'm not sure I'd ever had an orgasm. We rocked and rocked against each other, moving faster and faster, working our bodies deeper and deeper into each other's souls. Per-haps Paris has forgotten that first afternoon; he's never men-tioned it. But I've never forgotten it, not just in my memory, but in the muscles and nerves of my body.

I lived in that apartment less than twenty-four hours. Although my artist friend and I had had sex in that very bed, we'd never broken the bed frame. I didn't know the landlord, a dignified Italian widower, lived right below us. I believe my first orgasm coincided with the snapping of the crossbeam on the frame. I felt like I was falling, the way you do when you're asleep, and all the vertebrae in my backbone seemed to sing. The trees danced. We didn't hear the pounding on the door until we were both spent. We noticed the bed frame raised above us as we looked toward the door, which we had left open.

Grabbing Paris' shirt I assured the landlord there wouldn't be any more trouble and that we'd pay for the dam-age to the bed. That seemed to satisfy him and he retreated to his flat below mine. "Priorities," my tall, dark stranger said. He sniffed his armpit. "We need a shower."

"Shark," I said, and stepped into the shower with him. But twenty minutes later, the shower gone cold, water run-ning all over the floor, Paris and I foundering like fish in the overfilled tub, the landlord was standing in the bathroom shouting at us in Italian. He reached over Paris' naked ass and turned off the taps. "My ceiling," he shouted, pointing at the floor. "Out!" And he turned back into the main room and started hauling my boxes out to the landing and pitching them down the stairs.

I spent that night at Paris' apartment, only half a block from the pantry where I'd started in the morning. We didn't unload the van until the next day. Paris' bed was merely a mattress on the floor.

One of the most consistent things about Paris is that he always makes me feel young when we're in bed together, as young as I was when we first made love over twenty-five years ago. Twenty-five years, a quarter of a century. Silver jubilee. I never dreamed I'd know anyone for a quarter of a century or more. And yet no matter whether I'm overweight or in terrific shape, whether I'm injured or strong, Paris makes my bones feel young and my muscles supple. I wrap my legs around his neck and feel the sweet strength clenched in my thighs. My arms are smooth as they cross his shoulders, my hands delicate as the hairs on his chest brush my palms. I arch my back, my body pressed against his, and all my nerves fan out to encircle him, bind him to me. With other lovers I'm always aware of the two of us, enjoying each other. But with Paris, even all these years later, I never know where he stops and I begin.

Of course, that's because we could never stay with each other long enough to become disillusioned or bored. We hit a flash point very quickly. My dance-away lover. And like water to a fire, distance was the only way to douse the flame.

Successive moves became easier as more and more of our things were broken or abandoned. At one point everything I cared to take with me fit into three blue Samsonite suitcases Nina and Frank had given me as a high-school graduation present. I lived out of those suitcases for over two years. They meant packing and moving could be accomplished in a New York second.

My parents had taught me one thing: there's always a new place to go. I wonder about people who are raised in one place, settle in that same town when they're grown. Imagine having all those people know all those secrets about you. Imagine watching them as they age, going to their funerals when they die. The majority of funerals I've attended have been for people my own age. Vietnam, suicides, victims of car wrecks, AIDS. Victor told me there was one week when he attended five funerals. Imagine living in a place where there was an ice rink where you skated as a child, watching that rink being demolished just when your own kids were old enough to skate. Seeing a new rink rise on the same site when skating became popular again, even though you are too old to risk a fall on the ice. That's always been my image of a small town, the towns Frank and Nina took us through the way other Americans tour Europe. When Paris and I had trouble, one or the other of us lit out for new territory, like taking a trip. Three suitcases made traveling easy.

It's taken me a quarter of a century to understand the real attraction of chasing, and being chased, around the country. I'd grown up with the image of new territory as constant as a goal. But as a child I was completely powerless, dragged along in the wake of my father's jobs. I had no choices then. With Paris I had power. I could leave him. He could leave me. I could follow him. He could follow me.

"What do you want from me?" Paris was tossing his clothes into his old, battered suitcase. "You don't want a lover, you want a pet. Total, unthinking devotion. This is it, Emery. I'm telling you. You don't know how to love. Get a dog to keep you company."

"And I suppose you do. You know all about how to love. But you don't know anything about commitment. Why live with me if you can't show some respect for me?"

You cannot unlearn the lessons of childhood. I can walk through a house as quietly as a burglar. I used to think every-

93

one went through their homes with the stealth I use, even when I live alone. Paris couldn't sneak through an empty bed. Paris possessed everything he came in contact with. It would anger Paris to find me sitting quietly somewhere in the house when he thought I wasn't home. My sense of stealth and Paris' sense of possession. I had just walked in on Paris and a girl named Molly spooned around each other in our bed. I simply stood there and looked at them until Paris noticed me. "You know, Emery," he had said as he looked up shamelessly from the sheets, "when you sneak around like this you're bound to run into something you don't expect."

Paris was rifling the shelves for his books, slamming them into a box. "Love isn't possession," Paris said. "I mean, what the fuck do you want?"

"In twenty-five words or less, everything. I want to know when I come home I'm coming home to my house, my lover, my bed. I don't expect to find strangers getting laid."

"This is it," Paris kept repeating. "This is definitely it. You make me jump through hoops, over and over again. The same fucking hoops. I don't know why I do it. This whole relationship is built on your insecurities. I don't need this crap."

"Fine," I said, hoping to sound calm and collected, uncaring. That wrecking ball was smashing through my chest as I watched Paris pack up his belongings. I knew he had a point. My insecurities. Molière said the great ambition of women was to inspire love. But I still, to this day, don't know what I inspire in Paris.

"I'm not coming back this time," Paris said as he put his typewriter into its carrying case. "There are plenty of women who can give. All you can do is take."

"All you can do is cause pain. There's no joy living with you. I always feel I have to be ready for the other shoe to drop. You didn't have to sleep with her here. The point of any adultery is always the one who isn't in the bed."

Paris would leave me and I would be just about used to him being gone when one of our friends would call up and say they'd talked to Paris in Houston. Or I would leave, destination unknown, and once settled, as far away from Paris as possible, I'd get a postcard saying someone, someone who knew Paris, was going to be stopping through town. I thought of my friends as spies, friendly spies, since somehow I always believed Paris, or news of him, would turn up. We had unfinished business. We both knew that. For a while I thought Drew kept Paris informed as to where I was, but Drew has always denied this. "That man is a handful of air," Drew would say. "Why would I tell him where you are?"

It feels like I missed some lesson, skipped a crucial grade in the school of growing up. I was too busy leaving to realize what I was heading toward. The only concrete thing was the past, and that could be dumped. The future was open and clean, bright and shining, and could be anything I wanted to make of it. Drew has the best outline of the years I spent becoming who I am—the two pages in his address book solidly filled with my name, the addresses, the towns. Over two dozen different states. Over half the country. Moving was a goal in itself, a test to see how much of my past would catch up with me. A test of the depth of Paris' loyalty.

When I lived on a quiet street in a sleepy town in Maine I was surprised one Monday afternoon when the doorbell rang. Paris stood there bundled into an expensive fur coat, snow falling all around him as he clutched a picnic basket. I hadn't seen or heard from him in four months.

"Get your coat," he said. "We're going on a picnic."

"A picnic," I said, looking at him, the coat, the picnic basket. "A picnic." His eyes seemed to be the only thing that belonged to him. The coat and picnic basket borrowed from someone else, another Paris I didn't know. "Don't you want to come in?" I said. "It's cold, in case you haven't noticed."

"Get your coat," he said. "Damn straight it's cold."

"A picnic," I said. The temperature was twenty-three degrees.

"Well, if you're busy." Paris turned to go. "But a picnic's always more fun with two." He stopped midway down the walk. "Quit playing games, Emery. Get your goddamned coat. I didn't come all the way out here to freeze my ass off alone."

Some men bring you flowers when they want to make up after a fight. Some men take you out to dinner, or fly you off for a weekend in Hawaii. I've known men like that. But Paris, if Paris wanted to set right some previous wrong he'd fly up to Maine in the middle of a snowstorm and offer to take you on a picnic.

"I decided on stuff that was suited for the cold," he said as he unloaded the hamper beside a frozen stream. Popsicles, frozen yogurt, and ice-cream cake. We left most of the stuff on the ground beside the frozen stream and took turns pulling on the thermos of Irish coffee. We smoked cigarettes while we singed the fingers of our gloves.

"I've got a little place down in Virginia," he said. "Right outside D.C. Weather's a hell of a lot better. You still get the first snow, but don't have to deal with real winter." He patted at the snow beside him with his gloved hand. Eight inches were already on the ground. The weather forecast predicted twelve to fourteen more. "They say the cherry blossoms down there are terrific in the spring."

"The picnic was your idea," I said.

"As an idea, it was fine. Now, reality," he cocked an eyebrow up at me, "well, reality is a different matter. Another horse altogether."

That's when we thought of the trapeze artist snowman and tried to build a slim, arcing snowperson swinging from a low branch of a tree. It didn't have to be big, Paris said. Just big enough to be noticed, if anyone would be foolish enough to go traipsing through the woods in this weather. We argued about whether this was a woman trapeze artist, with a tutu skirt, or simply a slim male form. We opted for the woman since she would be more difficult. We built her on the ground, from the legs up, our gloved palms sculpting her calves and thighs. Up over the tutu skirt and budding breasts. Her arms were stretched above her head and we hoped to hang her by her hands from a low branch, pour water over her and freeze her to the tree. We chopped a hole in the ice with a broken branch and scooped water with the plastic container for the ice-cream cake. But she was too heavy to hang in the tree and when I held her up to the branch and Paris poured water over her he only managed to spill the brackish creek water down my sleeves. We left her leaning against the tree, her arms outstretched, hands sheared off, head cocked at a broken angle, dead brown leaves stuck to her skirt.

A trapeze artist snowwoman. "History is simply the story of conquering the impossible," Paris always said.

His ancestry is Scottish and Cherokee, an impossible combination, and I loved to fantasize about his great-grandparents. I would imagine a tall, rawboned Scot with curly red hair immigrating into the crowded ghettos in New York and immediately setting out for any place where he could see the deep green of heather. Paris' great-grandmother is always young in my fantasies, although Paris told me she lived to be ninety-four. She wears a beaded buckskin dress and her glossy hair is plaited in braids hanging to her hips. Paris' lineage, a chance meeting of the dispossessed. In my fantasies sometimes she finds him dying of thirst on the prairie. Sometimes he finds her starving in a decimated village. An impossible combination, Glasgow and Catawba. Paris' great-grandparents follow the Oregon Trail, then move down the coast to California. Paris is fifth-generation Californian, as far back as a homesteading family can go.

After twenty-five years I now believe Paris and I are partners in life, no matter who we are living with at the moment. And your partner in life affects every aspect of your being. For instance, every lover leaves you his music. I've had lovers leave me legacies of jazz, rock 'n' roll, rhythm and blues, classical, country and western, reggae. Once the relationship is over I can't listen to their favorite music because of a burning sensation in my chest, a ringing in my ears. I used to blame this on those lovers, how my dissatisfaction with them or their rejection of me ruined the music. One night a few years ago my new lover, Jerry, had taken me to a rock 'n' roll revival. I realized then that none of those lovers were to blame. I associated Paris with music. Each time we'd find each other across the vast spaces of the country Paris would have a new passion in music. "You want horns," he'd say. "Now, Art Pepper, that's horns." The quiet moments in those next few months would be filled with horns, pianos, whatever Paris' passion was at the time. And then we would separate, months would pass when the sound of horns would send spasms through my body like muscle cramps. Then, I'd see Paris. This time it would be classical. "Dvořák," he'd say. "He could see music in Niagara Falls. In 'The New World Symphony' you get the first real blending of a European style with something as American as 'Swing Low, Sweet Chariot.' He used sea chanties, gospels. Listen to the music in a John Ford western. Tell me that's not inspired by Dvořák." No matter who Paris was enthralled with at the time he presented each artist or composer with the same authority as citing the high temperature of the summer solstice in McMurdo Sound, Antarctica. Who's going to question that?

We were drawn to each other like iron filings to magnets. Heat lightning filled my hands when Paris was nearby. An animal awareness would overcome me, my mind trusting my body to respond. I'd feel my nerves tense and imagine a force field encircling me. One night Jerry and I were in a bar in New York, and I believed at the time Paris was living in

New Orleans. The bar was crowded and Jerry and I stood against the rail near the door. We'd been living together for about two months, but I'd still wake up in the middle of the night, surprised by the red-bearded stranger lying next to me, wondering what this man was doing in my bed, wondering what had happened to Paris. That night we'd just come from a movie when I felt my hands fill with electricity, then a tap on my shoulder. There stood Paris, with a woman. "I still have your electric blanket," was the first thing he said. And there wasn't much to say after that, Paris and I standing there staring at each other while Jerry and the woman ordered drinks and glowered at us. "Let's go," the woman said, and took Paris by the arm. "Yeah, in a minute." Paris shook her off like a dog flicking water from his coat as we continued to stare at each other. As the evening wore on Jerry and the woman eventually disappeared, but Paris and I didn't notice. At closing time we looked around for them. They were gone. Outside, Paris flagged a cab and opened the door for me. "I'm going to walk," he said. "I'll see you."

"In your dreams," I said.

"Always," he replied. "I'm the lord and master of your dreams."

I learned to ride horses with Paris, eat artichokes. He loved to read Faulkner aloud and over time I've listened to him read eighteen of Faulkner's twenty-five books to me. In Denver, Paris called me from the airport, a new tactic for him. Surprise was always one of his major weapons. " 'Sitting beside the road, watching the wagon mount the hill toward her, Lena thinks, "I have come a fur piece." ' And it's spelled like that," Paris said. "F-U-R. As in mink. Chinchilla. Silver fox. I thought I'd drop by. We still have the Snopes trilogy to go. We haven't read 'Spotted Horses.' I promise to leave when we finish the Snopes trilogy. You're only half-educated in Faulkner until you've done the Snopes trilogy."

Drew once asked me why Paris and I never married.

"There was never any time," I told him. "We were always too busy."

"Busy with what?"

"The strategies of war," I told him.

And it was during one of those wars that I told Paris I was going to Portugal. We were lying in bed watching the sun rise. I can still see the light breaking over his strong shoulder, the supple muscles of his arm stretched across my breasts. "That'll be fun," he said. "I'll go to Kenya and we'll meet in Tangiers. Compare notes on our travels."

"No, Paris," I said. And I meant it at the time. I thought then that I could never commit to him and he would never commit to me. "It's over. I'm not going to keep chasing you for the rest of my life." Paris seemed to listen with his eyes, the deep-blue pupils dilating and deepening following the cadence of my voice.

"Seems like I'm the one who has to do all the chasing. I'll tell you one thing, Emery. If I hadn't met you I might still be in California. I might have settled down, raised some kids. Hell, I might own my own business by now. It's been fun, but pointless, you know. See America first. But we can't keep doing this forever."

"Shark," I said. And I watched him, memorizing his body, the look in his eyes, the way his hair fell across his brow. I saw the sun rise over the crest of his shoulder, brightening the tangled sheets on the bed.

He rolled away from me, so I couldn't see his face. "Go wherever you like," he said. "You'll always have me, just a little bit of me, like carrying an old ticket stub in your pocket."

"The show's over. The ticket's been used. I'm cleaning out my pockets."

"Sure," he said. "Go ahead and try."

I never went to Portugal. Paris married the daughter of a dermatologist. That should be the end of the story. We all have our first great love. Our partners in life. They become the pieces we build our past upon. They are the nesting ground for the ideas that will govern our lives. They should stay buried, or maybe should be burned. But somehow it never seems to work out that way. Paris is a jumble of memory and fantasy. There were nights, alone in my apartment, when I would talk to Paris, the way Nina talked to Mrs. White, feel his hands running across my body. And those moments are as real to me as actually seeing him, whether he's sneezing or hoeing a garden or making love to me. In the last few years, when I see Paris, I forget that some of the conversations we've had exist only in my imagination. "Don't worry," Paris said. "I have the same problem. It makes you larger than life. My mythical love."

"I 'm Kiskejohn," the tall man said. I must have been still asleep and dreaming this man. He looked at me with transparent cinnamon-colored eyes, hollow as though I could see through them into the infinite workings of his brain. His long, carefully groomed gray hair was tied back in a bandanna. Faded jeans and a nondescript flannel shirt worn through at the elbows. He smelled like bananas. It was quarter to seven in the morning and I felt the same dislocation as if I'd pulled an all-nighter back in college. "This is Tree," he said, gesturing to a small man standing beside him paring his nails with a Swiss Army knife.

I heard Frank coming up behind me, the drag of his foot due to the brace on his knee. "What do you want?" His voice sounded caked with rust. When Drew hadn't come home last night Frank fell asleep on the couch, Nina locked in Drew's bedroom with two bottles of scotch. I wanted to be as far away from them as possible. The balcony was my only escape. So I bundled up in blankets, ignoring the cold, out on the balcony, looking out over the city, trying not to think.

It's amazing how difficult not thinking can be. Memory can be like a Chinese abacus, producing results with great accuracy and speed. But, like the abacus, it is unable to work backwards to search for a fault.

"I'm Kiskejohn," the tall man said again. "This is Tree." Kiskejohn looked at me as if expecting an order.

"What do you want?" Frank asked again. He focused on the two men standing in the hall as if he thought they would commit a crime right there, right now.

"Drew sent us," Kiskejohn said. "For that." He pointed into the room at the collection of goods Nina had acquired yesterday in her attack of consumer therapy. I'd kept my back to it all night but somehow constantly aware of the snakebite kit, the cherrywood china cabinet, the piano. It felt like a crowd of people waiting for me to jump from the parapet. "We have a truck," Kiskejohn said.

"Well, all right." Frank grinned at Kiskejohn and Tree as if he'd suddenly rediscovered them as old buddies. "Want some coffee?" He turned and limped back into the apartment.

"What the hell's going on here?" I wanted to know. "Where's Drew?" Kiskejohn instilled that paranoid feeling when you don't know if the person you're facing knows something about you or not. Knows something bad.

Kiskejohn's look was carefully couched to be as bland as an egg. "At work." His eyes followed Frank until he disappeared around the corner to the kitchen. "You're Emery," he said, as if telling me my own name would galvanize me into action. "Drew said you'd know what to do."

"If you've got a truck," I said, squaring my shoulders underneath the blanket I'd draped around me, "the best thing would be to take all this stuff back to the store." I hitched the blanket again. This man wasn't going to intimidate me.

Kiskejohn and Tree shouldered past me.

"Nina!" Frank hollered, loud enough to wake the whole building. "Let's get a move on!" He handed mugs of coffee to Kiskejohn and Tree. "First we'll load this stuff into your truck. We need to get ahold of Drew to find out exactly where we're going."

"I know." Kiskejohn dismissed the collection of goods with a wave of his hand. "You're not going to need most of that stuff."

Frank shrugged. "My wife." He ran his hand lightly along the keys of the piano. "I didn't even know she could play."

"I'm going to relearn." Nina stood in the small hall separating the living room from the bedroom and bathroom. The plain flannel nightgown I'd bought her the other day hung from beneath one of Drew's tweed jackets. "I bought a tape player." She picked up one of the boxes from the pile. "Sheet music. I used to play. My sister and I performed duets. There's going to be lots of spare time out there. I'm going to brush up my skills."

Frank shook his head and limped toward the bathroom. "If you want to start loading this stuff, I'll just get dressed." He was wearing Drew's only pair of pajamas, ones we'd found in a drawer still in their plastic wrapper some time around nine o'clock when Frank decided to 'nap' on the couch until Drew returned. "I'll just call the school and tell them I won't be in today."

"I'll handle this," Nina said, and I could see the light in her eyes, the same light from long ago that came over her when she had moving men to order around. Those days had been the high moments of her life because we usually moved without Frank, always ahead of us like a point man. She was looking at Kiskejohn and Tree as if she owned them. "You go on to school," she said to Frank.

"Get dressed," Frank said as he picked up the phone. He dialed a number, waited for a moment, then tucked the receiver between his bruised chin and shoulder. He began to sign.

"Dad," I said. "Dad." Kiskejohn and Tree were looking at him as if trying to identify some kind of road kill.

"Frank," I said again until he looked at me. "They can't see you."

He gave a sheepish grin. "Right." He began to talk into the phone.

Kiskejohn looked at me and I felt a tiny shudder in the base of my spine, nerves fluttering. I cut my eyes to the pile of goods cluttering the foyer. None of it looked real to me. The empty pizza box could have been a Frisbee. The open carton of liquor, a clothes hamper. The china cabinet seemed to change size, expanding and shrinking the way scudding clouds change form. I moved into the kitchen, past Kiskejohn, and poured myself some coffee. I thought of Nina's scotch, all that scotch. A nice stiff Irish coffee. A different slant on the world. An unspecified fear fluttered through me. Maybe I could buzz out on coffee, or sweeten it up enough to go into sugar shock.

Kiskejohn and Tree began picking up the cartons. They worked silently, in rhythm with each other, as if they communicated telepathically. "Who are you?" I asked.

"Drew sent us," Kiskejohn said. I wondered why this man made me so nervous. I was afraid I'd lapse into Chinese or Norwegian, languages I don't speak.

They padded the piano and china cabinet with the futons and Hudson Bay blankets Nina had bought. I began getting dressed. They knew how to load a truck and all my expertise in moving wasn't going to be needed. One thing about being burned out in a fire: There's damn little to fool with.

Nina decided to wear her new fur coat, although the day was turning Indian summer warm. And then I realized what had been bothering me since Frank and Nina came back from their separate shopping sprees. An animal sense, an electricity in the air. The feeling of holding your breath underwater right before panic sets in. All yesterday afternoon and last night I'd been waiting for Frank and Nina to have a fight. The potential topics bobbed on the surface of the conversation like so much driftwood. Nina's houseboat fantasy. The fact that Drew hadn't come home. The decision to move to Drew's cabin, certainly a topic which deserved some discussion, and discussion between Frank and Nina always translated into a fight. They could have fought about their purchases, or items still to be obtained. But they hadn't raised their voices to each other once.

I called Drew's office, but his secretary refused to put me through. She gave me a message instead. Drew would pick me up at the hunting lodge at six o'clock that night.

I began biting my nails, a habit I detest. After taming every emotion with alcohol for over thirty years I feel unmoored when I'm in a strange situation and know I can't drink. HALT, an AA cliché meaning you should never get too hungry, angry, lonely, or tired. Another nice theory that just doesn't work out in real life. I was all of the above, plus scared and nervous. As we followed Kiskejohn's pickup in Frank's new turquoise Buick sedan, complete with car phone, I could see myself saying: Hey, Frank, call up AA. I want to talk to somebody.

"Water," Frank said. "We'll have to do something about the water."

Nina stroked the fur of her new coat.

I sat in the back seat and let them indulge their new fantasies. Who was I to tell them people don't take up wilderness roughing it in their seventies? I tried to imagine what Drew really had in mind, why he let things go so far. But after he left with nothing but his blueprints it was as if I could no longer see his thoughts.

As kids we'd always believed we could see each other's

thoughts. Physically see them. Drew claimed my thoughts were always shades of blue and when he wanted to look into my mind all he had to do was look at something in any shade of blue. Bodies of water were good touchstones for this, he claimed, and that made a certain kind of sense since I've always felt most comfortable around oceans, any body of water where I couldn't see the other side.

I believe Drew's thoughts run the spectrum from gold to sandy-beige, nothing as dark as chocolate brown, just light and floating hues. I don't need a touchstone because I can't control when I see what he's thinking. His thoughts come upon me as suddenly and unexpectedly as finding money on the street. I knew he was coming to visit me in San Francisco two weeks before he called. A month later, I was watching the clouds float across the moon, Drew asleep on the hide-a-bed in my living room, when I knew he would leave. I'd been remembering the night Paris and I watched the deer in the moonlight, their shadows like etchings moving over the barley tops, when the clouds became golden. "Drew's leaving," I said to my cat. "He's already gone."

When Drew picked me up at the airport the other night he looked startled when he saw me. "Did you always have such green eyes?" he asked. Imagine not knowing the color of your sister's eyes, yet knowing the color of her thoughts.

Frank and Nina chattered like birds while Kiskejohn and Tree unloaded the pickup. I idly inventoried the canned goods and the sticks of battered furniture left by the hunting club. It would have been a passable place to park yourself for a week or two, if you weren't my parents' age. Even I don't sleep on the floor anymore. Kiskejohn and Tree worked silently, the way people who've known each other for a long time can anticipate each other's actions. I sat in an old rocker, one arm broken away, and watched. I could feel the wind drifting through the walls.

They placed the china cabinet, the last piece, near the

fireplace, on the other side of a cord of split wood and Kiskejohn came over, placed his hand on my shoulder. I felt a run of electricity through my body. Nina and Frank were tearing open boxes, throwing the paper into the fieldstone fireplace. I rose and followed Kiskejohn and Tree out the door and into the cab of the pickup.

I'm not sure my parents even noticed us leave. Tree pulled a beer from a cooler at his feet, popped the top, and took a long swallow. Kiskejohn fished a joint out of his shirt pocket and fired it up. I realized we were driving along the road leading to Drew's new house.

Kiskejohn parked the truck between the house and the lake and I followed them, silently, until they stopped at a boulder perched out over the water. Kiskejohn handed me the joint, and I passed it on to Tree. Kiskejohn already had my nerves singing. I wanted to stroke his long, lean bones, run my hands through his shining hair. It would feel soft, expensive.

"How do you know Drew?" I asked and watched as Kiskejohn's eyes seemed to look through me, undressing me the way men in pick-up bars do.

"We work for him. Tree knew your sister."

I looked at Tree, who stared dreamily out over the lake. The sun sent bright chips of light over the still surface, as if clouds were bouncing, skipping off the water. "Where?" I asked Tree, who continued to look away from me.

"Vietnam," Kiskejohn said.

"Doesn't he talk?"

Kiskejohn gave a vague gesture, still looking at me as if I were standing naked before him.

"So what's going to happen?" I asked Kiskejohn. "What's Drew got in mind?"

Kiskejohn stretched out on the sun-warmed rock and I felt all my energy collect in the ball of my belly. My breathing was shallow and beads of sweat broke out around the fine hair on my neck. I wanted to run my hands along the long bones of his legs. I clenched my teeth, grinding them together. I sat down facing Kiskejohn, my eyes squinting against the strong sunlight.

"Drew says your parents are gone to the zoo." He gave a thin smile, strong, even white teeth. "He's right. Pianos and china cabinets. So Tree and I are going to camp here." He indicated the skeleton of the house rising behind us.

"Do they know about this?" During our drive out here yesterday Drew hadn't mentioned his new house or the size of his property. He'd carefully given the impression the hunting lodge was the extent of everything he owned.

Kiskejohn shook his head. "Drew's worried they'll set the place on fire." He looked back toward the hunting lodge. "If they do, we'll know."

"This is crazy," I said. "Fires are the least of it. Heart attacks. Falls. They're retired, for god sakes. And they have less idea what to do out here than I do."

"Drew's pretty sure this won't last long. Tree and I can use the extra money." He jerked his head toward the new house. "There's plenty to keep us busy. We've got to raise at least a temporary roof before the snow falls."

"This is nuts." I stood and began pacing the small platform of the boulder. The skin along my back crawled, feeling Kiskejohn's zircon eyes on me. "Completely out of hand."

Tree turned and faced me. "Heredity," he said, the first word I'd heard from him all morning. "Craziness runs in your family."

"How did you know Julia?" There was a hardness to Tree's face, a stony wall I couldn't penetrate. Suddenly, I felt afraid. What was I doing, out in the woods with these two? I should be home, back in San Francisco, trying to find a new job, snorting coke with Victor, drinking alone, safe in my apartment. I was not safe with Nina and Frank and flashed Nina wading into this lake in her fur coat, Frank biting into his foot with an ax. And I knew I would somehow be held responsible. That was my role in the family game plan. I was responsible. I was the oldest.

"Vietnam." Tree turned and hopped down off the boulder, sauntering back to the pickup. He favored his left side.

"Tree doesn't talk much," Kiskejohn said. "Be flattered. That's a pretty long speech for him."

"What the fuck is going on here? I don't know who's crazier, you guys, my parents, my brother, or me, for letting all this get set in motion." We were all locked together in a mental ward, the hills, the lake, the trees around us the bars holding us in. I was twelve years old, old enough to realize what was going on, too young to do anything about it.

I scuttled down from the boulder and headed for the water, tearing my clothes off as I trotted across the rocky beach. I flung my new shoes over my shoulder, dropped my sweatshirt and jeans on the sand. I tossed my underwear away as if it were irredeemably filthy. My toes went numb as my feet hit the first freezing lapping waves. I had no idea how deep this lake was, but needed some shock to pull all this madness back into a definite shape I could hold. Skimming across the water in a shallow racer's dive, the chill water knocked the breath out of me. This must be what it feels like to be electrocuted, I thought, as I surfaced and raced back to the shore.

The air didn't feel any warmer than the water and my tension, anger, fear, all balled up in my belly like a stone. I stood there shivering, naked, Kiskejohn looking down at me from the rock above. I wanted to expel every feeling from my body, blow it out like an orgasm. The muscles in my pelvis clenched. I shook all over and my teeth clattered against each other.

Kiskejohn watched me. Tree had disappeared. Drew was at the bank in town. My parents were lost in some wilderness fantasy that would probably kill them both. No, they wouldn't be lucky enough to die. That would be too easy. Something would happen, something bad. An injury, an accident. I felt the fire, the destruction of their home, not as an end to anything, but the fabled tip of the iceberg. Wrapping my arms around my knees, I sat down on the sand, rocking my body back and forth, trying to dislodge the pain and fear. But it grew, pressing into my spine, against my thighs. The midmorning sun beat down on my back, water streamed off my hair. I held the pain and fear against me, unable to release it.

I watched Kiskejohn pull out another joint and light it, then lie back, basking in the sun. I wanted to lie next to him, his arm around me. I wanted to be under him, his body pressing my back into the rough surface of the stone. I wanted to stop the images racing like storm clouds. I wanted my mind to be pure and blank. I continued to crouch on the sand of the small beach, until I heard footsteps behind me, crunching through the rough sand.

A whoosh, and then the cold nylon of a sleeping bag fell over my shoulders. Tree had dropped it on me and continued on up the beach, turning toward Drew's unfinished house. Kiskejohn raised himself, as slow and luxurious as a cat stretching after a nap. He followed Tree toward the house and presently I heard their hammers falling rhythmically.

Who were these men? Drew's workers? Our bodyguards? Definitely crazies, like the rest of us marooned out here in the wilderness. Gilligan's Island. I rubbed myself dry with the sleeping bag and got back into my clothes. The ring of Kiskejohn and Tree's hammers filled the air. Leaving the sleeping bag on the beach I began to walk back toward the hunting lodge. What else was there to do?

The woods sparkled with bird cries and bright splotches of fall colors. The maples were more red and gold than green and I knew there would be snow soon, perhaps not much but just enough to frighten us all back to reality. But what was reality in this situation? The tables had turned. Drew was now the towering parent locking us in our room because we were bad. But what had we done? Why was I involved in all this? Although we all seemed to be moving quietly, slowly, an avalanche was occurring, sweeping us along toward a crevass. Inertia can become its own force field.

I followed the old dirt road toward the hunting lodge and as I topped the rise I realized I could no longer hear Kiskejohn and Tree as they hammered away at the struts on Drew's new house. About a quarter of a mile ahead of me I could see the tall chimney of the hunting lodge. Nina and Frank might never realize Kiskejohn and Tree were so close. Or maybe they'd stopped work and sailed away across the lake.

But when I found myself in front of the hunting lodge, I discovered Frank's new Buick was gone. I walked through the open door and stood gazing at the interior of the cabin. Three futons were neatly made up with the Hudson Bay blankets, and I felt like Goldilocks peering into the home of the Three Bears. One of those futons was for me. Did Nina and Frank expect I'd stay with them through this whole charade? Boxes were stacked neatly in one corner and when I looked into them I saw parkas and thermal underwear, wool socks, twill pants, sweaters, all folded inside. The tags were still on them. In the cupboard, the pots and pans were stacked together, the canned goods turned with their labels facing forward. Sheet music sat on the piano. The cherrywood china cabinet was empty.

Sitting in the rocker I tried to calm myself, but the pain and fear felt like a live thing in my body. I rocked, and felt the tension rise as if I were horny and my pelvis was the only focus for my body. It throbbed and my upper thighs burned. I wanted Paris to reach in me, explode the terror, expel it from my body. I kept seeing Kiskejohn's long legs, felt Drew's arm draped over my shoulder. I rocked. I rocked. My belly swelled against my jeans. With my head tucked between my knees I smelled the sweet stickiness collecting in my crotch.

My mind let go, snapping like a rubber band under too much pressure. It had been a long time since I'd been this aroused, since Paris. They say when your life is in danger you have the fullest sense of being alive. But my life wasn't in danger. Not even during the fire the other night did I feel as if I was about to die. I never even thought Frank would die, was merely concerned as to his whereabouts until I saw him in the tree. So why now?

I rocked, listening to the old wood chair scraping against the wooden floorboards. I placed my hands inside my jeans, coaxing myself, not as erotic desire, but trying to lure a caged thing out. The bones of my ass pressed against the wooden seat of the rocker. Gaining momentum, my thighs clenched and released, clenched and released.

It was over with a great sigh, a flash of blue, honey-scented air escaping my body. I felt my shoulders sink back into my skin. It wasn't pleasurable, it wasn't unpleasurable.

The satisfaction in a moment like this is that your mind stops. Everything weighs equally. The zipper of my jeans was pinching my soft belly, and that was as important as arranging to get myself back to San Francisco, or finding something to eat. I felt nothing. Safe harbor, like a boat riding gently at dock. Casting my eyes around the room I noticed each corner hung with intricate spiderwebs, the bright blue, red, green stripes of the Hudson Bay blankets. The way the light caught the bevels in the glass in the china cabinet. I felt the hard wood of the rocker bite into the bones of my ass, the way my ligaments tied into my hip sockets. Nothing mattered. Time stood still. I expected the colors in the room to fade to black and white.

I heard the whine of an engine, then the crunch of gravel, as my father's new Buick pulled up outside. The doors slammed, but I continued to sit in the rocker, pushing off with my toe. My mind was as empty as air and I wouldn't have stirred if Nazis or desperados charged in waving pistols.

"Oh Maura," Nina exclaimed as she came through the creaking door. "You should have said something. Your father and I just went to get something to eat. There's a little café a couple of miles down the road. I had corned beef hash. Imagine that, way out here. Corned beef hash."

I sat there looking at her, still in the new fur coat. That gorgeous blush mink, the color of champagne, that set off her white-blonde hair nicely. If you could just catch a fleeting glimpse of her through your peripheral vision she would strike you as a stunning woman. There seemed to be more bounce in her step, as if the fire, the loss of everything she'd saved, balls of twine to broken crystal, had invigorated her somehow. Frank limped along behind her and lowered himself gingerly onto the musty sofa.

"We should have done this years ago," my father said, as if this cabin was his idea, a dream planned for over the years. "The nice thing about a situation like this is that you have to make a value judgment about everything now. Nothing taken for granted. Do I really need a copy of *The Rise and Fall of the Third Reich*? There was a woodworking kit I bought when I retired. I'm no good with my hands when I'm making strictly ornamental stuff. I might have used that thing maybe twice, botched each piece of wood I touched. And yet we must have hauled it through three moves. I'll have to go to the hardware store and get some caulking to shore up these windows."

Maybe he would build a sauna, reshingle the roof. I got up from the rocker and looked through the cabinets. Vienna sausage. Baked beans. Breakfast.

They should have bought a Scrabble game and we could waste the afternoon with that. Until six, when Drew would pick me up. I knew Drew had something in mind for just the two of us. Perhaps he was out buying them a real house, and wanted my approval first. Or he could show up buck naked. I couldn't predict anything.

"I'll need a cookbook," Nina said. "Maura, you cook. What's the best cookbook to learn from?"

"Why bother to learn to cook now? It's not like you're going to stay here forever."

Nina looked lost for a moment; I'd punctured her dream. "A hobby," she said finally. "I've been thinking of taking up a hobby for some time now."

That's what old age must do to you. You become skilled in 'thinking' of things you're going to do. Nina was sixty-eight and decided she needed to take up cooking for a hobby. But more likely she needed to go back to the stores, buy a wok, bamboo utensils, which would be left in a corner or a cabinet, the beginning of a new collection of junk.

"We should make a list," Frank said. "That way we don't have to worry about hobbies."

"Right. A list," Nina said. "Does anyone have any paper?"

Frank rose stiffly from the sofa. "Come on, Maura," he said. "Drew's bound to have some paper at his place. We'll take a little ride into town."

Nina was at the counter, mixing herself a drink in a plastic tumbler. "You go," she said. "I have things to do here."

As Frank and I got back in the Buick I could see the pattern of the next few days. Of all the things they'd bought, only Frank's car would be essential to them. What did they really need? An answering machine for their car phone? If they managed to sleep comfortably through the night in the hunting lodge, they would spend their days ferrying back and forth in the car from the cabin to town. There would always be something, some paper, a spoon, that would enable them to go to town. Who knows how long that would keep them occupied? To hell with the insurance, the arson squad, realtors offering new houses. When your life is unmanageable a small goal, like finding some paper, can become a major triumph.

The first thing Frank did was to show me how to use the car phone. "You press this button here," he said, and went on to explain how the thing worked. My father loves to explain how things work, as if that knowledge accords him a small step up on the world. But so much of it is useless knowledge, esoteric at best. He knows it's a myth that you can balance an egg on its end during the spring equinox. You can balance it any time at all. You just shake it until the yolk settles to the bottom. He knows if you want to use an animal in a performance or parade you have to give it an enema an hour before showtime. "You try, " he said. "Call time."

But it wasn't paper we were after, the real reason for our trip to town, back to Drew's apartment. In Frank's own elliptical way he wanted to tell me something, something more important than how to use the phone. Something either too abstract to be of any use or too couched in subtlety to be understood. When I was in high school Frank once asked me to take a ride like this with him, as if the car provided the necessary environment for him to talk. 'You're getting to the point where you should know about sex, Maura,' he said on that ride. There was a long silence as the city streets sped past us. 'Do you know why men's balls are different sizes?' And assuming this would lead to a larger discussion of sex I dutifully said 'No.' After another long pause Frank said, 'So a man can cross his legs more comfortably.'

That was all my father ever told me about sex.

Now here we were again, the countryside speeding past us. Although there was a radio and a tape player in the new Buick Frank preferred to travel in silence. I smoked and found myself engaged in an old game from childhood—counting the cows we passed. But it wasn't as if knowing how many cows we drove past would prove something. I wanted my mind to stop. I wanted to tuck all the racing images away in a box. Sudden Adult Brain Death.

Finally Frank said, "You know, Maura, I'm considered an expert in my field. But becoming an expert isn't the result of age. It's the result of what you know."

"Yeah," I said. How can you argue with that? My father knew facts, how to fix things. He knew how to hypnotize an alligator. My mother's knowledge and world came from what she read in books. They saw life as if their minds were clouded with cataracts.

"So you see," he paused and studied the road for a moment, "there's really only one thing I'm truly an expert on."

"Oh," I said. "And what's that?" I never liked these talks with my father. In my father's company I wasn't a woman with my own life. I became his child once again.

"Your mother." He watched the road, flexing his fingers against the wheel. "I probably know her better than I know myself. This is upsetting her more than she's letting on. You have to look at the big picture. I wish you'd known her before we had you kids. She was all right then. For a couple of years there life was an adventure for us. Everything, whether it was scraping together enough pennies to pull off a party or taking a trip just to see what was there. I don't know why we decided to have kids. We were pretty happy then, in our own way. When you kids came along it was like she lost part of herself. Like a car losing its brakes going down a slick mountain road. You still have the car, but it just doesn't work right."

I nodded and took a deep drag on my cigarette. "Yeah. Like a sail or a rudder. You've got them when you leave the harbor. But you can lose them in a storm."

"I guess we didn't think of you as people, potential people. Maybe we saw you more like living tables and chairs, necessary but nothing you took special pains with. You know, in our day kids were taken for granted. It had been like that since time immemorial. There wasn't all this crap about 'quality time' and 'role models.' Kids were kids. Everybody had them."

"That's lovely," I said. "Sure makes me feel great."

"Don't get me wrong. I'm not telling you this to make you feel bad. I'd sort of like to square things with you, with Drew. I didn't know this then. And it's too late now to change anything. But I thought it might help if you knew."

"Your logic," I said. "Don't you realize other people grew up at the same time we did? Baby boomers. The largest demographic block in history. And somehow a lot of those folks managed to grow up to be regular people. Because they didn't start out being thought of as tables and chairs."

"Don't forget. You left home at fifteen. Anything after that is your own doing."

"You guys gave us a foundation as sturdy as Jell-o. I've spent almost thirty years trying to nail that Jell-o to the wall."

In his silence, his steely-eyed stare at the road ahead of us, I realized I'd hurt him, a rare accomplishment. As a child I could only recognize one emotion in my father: rage. But I hadn't seen my father, except for the visit home for Julia's memorial service, in over twenty years. Maybe I could see more now, with the distance of those years. Maybe he had more to show. "How would you have liked it to have been?" I wasn't hostile, merely curious.

"When I married your mother I guess I thought we'd embarked on a great adventure. I saw us hopping from one exciting situation to the next. I'm trying to be honest here, Maura. When you were born, I felt having a kid was exciting, like visiting Cuba used to be. Exciting in the same way. I didn't stop to think the two situations might be different."

"Well I'm sorry I'm not as exciting as visiting Cuba." The backs of my ears began to ache.

"That's not the point now. I've learned a few things in all these years. And mostly I've learned about your mother. You know, she's not right." He tapped his skull with his index finger.

"I'm beginning to see that," I lied. I'd always thought there was something wrong with Nina's mind, even before she proved it to me when she thought I was Mrs. White. Did she ever tell him about her visits with Mrs. White? But more importantly, why hadn't I told him? Why did I keep her loneliness such a secret? Why could I never approach my father and tell him about her other life in the night?

"So we have to watch her," my father was saying. "That's why I'm glad you're here. Drew tries to look out for her. But he's awfully busy. She's more than a full-time job."

"Then why are you gone all the time?" The School for the Hearing Impaired, the SPCA, his candy-striper work. He's very proud of his work, but that surely didn't leave him much time to keep an eye on my mother. My mother with her Eskimo mind.

"So she won't think I'm spying on her. She can be very paranoid. We have to be careful with her."

"This pisses me off. We have to be careful with her. Yet she doesn't have to be careful with us. Throughout my whole childhood she ran over Drew and me like a herd of stampeding cattle. And you passed through our lives as if you were living on another planet. A close encounter of a different kind." There is no map for the heart. Why couldn't I put these people behind me?

"You can be as bitter as you want, Maura. It won't do any damn good now."

This, like most of my talks with my father, wasn't going anywhere. "Oh, Christ Frank. You're no different than she is. I mean, this whole camping-out business, come on. It's not like you're approaching this head on."

"I'm trying to buy time, Maura. I don't know what your mother's going to do. This way, I can watch her. See what's best for her. You have to help me."

"Help you? It's pure fluke I'm even here. Do you know why I'm here? Mother says you're dying. What about that? Is that true?"

"Dying?" He cut his eyes toward me. "Dying. Well, I suppose I am. There's nothing special about that." And then he gave a secret little smile I couldn't read.

"Well, what about it?" But I knew he wouldn't answer, any more than I could acknowledge that I would die. Drew said half his life was over. Death is comprehensible, a finite end. But dying is a process, changing from minute to minute.

"That's not important." And then, like a curtain drawn over a window, he became totally involved in driving the car. He hunched his shoulders forward, his hands tightened on the wheel, and he appeared to be piloting this car through a thick fog, late at night, with no lights.

We would drive a total of fifty-some miles, into the city and back out to the hunting lodge, to get to Drew's apartment, rummage through his drawers and retrieve a notebook and a couple of ballpoint pens. A fire reduces everything to basics. Up in smoke. Vanished as a whisper or last night's dream. We didn't really even need the paper: the wrapping from all their boxes would have done. But our empty pockets contained no pens or pencils to begin their list of things to do.

We were riding back in the silence of the late afternoon when the phone in the car rang. "You get it," my father said. "It's probably Drew."

Although I'd seen car phones I'd never talked on one in a moving car before. A lawyer friend of mine was engaged in a running fight with the Port Authority about using the Diamond Lanes during rush hour if he was on the phone. 'It's a conference call,' he told the patrolman who pulled him over, 'so there's more than one person in the car and therefore I can use the carpool lanes.' He's still fighting that ticket.

"Hello," I said into the beige handset positioned between the two bucket seats.

"This is Myles Hung Long," the voice said, an American voice. "Are you familiar with Tale of the Times?"

I thought it might be a bookstore, or someone selling magazine subscriptions. "No. What can I do for you?"

"It's what we can do for you, lady. Wade Deep and I are the organizers of the Society of the Best Equipped Men in America. Are you interested in pornography?"

"No." And I wasn't, no matter that my father was sitting next to me piloting the car back to my brother's cabin. I've always loved sex, but somehow pornography strikes me as sterile.

"Well, that's too bad," the voice went on. "Or maybe you never really gave it a try. We have tapes guaranteed to turn you on. You can play them in the privacy of your home on your VCR."

"How did you get this number?" What a joke. Privacy of your home. Your own VCR. I watched the swirl of the yellow leaves drifting along the roadside.

"Random selection. For $39.95 you can audition four tapes. We also have a follow-up service, should you find the tapes arousing, and would like more."

I smiled and shook my head. My father was casting glances at me out of the corner of his eye. "I'm eighty-four years old," I said. "I've seen all of that I need for one lifetime. Please don't call again." And I hung up.

"What was that?" my father asked, his eyes back on the highway as we turned into the dirt road.

"A survey," I said. "You've had this thing less than a day and already you're on everyone's soliciting list."

"So much can happen in one lifetime," my father said. "I remember when we got our first phone, with a hand crank to ring up the operator. Now strangers can call you up while you're driving down the highway."

When Frank and I returned from town Drew was already there. He and Nina were unloading a bag of groceries. Juice, danishes, cookies, potato chips, nothing that required cooking. The staples of life in my parents' home. A big bucket of Kentucky Fried Chicken sat on the counter. My mother had been a truly modern woman in her day, embracing all the great inventions of her time. Unbreakable Melmac plates. Swanson's frozen TV dinners. Wonder bread, with its sprayed-on vitamins. Consequently, everyone in my family is an expert on the nutritional value of junk food. A small can of fruit cocktail gives you all the daily allotment of vitamin C an adult needs. Oatmeal raisin cookies supply adequate fiber. Chocolate contains a natural tranquilizer. Beer has almost as many nutrients as milk and, with practice or necessity, can be enjoyed at room temperature.

"Build a fire, Emery," Drew said. "Get the chill off the room."

The wrappings and boxes from Nina's purchases provided a good base. Drew had already laid in dry twigs and small branches, lathing, split logs. As I built the pyramid in the grate I kept reading the cardboard boxes: This Side Up, Sony PH-W402 Operating Instructions. Building a fire, like fishing, is essentially a meditative activity. As I arranged the elements of the fire I could see Nina racing from department to department, deciding on her purchases as quickly as a snap of her fingers. No comparison shopping here. In the space of a couple of hours she'd decided on dozens of various items ranging from fur coats to pianos. Yet during the same time Frank had made only one purchase—the Buick with the car phone. They'd spent more in one day than I spend in a year. These were the two poles I'd grown up with and I still feel myself swinging between them, ping-ponging from one to the other, never settling on the net, the way a quarter will always land either heads or tails, never on the edge separating the two.

Drew, in his business suit, looked like a realtor chatting with Frank and Nina. I was impressed by his graceful movements as he circled through the cabin. I don't know where he picked up such elegance. My father, when he was younger, was a powerhouse, a steam engine, swift and thorough. He could destroy anything in his path. My mother either floated or fell, nothing graceful in either of her modes. And this woman had wanted to be a dancer. When she floated she bobbed about the room like an untethered helium balloon. When she fell she was all joints, wrists, elbows, knees. But Drew could glide through a minefield with a sprightly Fred Astaire dance step.

As he talked he tucked his hands into his pants pockets. I noticed the softness of his belly tipping over his belt. Why hadn't I noticed this before? Perhaps I've always suffered a selective blindness about my family, seeing only what I want to see so that their idiosyncrasies and inconsistencies won't confuse me. Maybe this was a family trait. When he picked me up at the airport Drew had been surprised my eyes were green. He was explaining the deco bathroom again, but listening to them was white music to me, a foreign language I couldn't understand. I concentrated on the fire, building it carefully, fanning the flames, watching the dry twigs catch and burn.

"You know," my father said, "at the South Pole toilets flush counterclockwise. It's called the Coriolis effect. It has to do with the earth's rotational direction. In the Northern hemisphere it's to the right, in the south, to the left. It reverses the direction of hurricanes and tornados. I've always wondered if that would make it physically impossible to have a hurricane exactly on the equator. If the equator might be the most meteorologically stable place on the planet." Where does my father learn such stuff?

"Come on, Emery," Drew said. "We gotta go."

I didn't question this but was surprised Frank and Nina made no objection. "Better take one of these parkas," Nina said. "The blue one would look nice with those jeans." Perhaps they'd already discussed all this, but I hadn't been listening.

In the BMW Drew took off his tie and stretched himself behind the wheel. "What the fuck's going on?" I asked. "Who's orchestrating this symphony?"

"Symphony? This here's cacophony, sweetheart. If anyone's in charge of all this they must have a wicked sense of humor."

"Okay," I said. "Twenty questions. Who are Kiskejohn and Tree?"

"They work for me."

"*That* much I already know. Where were you last night?"

"At Quinn's." He kept his eyes on the road and I had the paranoid notion he was keeping something from me.

"Quinn? Who's Quinn?"

Drew shifted through the gears. "She's my friend, a woman I don't really understand, my main squeeze, someone else's wife, a teller at the bank, a member of the Sierra Club, a redhead, a coke dealer, a liberal Democrat, an Aquarian, the owner of two hamsters."

"Oh," I said. "So that's Quinn. I see. Does her husband mind when you spend the night with her? Your main squeeze?"

"He's a software salesman. Drives an Audi . . ."

I held up my hand. "Spare me. Where are we going? To Quinn's, perhaps?"

"To Coleman's. You have to meet Coleman."

"Coleman?" I said. "Drew. What's going on here? What are we doing?"

He looked at me briefly, then cut his eyes back to the road. "I honestly don't know, Emery. We're all playing this by ear. I've given up trying to figure it out. I'm just going with the first thing that hits my mind. Intuition, flights of fancy. You name it. I can't."

"Somebody has to be in charge here." My spirit was sinking, slipping like mercury down my spine to pool in my instep. Yet I knew I could change it all, if only to demand Drew take me to the airport and get me on the first plane back to San Francisco. Why not? Why stay? What difference did it make where I was?

"Emery, love. Since when has anyone ever been in charge? We've been running on blind faith all our lives. Running on empty in the fast lane. So what's the difference now? Go get the gate."

We turned down another dirt road, away from the city. Indian summer was just leaving the land, the maples tipped with yellow from the first frost. My blood felt thick as honey and just as slow. In the twilight we skirted the edge of the lake. In a flash I could imagine this farmland sectioned off into fancy tract houses, a bedroom suburb. Aquamarine swimming pools.

Since I've made a profession out of moving around I've

developed a good sense of direction, but, like a superimposed image, I still see other places beneath, behind, pasted over, the actual terrain. A curious thing began to happen to me after the seventh or eighth move. All the cities began to look alike. On the first day of school when I was in the fourth grade I got up, got dressed, and began walking to school in the direction I'd walked to school when I'd been in third grade, Drew trailing at my side. Drew kept questioning me. 'Are you sure we're going the right way? I don't remember railroad tracks when Mom took us to meet the teachers.' I kept walking, taking the same turns in the same direction the way I'd done when I was walking to third grade in Elgin, Illinois. But by the time Drew and I entered school in the fall we were living in Elmira, New York. I walked until the exact amount of time had passed to get us to school in Elgin. Then I stopped, surprised to find we were in the middle of a railroad yard. 'What are we doing here?' Drew asked. 'Going to school,' I said.

We kept going to that railroad yard for almost a week, thrilled at the sight of the massive trains pulling in and out of the yard, until an old man who had something to do with the trains became suspicious of two little kids hanging around the tracks day after day. He must have called someone because the next day a woman in high heels made her way across the tracks toward us. She asked who we were, and we dutifully told her. She asked where we lived, who our parents were, and like good children we told her. She led us back to the car and we got in. Once we arrived at the school where our mother had taken us a few weeks before so we could meet our new teachers, she told us to sit in the principal's office. Drew and I scribbled pictures of trains in the railroad yard until Nina and Julia showed up.

After that the woman in the high heels picked us up every morning for school. She was waiting for us after school and drove us home. She was our truant officer. She did this every day until we moved, in the dead of winter. I was still in fourth grade. Drew was in second. But the new place we lived had a school bus that stopped right at our corner so Drew and I didn't have a chance to get lost.

We pulled into a yard surrounded by haphazard buildings and long chicken wire runs. A woman in army fatigues came out and greeted Drew. "This is Coleman," Drew said.

I looked at her closely, the veins in her hand as she shook mine, the lines surrounding her eyes. She was about my age, although from a distance her thick shock of pure white hair made you think she was older. She ushered us into the house and poured coffee.

Her voice was melodic, dainty, feminine. "Drew said you were visiting. Too bad about the fire." The sound of her army boots banging against the hardwood floor as she puttered around the kitchen almost drowned out her soft voice.

"The fire's the least of it," I said. "Drew's got us living in an abandoned cabin." And then I felt stupid; she probably knew more about what Drew had in mind than I did. There was a relationship here and for just a moment I could see myself as Coleman, Drew's confidante and friend. Picture a place in the country, your banker brother dropping by to talk on long Sunday afternoons. A pot roast in the oven. I realized I didn't know a damn thing about my brother, not his thoughts or his feelings. His thoughts might be turquoise colored, not gold. I couldn't decide if I was shocked, or hurt. Imagine, shocked or hurt over the loss of a fantasy, as insubstantial and intangible as the feeling of touching a cloud.

"My husband left me three years ago," Coleman said, as if that's what we'd been discussing. "It's really quite wonderful. This was Bo's family's place for the last couple of generations. Now it's mine. He went to Las Vegas to become a gambler. He only gave it to me because he was afraid he'd lose it at cards. He didn't like the thought of a stranger owning it. Come on, I'll show you."

Coffee cups in hand, we followed Coleman out to the pens in back. In the dying light of the day I noticed a large barn and heard horses whinnying. And the long chicken wire runs. The first one was filled with pink flamingos.

"You won't believe some of the animals out here," Coleman said in her soft voice. "These guys were in the Pittsburgh zoo. A bunch of kids broke in and started snapping their legs." I looked at the flamingos, the long wand-like legs, feathered wings arced away from their bodies as they fled to the corner of the pen, squawking like children. "I'll be returning them soon. You can see," she gestured toward the pink birds, almost as tall as I was, "they're in pretty good shape now."

"Why?" I asked. "Why would anyone do that?" I imagined the flock of splay-legged birds, crying in pain and writhing on the ground.

"Vandals," Coleman said. "Delinquents looking for kicks. Flamingos are very sensitive to shock disease. You upset them and some will just drop over dead. These are the survivors, but they were pretty badly shook up. They shipped them down here to cool out."

"Cool out," I said, watching as the flamingos huddled in a corner of the pen. Flamingos cooling out, R & R for birds. Shock disease.

"Coleman runs a sanctuary," Drew said. "Her husband raised Arabians. Once Bo left she started taking in birds."

Coleman waved her hand at the rest of the cages. "They all have a story. This one has a happy ending. Most don't." We followed her out of the cage and across the dirt track to the next one. A crabapple tree grew in the center, the topmost branches poking through the chicken wire. Coleman began to cluck and call, and birds in the branches answered back, booming 'hooo's, buzzing, clicking, warbles, and whistles. "Most have just gone to roost for the night," Coleman said. "Except for this fellow," she reached up and grabbed a white, fluffy ball, which I'd assumed was a cat. A cat in a bird sanctuary? The owl blinked luminous platinum eyes at us. "He's an albino, abandoned, or maybe pushed out of the nest. And he's blind. A farmer in the next county found him and brought him over. We keep him here or he dies. There's something wrong with all of them." She pointed to a big parakeet-looking bird, blue-gray and orange, tottering across the ground, making for the safety of a shrub. "Kestral," she said. "A small falcon. But it's got rickets. Too slow to catch anything on its own. Can't fly. So we take care of him."

Although there were several pickups in various stages of decay parked around the lot there didn't seem to be anyone but Coleman here. "Who's we?" I asked.

"Kiskejohn and Tree. They're as helpless as these birds. This way they can at least earn a living."

"Who's paying for all this?"

"Emery," Drew said, "that's none of your damned business."

"It's okay," Coleman said. She looked back and forth between the two of us. "She's your sister, right? She's only asking the same questions you did when you first came out here." She pointed up to the top of the crabapple tree. "See him?" she asked. "That white spot. That's Jason. He started all this. He's a bald eagle found in Idaho with both his wings broken, as if someone tried to tear them off him. Through my husband and his horses we knew the state senator from Idaho and somehow, since he'll never fly again, he ended up here. He's too pathetic to keep in a zoo, the national bird, crippled and crawling around. So when we got Jason we got some federal funding. Now we've got flamingos. And pelicans with their bills sawed off. They never caught the guy who did that. I'd rather have these dudes than my own MX missile."

"Yeah, I guess," I said. As the silver-blue dusk slowly enveloped the yard I felt the taste of brass in my mouth. A place in the country for battered birds, a husband who wants to be a gambler, employees who can't take care of themselves. An idyllic country setting filled with flaws. Paradise on a seconds table, reduced for quick sale.

"It's perfect," Coleman said. "I get up in the morning and know exactly what I'm going to do, every minute of the day. It feels good to be doing this. Nothing scary about any of it."

"Nothing scary?" I was amazed. "I'd be terrified if I was shipped a bunch of pelicans with their bills chopped off. How can they eat? Where would you get the fish?"

Coleman shrugged it off. "You learn. I guess you could say I've become a paraveterinarian. I'll tell you what's scary. Going to work like Drew does. Just putting on a suit like that every day would terrify me."

"You always say that," Drew said. "It's really not as bad as you think. I get up every day and know exactly what I'm going to do too."

"But it's not perfect," Coleman said. "You've got to adjust your problems to your life. You're doing someone else's work. Me, I just do what's good for me. And that's what makes it perfect. There's not a thing I would change."

I just stared at her. I'd never entertained the idea anyone's life could be perfect. Adjust your problems to your life? Life was nothing *but* problems. How can you adjust what you can't control? You could as easily predict the timing of a heat wave.

"You don't get it, do you?" Coleman looked at me like a math teacher trying to explain a simple theorem. "The Zen Buddhists believe a perfect bull's-eye is the result of ninety-nine misses. Yet none of us live long enough to outlast the time it takes to miss ninety-nine times. So I'm not aiming for a perfect bull's-eye. I'm aiming to keep one bird, or horse, I've even got a raccoon, just keep them alive from day to day. That's all you can hope for."

"She gets all that Buddhist shit from Kiskejohn," Drew said.

No matter where she got it, this woman had hope. Hope, that most faithful of lovers. Perhaps hope is contagious. I wanted to see the eagle fly away, the owl swoop down upon a mouse, the kestral floating on a thermal. Not just any eagle, or owl, or kestral. These birds, healed. I've always longed for the impossible. Macondo. Egyplosis, where living things are created through spiritual power. Camphor Island, the home of the unicorn.

"Come on," Coleman said. "We'll finish the chores and I'll feed you. Kiskejohn and Tree have already eaten and gone. But there's some chicken left over."

"So Kiskejohn and Tree live here?"

Coleman was moving toward the barn, and the horses seemed to sense this. I could hear whinnying, stamping, snorting. "Yep. Grab that bag of oats."

Drew was ahead of me and reached for an open sack.

"Not you," Coleman said. "You'll ruin your fancy suit. Honestly, Drew, if you're going to hang around out here, you ought to dress for the occasion."

"Leave it alone," Drew said. "I've got more than one suit."

There were seven horses, five Arabians and two Thoroughbreds. Paris and I once managed an estate where I became especially involved with one Thoroughbred, Love & Money. I used to challenge Paris to race me. That was years ago. I haven't been on a horse since.

Coleman recited their names and pedigrees, stroked their muzzles, and gave me apples to feed them. For the first time since I arrived in this strange inland city, I began to feel calm, secure beside the massive, warm presence of the horses.

"Did you find the bell?" Drew asked when we finally closed the door on the barn.

"It's in the shed. But you're going to have to figure out how to hang it."

"Let's see it." Drew strode toward a pre-fab tin box.

In a welter of ropes, tack, saddles, car parts, and other unidentifiable objects, Coleman pulled out a large iron triangle. It looked exactly like a prop in a western. The whole shed looked like something Nina might compile. "You can use this for emergencies," she said to me.

"Look here," I said. "I'm going back to San Francisco. And I don't know how a goddamn dinner bell is going to help out in emergencies."

"The lake's right over that ridge," Coleman said, pointing at the treeline as we headed toward the house. "And the sound travels like you wouldn't believe. During the day I can hear Kiskejohn and Tree working on Drew's house. You hang that bell and if you need something, I'll be able to hear it."

"Listen," I said. "I can't stay here. There's nothing I can do for them. I should go back home." I thought of my kitchen, a little galley affair, and then looked around Coleman's kitchen, a big, warm, farm-style room. You could put a couch in that kitchen, lay back, and watch soup simmer all day.

"You can stay here for me," Drew said. "I need you. Someone has to keep an eye on them out here. It would have been different if they'd taken the apartment."

Coleman put cold fried chicken, potato salad, and biscuits on the table. Drew went to a cabinet and pulled out a bottle of rye. I tried to concentrate on eating, but Drew and Coleman seemed determined to convince me I should stay and watch over Frank and Nina. "What else have you got to do?" Drew kept asking.

"Look," Coleman said. "I don't know why I have to tell you this. But this is a bad spot. You can make a difference, you know."

I resented all this pressure, particularly from a woman I

didn't know. "I don't see how any of this is any of your business."

"Fucking A it's my business." Coleman took out a cigarette, lit it elaborately, theatrically. "I'm feeding you. You'll stay here tonight. And if you don't help Drew all this shit will fall on my shoulders. I don't need that. Drew's my friend. But I don't see why I should have to take on your whole damn family."

"No one is asking you to do jack squat." Suddenly the meal turned sour in my mouth. My center of gravity shifted as if I'd swallowed a rock.

Coleman blew a smoke ring at the ceiling. "There are things you do for your friends."

"I wouldn't know about that," I said. "I'd have to read a book on how to make a friend. My friends have always come to me as gifts. I'd have no more notion about how to go out and make a friend than I have about quantum physics or nuclear disarmament. I know those things exist, but I don't know how they work. We moved around so much the word 'friend' never made it into our vocabulary."

Drew corrected me. "*You* move around so much. My moving days are over. I'd do the same thing for Coleman."

"I already owe you," Coleman said. "From when Bo left."

Drew shrugged. "The point is, Emery, they're our parents. You're here and there doesn't seem to be any burning reason for you to leave at this very moment. Having you here makes a big difference."

"I'm not sure I want to make a difference. To tell you the truth, I'm scared. I know they're just an old man and an old woman. But they still terrify me the way they did when I was a kid."

"Well, sure," Drew said. "I'm scared too. Those two are as unpredictable as a bank robbery. I mean, my god, they've burned their house down. They've decided on this camping in the woods shit. Nothing's changed since we were kids, sweetheart. I just need you to help me watch over them until they get resettled."

"You said that could take months. I can't stay here for months."

"It won't take that long," Coleman said. "I mean, I'd put them up here except I've already got Kiskejohn and Tree. Besides, living in that cabin's going to get old. They'll get things straightened away and into a regular house before too long. In the meantime, why don't you help your brother out? You're here after all."

Drew patted my thigh. "Listen, kiddo. I'm the baby brother. I depend on you."

I had the feeling this was some kind of interview. BABYSITTER WANTED FOR ELDERLY COUPLE. WAGES TO BE GIVEN AS CREDIT FOR COSMIC DEBT. "I'm going to be about as useful as an elephant out here," I said.

"You don't understand," Drew said. "I've always depended on you. When I visited you in San Francisco you'd go off to work in the morning and I'd get so damn pissed, or scared, when you walked out the door I thought I'd spit nails. I'd sulk around your kitchen throwing toast at the walls. I'd toast the whole loaf, two by two, and pitch them at the wall as soon as they popped up. Then I'd clean up the kitchen so you would never know and spent most of my time in the Park, in the Garden for the Blind. I'd eat the spearmint, crush the nettles between my fingers, and think about being blind."

"Blind? Why would you think about being blind?"

"It seems I can only see far enough to establish my own cozy little nest. Everything gets fuzzy outside of that. The whole time I was in San Francisco, except when you were around, I felt like I was dizzy, like I would pass out on the street."

"I sort of knew you would never really make the break

and stay in San Francisco. But I didn't think it would make you dizzy."

"San Francisco's one crazy town," Coleman said. "Second only to New York and Tijuana. That's why I don't like to travel. You run into too much weird shit."

"You've just got to turn it around," I said. "Traveling can remove you from a lot of weird shit."

Drew snorted. "Right."

I walked out on Drew when he was fourteen. I didn't think of myself as abandoning him, only of shutting out Frank and Nina. When I was young I was invincible. I didn't know how flawed I was, what my limits were. Anything was possible, I would live forever, nothing was irreversible. The past consisted of only what I chose to remember. The future was anything I could imagine. And Drew wasn't really part of that picture, he was a given, my brother, assumed and never questioned the way we never question our breathing.

Over the years Drew, not my parents, anchored me. He went to the same university to earn both his degrees, lived in the same town, had the same phone number. I could always call him and as I remember it, he was always home. As I bounced around across the country, trying to shed my past, myself, which followed me like an animal's tail, I could call Drew. Several years would go by between visits. I can only remember one or two Christmas cards, no letters. But I always had a sense Drew was there. It wasn't until that very moment, sitting in Coleman's kitchen, I realized how much I'd taken for granted.

"I give up," I said. "At least for tonight." Maybe all along some part of me wanted to be asked, begged, to stay. That's one of the goals in the game of Come and Get Me, the game Paris and I played so well. I was waiting for an acknowledgment, a physical demonstration, that I was needed, wanted, loved.

I eyed the rye, knowing I had been deceiving myself

about not drinking while I was here. As talismanically and childishly important as counting cows along the roadside. I rose from the table and got myself a glass.

And then it all seemed to be settled and we were free to move on to other topics. I was curious about Coleman. She seemed the only one capable of stringing more than two sentences together. Tree couldn't come up with more than two words in a row. Kiskejohn spoke in ellipses. Maybe Coleman could give me some idea as to what these people, these people who were supposed to help me out, what these people were like.

"I couldn't hack the city." Coleman lit up her second cigarette, more casually this time. "My mother shipped me off to Philadelphia to study music. I still play a little from time to time. Flute. But in Philadelphia I didn't have enough confidence to get on a bus. At one point I had to go out and get a job, a real job like Drew here. My bedroom faced the street and about seven o'clock every morning I'd hear people going to work. I'd get up and practice getting dressed, but I could never finish the whole procedure. I'd get my makeup on one eye, but couldn't do the other. That kind of thing. So instead, I married Bo. I knew it wouldn't last long, which made it even better. I'm not good with people. They frighten me. I just want you to know that. But I'm good with animals, the way some people have a green thumb with plants. I always think of animals as the true beings in the world. Pure. An animal has never driven me to drink, to move, to quit my job. Never driven me to self-pity. An animal can make me humble, but an animal has never humiliated me. So I'm doing the right thing here. And Bo was sweet enough to just leave after a year or so. Everything is perfect now."

Perfect. I tried to picture myself splinting a broken bird wing, breaking Arabian horses to saddle. I would be as helpless as Nina in a kitchen. Perfect.

"Bullshit," Drew said. "Life's not perfect. It's a process."

He poked absently at the chicken bones with his fork. "It's just that you never completely finish, you never heal." He gave a bitter laugh. "You no sooner get over one accident or injury, you break your leg, or your heart." He smiled, his face falling into harmony around his lovely aquiline nose. "You know my favorite cartoon? The king and his jester are walking down the hall. The king's pissed off and turns to the jester and says, 'No one thanks me for the heads I *don't* lop off.' Life isn't like money. You don't get any emotional credit."

I could feel my whole body becoming loose as the rye worked its magic. Emotional credit. Adjust your problems to your life. "Everything is looney tunes here," I said. "I don't see how I can help right now. I should go home."

Drew's voice became suddenly strident. "Let's not start that again. You've got to stay, even if only as a favor. It's that imaginary car wreck I was telling you about. Floating over the retaining wall. Suspended motion."

I was surprised at his sudden anger. Drew, who always seemed so together. "You should have made them check into a motel."

Drew shrugged. "I'm flying by the seat of my pants, blindfolded. Frank wasn't about to do anything. I knew anything I didn't want him to have would be the one thing he would go for. So I gave him a choice. Either way, I knew I was going to lose. That's the way it always is with us."

"I'm going to bed," Coleman said. "I'm glad to help out, but I don't want to know the details. Drew, you know where the sheets and stuff are."

We said goodnight as Coleman, a large glass of rye in hand, left the kitchen and mounted the stairs.

Drew moved into the living room and opened up the hide-a-bed in the couch. "Julia," he said. "I sometimes wonder how things would have been if Julia had come back from Vietnam."

"I never knew her. I can't remember ever talking to her,

playing with her." My strongest memory of my younger sister was a night when our parents had gotten into a physical fight. Drew and I were under my bed upstairs, listening to glasses being smashed, thuds, shouts, slaps, cries, and screams. I decided we weren't safe in the house and Drew and I crawled out from under the bed and decided to sneak down the stairs. If I remember correctly, our plan was to go to the bus station, since it was open twenty-four hours. I took twenty dollars from my mother's purse. A fortune. Maybe we planned to stow away on a bus, end up in Chicago or Reno. Julia was lying in the big double bed in my parents' room. 'Come on,' I whispered, pulling her arm, jerking her thumb out of her mouth. She shook her head 'No,' bit my hand like an angry dog, and popped her thumb back in her mouth, her eyes so wide and round the whites seemed to glow. 'Come on,' I hissed, and tried to pick her up and carry her away from the house with us. She squirreled and squirmed and kicked until she wriggled out of my arms and fell to the floor. Immediately, she jumped back up on the bed, burrowed under the covers and pillows. 'He'll kill her,' Drew said. 'Let him,' I replied, rubbing my sore hand. Grabbing Drew's hand we made our way down the stairs and out the front door into the night. But we lingered on the front lawn, watching our parents slap and pummel each other through the big picture window until a police car pulled up.

"That's cause she never talked or played." Drew opened a closet and took out some bedding. He threw me a couple of pillows and some pillowcases. "After the service I went into therapy for a while. Did I tell you that? I went in because I didn't feel anything about Julia's death. I just knew she was gone. I felt maybe she'd always been gone. Ginny kept telling me that was sick. That I was supposed to be overwhelmed by grief at the loss of my sister. That's what I told the shrink on my first visit. I said, 'My sister's dead. I'm not even surprised. It's like if you just told me your brother had died. I'd be sorry, but not deeply because I don't know your brother. I suppose I'm underwhelmed.' That's what I told him."

"Underwhelmed," I repeated, stuffing a pillow into its case. "Flammable and inflammable. Valuable and invaluable."

"Sort of like that," Drew said.

"So what did this therapist do for you?" I couldn't imagine Drew unveiling his soul to a therapist. I always thought of him as too independent to take anyone else's ideas as his own.

"Not much that I could see. It was like spending all this money to talk to a wall. A very nice wall, well decorated, nothing splashy. But just a wall nevertheless."

"Tree said he knew Julia in Vietnam."

Drew nodded. "You got Tree to talk? You must be some kind of wonder."

"He's not much of a man with words. But he wouldn't tell me any more than that. Those two are a weird pair."

"Definitely. They're still in Nam. They've got the buddy system for life."

"You ever regret not being in the war?" Drew missed the draft by one year, spent the whole war studying money in college.

He smoothed the sheets around the corners of the mattress. "Only when I'm around Kiskejohn and Tree. Even though they are terminally fucked up, they know something. They're closer to knowing about life than I am. I'm a spectator, compared to them."

"You don't have to kill a bunch of people, become terminally fucked for life, to feel alive. Look at Charlie Manson. Now there's a role model for you. Every year he tries to build a balloon and sail over the walls of San Quentin"

"Emery, love. Women have a whole different orientation to the problem than men. I thought you'd have figured that out by now. Especially since sometimes you seem more male than female."

"More male than female? Why? Because I don't have kids?"

"Naw. Just look at the issues you get involved in. You've been to jail because of Vietnam. Now you say half your friends have AIDS. Very male issues. I've never heard you get worked up over abortion or day care. You always toss those issues off. 'Since birth control, you shouldn't have a kid if you can't afford it.' You must have said that a thousand times. You act as if those aren't issues at all. *Finito*. And for you, they aren't. Anyhow, if you had a kid it would probably turn out to be a terrorist or a murderer, an arsonist or a rapist. You should get a tax break, maybe a medal, commending you for saving the country from another psycho. Same for me. You know, that's why Ginny left me. I had a vasectomy. Whether it's heredity or environment the only thing we can pass on is madness, craziness. Fucked-up-ness. Ginny wanted a kid."

"A vasectomy? You never told me. Jesus. That's definitely making a statement." A slow sensation, like goose-bumps. My brother, a given that I'd never questioned. But in truth, my brother was a stranger I just happened to know.

"I don't want to be responsible for another miserable life. I've never really learned how to trust anyone, anyone except you. Even Ginny. I knew she could hurt me, and I could never completely trust her because of that."

And I knew exactly what he meant. Paris and I had spent twenty-five years proving we couldn't trust each other. All our vulnerability, defensiveness. And how we used it against each other. Paris and Molly spooned together in my bed. Paris had been right, all those years ago. I could love a pet, but I had nothing left to give a person, a child.

"Maybe we're overreacting," I said, but I wasn't sure even I believed what I was saying. "Maybe we've overreacted all our lives. There's probably not an individual in history who didn't have a rotten childhood."

"We won't know that, now will we? If Julia'd lived, and had her kid, we might have been able to field test that idea. But," he snapped a blanket over the bed, "Julia, well, sometimes I think of Julia like a dog, a very expensive, pretty, smart dog, hit by a truck and left to limp off to the side of the road and die or recover on its own. Only it's kind of all turned around with Julia. She didn't get hit until she stopped being a baby. She limped along, and then suddenly got this burst of life. And once she did that, she was shot down for sure."

I let out a long sigh, took another sip from the glass of rye. "Pretty cynical, Drew. Nice talk." I was getting drunk, 'Zippedy Doo Dah' kept running through my head.

"You know, Emery, sometimes I feel I've got a hole in my soul. What I can't figure out is how you can have a hole if you never had what should have been in that hole. So there's something I don't even know about that separates me from everyone else. From the rest of the world. When I die I'll probably be put in a cage situated so I can watch what's going on in Heaven and Hell."

"Cut the self-pity," I said. "With ordinary luck I'd be in a cage right along side of you. If we stuck our arms through the bars we could hold hands." I thought of us holding hands through eternity, and that seemed right, calming. A sense of justice.

"Naw, not you," Drew said. "Women are supposed to know they need partners. Only men are spoiled enough to think they're so powerful they can go it alone. Is there a Ms. Robinson Crusoe?"

"Bullshit. The Lone Ranger had Tonto. Sherlock Holmes had Watson. Abbott had Costello."

"And I suppose you can tell me who's Rambo's best buddy?"

"I don't watch Rambo. Vietnam was too real for those kinds of cartoons."

Drew laughed. "See? You've got a man's mind inside a woman's body. Kiskejohn and Tree say the same thing. And they should know."

"Fuck." I stretched my arms and back gingerly. I still felt achy and itchy from the fire the other night. 'Zippedy Doo Dah.'

Drew came up behind me and started rubbing my back. He put his arms around me, holding me tight. I rubbed my temple against his chin, felt the whiskers just under the surface. "Think we're any worse off than anyone else?"

"It doesn't matter," Drew said. "Nobody thanks you for the heads you don't lop off."

He let go of me and went over to smooth the blanket across the bed. "Listen, Emery." He busily straightened the bedding. "There's something I suppose I should tell you." He concentrated on the bedding as if it were to become a work of art.

"Spit it out, Drew."

He plumped the pillows vigorously. "We're about to have a big fight."

"We are? What about?" I wasn't even very curious. Maybe it was the rye, but it seemed there was nothing Drew and I could seriously fight about. I'd agreed to stay. There weren't any other issues outside of that. 'Zippedy Doo Dah.'

He wouldn't look at me. "I talked to Paris today."

I choked on the rye. "What? What? Paris?"

"He called the bank. Said Victor gave him my number. He said he's going to New York, but that he wants to stop by and see you for a few minutes. Something about Victor." Drew wouldn't look at me. He kept smoothing the blanket.

I couldn't breathe. Paris? Here? "God damn you, Drew. What the fuck do you think that's going to prove? That's all we need, one more clown for this circus."

Drew threw up his hands. "He said it was about Victor. He's just stopping by. He's going to New York." He sat on the edge of the bed and began taking off his shoes.

I took a long gulp of the rye. Paris. Here. I should have known. This was a perfect situation for Paris to appear. Perfect.

"Come on," Drew said, patting the bed. "I stand to be the big loser here. You and Paris always cut to the chase."

"I'd like to shoot you in the elbows and the knees for this, Drew. I'd like to pull out all your teeth with pliers. Wrap your heart in barbed wire."

He took off his shirt and tossed it across the room. "Do it while I'm asleep. It's late. I've got to go to work in the morning."

I shucked out of my clothes and crawled into bed next to Drew. He wrapped his arm around me and we nestled together like lovers. "Listen," he whispered in my ear. "He said it was something serious about Victor. I know how you care about Victor. Normally I wouldn't have told him a thing."

"There's an Afghan blessing," I said. " 'May God deliver you from the venom of the snake, the teeth of the tiger, and the vengeance of the other.' You have just run afoul of the vengeance of the other."

As I curled up in Drew's arms that night I wanted to be high, to snort coke or speed, to be drunk, or at least to fall asleep. I felt my whole body fluttering, on the edge of something but not into the abyss yet. The closer you are to the precipice the faster you dance. Yet Drew snored, his breath blowing gently across my back. I could feel his cock hardening, pressing into the hollow of the backs of my thighs. I've always believed men can sleep through anything. It's a wonder they stay awake during sex. But I have been a career insomniac and no matter how hard you try you can't escape your life. I'm an expert in that field, as expert as any battalion commander who's just surrendered to the enemy. And that surrender always occurs during the deepest hours of the night. No hope for a new beginning with the dawn.

Paris was coming. Just stopping by on his way to New York. Something important about Victor. Reinventing the past is as impossible as skating on hot water. When there is no home to return to, you carry it with you, just a change in the climate. Paris and Drew were the only constants in my life.

Paris and I had been together on and off for over twenty years. But five years ago when Paris told me he was getting married, I felt the loss I didn't feel when Julia died. I never thought Paris would marry. Maybe I'd been saving all my emotions for that one crash to the bottom. And that's when Victor stepped in.

Five years ago we were lying in bed when Paris announced he was getting married. "Don't worry," he told me. "It won't change anything between us." I discovered I really didn't miss him too much if I kept high on coke, and cut the jitters with vodka. It was a useful solution, for a while. When I was low on money I'd substitute speed and wine. I was too much in love with my own solitary solace. The days had a nice, chemically predictable pattern to them. A line of coke before I got out of bed, vodka and grapefruit juice for breakfast. At work Pepper, who ran the camera room as her private domain, would give me a line of speed a couple of times a day. My metabolism is screwy, like that of a hyperactive child who needs to take Ritalin, an amphetamine, to calm down. While Pepper would zip around the ceiling after a hit of speed, I'd sit back with my feet up on the light table and savor the buzz while listening to blues or jazz on the radio. Pepper and I made a good team: my calm would bring her down and her speeding would get me up.

The rhythm of the evening was usually determined by Victor. Since Victor had tested positive for the AIDS virus he was trying to give up sex the way I was trying to give up loving Paris. I'm a careful druggie. I've never dealt, don't keep any more than I need in the house. As a dealer, Victor was an ideal partner. I'd go over to his house and we'd watch old movies from the 40s on his VCR between customers. We'd talk about love, the pleasures of sex, always in the past tense. Much as he'd try to abstain there would generally be a customer at some point during the evening whom Victor just couldn't resist. He'd give me a little coke for the morning and send me home, a bribe perhaps, or maybe just a kind gesture on his part.

It was a nice arrangement for a couple of months. I love gay men because they are frequently more entertaining and polite to women than straight guys. We generally enjoy the same things: gaudy women's clothes, antiques, houseplants, silk sheets. Victor and I liked the same type of man. And there was never any pressure to have sex. I believed sex was like any other addiction: with enough will power you can give it up. But, of course, this was before I tried to give anything up. Except Paris. Victor and I argued about this.

Besides, by then, somehow, the whole world seemed paired off. Married men carried their babies like trophies on their backs. Their women walked slightly ahead of the men, loaded down with chic diaper bags. These couples, which seemed to be everyone except gay men, had about a fifteen-minute attention span, the amount of time it takes a child to die of Sudden Infant Death or get into trouble. Their infants terrified me. I expected an ear or arm to fall off at any moment.

Summer came and Victor found a boy he really couldn't resist. They decided to spend a couple of weeks up on the Russian River, try out some real summer weather and escape the cold and fog of San Francisco. 'The coldest winter I ever spent was a summer in San Francisco.' I forget who first said that. I always break out my furs in August and wear them to the Giants games in Candlestick Park.

Victor had left me a good stash of coke, and if I'd been three IQ points smarter I would have remembered why I never keep drugs around. In five days I'd finished the coke. I figured I'd hit Pepper for some speed to get me through the next ten days until Victor returned. And that worked out quite well until the middle of the following week when Pepper got busted for dealing. Big time bust, made the TV news. The next day at work I started getting pretty sick and shaky and had to go home. I tried to pull myself together to see if I could help Pepper. But someone raised her bail and she instantly skipped town. In that whole period the one thing I'm proud of is that I didn't call Paris.

We all have our own get-well cures, our personal equivalent of chicken soup. I figured I'd coast down on wine until Victor returned and since I was too sick to go out I called various liquor stores each day, charged enough wine on my credit cards to keep a trainload of soldiers drunk for a week. I told the clerks I was having a party. My only criterion was to have the wine delivered. By the time Victor returned my apartment was scattershot, wine bottles littered around like giant confetti.

When Victor found me I hadn't eaten in over two weeks. Anorexia can be quite pleasant. After a certain point food is nauseating, even a piece of cheese can feel like a rock moving through your system. Twenty-eight feet of intestine, and you can feel every painful twist and turn. But your mind floats light and free, as if it is sailing before a strong wind. I was sprawled across the couch when Victor let himself in with his key.

"I haven't called Paris." That was the first thing I told him.

Victor, bronzed as a sun god, his curly hair long and boyish, looked at me sadly. I was confused. He might have been Mel Gibson. Bruce Springsteen. Raul Julia. He waved his hand at the dozen or so wine bottles flanking the couch. "Maybe you should have," he said.

"Paris doesn't care about me."

"You got that one straight. Looks like you don't care about you either."

I laughed. "I'll be fine. You know how to make me fine."

"Right." Victor laid out a line of coke. "But this time it's going to cost you."

I struggled to sit up on the couch. "You going to make

me pay because I'm not a very good housekeeper?" My eyes really didn't see the room, only the coke on the mirror as Victor chopped.

"Yeah," he said. "You're so far gone I got to get you up to get you together. There are very few rules in this business but one of the rules I've got is that I never give coke to hopeless cases."

The coke made me feel better, even gave me enough energy to help Victor take thirty-some wine bottles out of my apartment. We snuck them into my neighbors' trash cans up and down the street. Then he pulled my suitcases out of the closet.

There was an edge of paranoia coming on when I saw the suitcases. "We taking a trip?" I tried to sound excited, but the little voice in the back of my head was telling me this wasn't going to be a weekend in Mexico.

"Yeah," Victor said, as if the idea was new to him. "We're taking a little trip. This very afternoon."

As I watched Victor going through my closets and drawers I felt less and less elated by his tone, flat with the false enthusiasm of a liar. "I got plastic," I said. "Scratch the luggage. I'll just buy new."

"Get in the shower," Victor said. "You smell like formaldehyde."

Getting into the shower meant stepping over the rim of the tub, a dangerous idea in my condition. Victor helped me; he scrubbed my back, massaged my head as he shampooed, stroked my legs. "You're going to love this," he kept saying. "You're really going to love this."

Even though Victor is a connoisseur of women's clothes I discovered later he'd packed a bag full of bricks. No belt, three socks, none of them matching. My burgundy fuck-me teddy. Five sweatshirts. No jeans. He kept loading me up on coke until even the paranoia disappeared. Holding my arm as if I were an old woman, he guided me down the stairs and into his car. He opened a bottle of wine and gave me my own vial for the trip. I remember it was a beautiful day once we got out of the city, warming up as the bright afternoon sun played across the fields.

"Oregon," I said when I noticed we were heading north.

"Not quite," Victor said.

"There's something you're not telling me." The suspicion was back, but I couldn't believe Victor would hurt me.

"Yeah," he said. "Don't forget to keep that bottle down. The police don't want our number. Let's walk out like movie stars."

At the dryout farm sobriety worked only until I realized what sobriety really felt like—exactly the way I'd felt in high school before serious drinking and drugging began. Before those days when sex, drugs, and unemployment were truly recreational sports. Pain heals in just the same way a broken bone in an eight-year-old will heal faster than a broken bone in an eighty-year-old. There must be some mathematical formula to predict how much pain you'll feel as the weight of the years accumulates. Suddenly there were those quiet moments so searingly painful I would wonder why people weren't hurling themselves from buildings with the regularity of falling leaves in autumn. The world felt stopped, the sun would never set, birds would hang suspended in midair. And yet I knew somewhere the world didn't feel like this, day after day. When I was twelve I found the answer. It was easy, right at hand. I believed that if I'd had an unhappy childhood it was because I neither smoked nor drank. My parents had found this answer decades before, and for years I believed smoking and drinking were the only good things they'd bequeathed me.

But sobriety wasn't the answer either. It attacked the symptom, but not the problem. After the dryout farm I joined AA for a couple of months. But I didn't feel all that fabled fellowship. I felt I'd been ostracized to a leper colony. Here are all these very nice people. They didn't ask to get leprosy. They try to help each other as much as they can. They fight against their disease every day. Very brave people in a lot of ways. Locked in a leper colony. Alcoholics. The only thing holding them together: their disease.

But, years after the fact, it gave me a window into my mother's loss. We all live with ghosts. Paris is my ghost, Julia is my mother's. Julia was ten the last time I saw her. A generation used to be counted as twenty years, but I recently read a statistic that claims, due to the saturation of media, generations are now counted by intervals of seven years. That made an intuitive kind of sense to me. Drew and I are of the same generation, Julia belonged to a different generation, or perhaps generation isn't the right word for how I feel about my sister. Julia belonged to my mother. I've never been able to think of her as my sister, the way I think of Drew as my brother. When Julia vanished she was Nina's loss. My world hadn't changed.

I went home for the memorial service in 1976. When the Vietcong attacked Da Nang hundreds of bodies, mostly children, were lost when the orphanage was hit. My parents received a letter stating Julia was dead and had been buried in the church cemetery. I hadn't really been back since I'd left for college ten years earlier. My parents looked the same; they just acted differently. Frank spent a lot of time sitting in the backyard while Drew managed the household and the service. Nina had vacated the couch, locking herself in Julia's room and I only saw her once, the afternoon of the memorial service, during the three days I was there. She didn't speak.

Memorial services are sadder than cemeteries. No one knew for certain Julia was truly dead, yet none of the few people gathered in the church believed she was alive. I longed to *know,* to stand by the memorial plaque in the cemetery and watch as a vampire stone was placed over the length of her casket, sealing in her soul.

But it was difficult for me to imagine who this person was who had disappeared, died. Julia to me is a baby, sucking her thumb while curled up next to my mother. When she was too old to stay cleaved to my mother I would find her sitting under chairs, eating Ajax's dog biscuits. She had very large, round blue eyes which followed you the way the Mona Lisa's eyes seem to focus on you wherever you are in the room. I don't clearly remember the sound of her voice, or her laugh, but I suspect it was thin and breathy. When I think of Julia in motion I see our dining room in Coltrain, a small alcove really, one wall of which was a mirror, to make the room feel larger. Julia sits across from the mirror, her reflection bouncing back at her, small, and with the ethereal quality of an imp or wood sprite. At some point she lifts the pork chop from her plate and heaves it at the mirror. Thick, whitish grease sloughs down her reflection, distorting her features like a fun house image.

Sometimes I imagine she shared my fantasies of escape, and pulled it off completely. Julia traveled halfway around the world and walked off into the smoke and burning air. She is someone else now, living in Hong Kong or Budapest. Like a character in a spy novel, Graham Greene or John le Carré, she has no past and spends her days involved in love affairs or international intrigues.

Julia's life had more substance than my memories of it. She graduated from high school and enrolled in nursing school. By 1973 she was working with the Medical Volunteers at an orphanage in Da Nang. Perhaps in my family a generation spans only six years, the six years difference between Julia and me. By 1973 the war was over for me. I'd been tear-gassed too many times. I'd spent too many nights in jail. One too many friends had died. I walked away because it no longer made any sense. We couldn't win, the whole country was aware of that by '73.

Watching movies about Vietnam I think of Julia, imagining her as an actress in the film. Sea gulls must have soared over Da Nang, rain must have fallen on the roofs. I can't say exactly how or why she died. Sheaves of paper, Nina's files, now lost along with everything else in the fire. My mother kept those papers like a memorial, detailing in dry language what the last two years of Julia's life were like. She volunteered to work in Vietnam and her paperwork shows her touching down in Cam Ranh Bay, Saigon, Da Lat, Da Nang. Moving north toward the DMZ. Her last physical, three months before her ID was found, stated she was in good health and four months pregnant. No name for the father was given. Rape? Immaculate conception? Imagine a nurse seven months pregnant working in an orphanage as the Communist troops overran Da Nang, March, 1975. Julia vanished like a wisp of smoke. Only her ID, some cosmetics and clothes, a few letters, were returned.

Drew tells me Nina spent two months in a sanatorium after the memorial service. Frank seems to mourn the unborn baby more than Julia. "That might have been my only grandchild," he always says. Julia was Nina's child and she would call me up and talk to Mrs. White about her grief. Read to me from her files.

When I left Julia she was a small child, even for ten, and her most expressive form of communication was to smile sometimes. Drew can't seem to remember how Julia drew away from our mother. But then, Drew left shortly after I did, to start his own life, anchored to this inland city. The memorial service, sparsely attended in another new city where Frank and Nina lived, was over fifteen years ago.

I can't make Julia grow up. She's still ten years old, Nina's baby. I can't imagine that baby caring for Asian babies, having a baby of her own. I can't see her with her hand on her belly. I don't know what she looked like with breasts.

Some Vietnam vets suffer from post-traumatic stress syndrome, a delayed reaction to their experiences in Vietnam.

Yet sometimes I don't think post-traumatic stress is confined to those who were in the war. The symptoms are so general: inability to hold a job, maintain a relationship, make a commitment. A few years after the memorial service, I began to believe my parents were dead. Somehow, in my mind, they died with Julia. There was a space of about four years when I refused to answer their letters, hung up on them and left the phone off the hook. I remember telling my therapist that all the good things about myself resulted from what I had done to change my life, and all the bad things were the residue of sixteen years of living with Frank and Nina. Simplistic, I know, but consoling at the time. I believed my family consisted of my friends. Paris. Drew.

This lasted for a couple of years until I got a telegram from Nina on Wednesday, May 23. FRANK WILL DIE MAY 25. LOVE, MOTHER. This telegram signified a real problem: my fantasy was simply that, a fantasy. I'd put off facing the dregs of my past. My mother could be planning to murder my father in two days. Or she could have sent that telegram to spark some reaction from me. I called Drew, as I always do, and he said, Yes, our father was sinking fast after an operation to remove a cancerous part of his spleen. They hadn't told me he was sick, but then, I hadn't given them the chance.

I didn't go home. And Frank didn't die because, according to Nina, she threw herself on his body lying in the hospital bed at the moment when she felt his spirit slipping away from his life. Who knows? Maybe that's why I came home when she told me he was dying again. Lightning doesn't strike twice.

My ghost is Paris, and unlike Julia, Paris will appear. He's on his way to New York. I'm afraid I know what it is he will tell me about Victor. But Julia will never appear for my mother. Before this visit is over I'm sure she will have something to tell Mrs. White about the years since Julia vanished. The years of her deepest loss.

I curled deeper into my brother's arms, listening to him snore, feeling the power of his thighs against the backs of my legs.

Coleman wasn't around when Drew and I woke the next morning, but there was coffee on the stove and something baking in the oven. I imagined her out feeding the bears, rounding up wild mustangs. There was no time to look for her though, since Drew was late for work. He seemed still half asleep as he dropped me back at the cabin.

Our father was raised on a hill farm outside Nitro, West Virginia. So it shouldn't have surprised me to find Frank and Nina discussing buying a gun. Nina was once again wearing her new fur coat, sipping from a purple plastic tumbler. Frank stuffed broken boxes and wrapping paper in the old wood stove. "We should have done this last night," he was saying as I stepped into the cabin. "My mother always kept the stove going, even in the summer. I don't know why I didn't remember this last night."

"I think a gun's a good idea," Nina said. "My mother kept one. After my father died. You never know who's prowling around out here. And you," she said, pointing at me, "since you're not around, who's to know if something happens to us?"

The thought of Nina, in her fur coat with a drink in one hand, a gun in the other, is quite frightening. Imagine Nina nursing her eternal glass of scotch and my father stepping into the cabin after taking a leak. Like a movie, I see a bright splot of blood fanning out over my father's waist after Nina pulls the trigger. My father sprawls across the floor as Nina, slowly and fluidly, rises from her chair and goes over to inspect him. 'Oh, it's you,' she says. 'I'm so sorry. I wasn't expecting you. Are you okay?' All the while my father's eyes glaze over as Nina flutters around asking if there's anything she can do.

A drunk with a gun. A swell idea.

"You're not going to live here forever, you know," I said. "Rather than worrying about buying a gun, maybe you guys should get on the stick and start looking for a new place to live. Get your insurance stuff straightened out."

"Isn't that just lovely, Frank. Our little Maura telling us how to run our lives. You know, your father was raised in a cabin like this. Weren't you, Frank?" Her voice was mocking, slurred just a bit, her eyebrows arced. She looked as if she'd been up all night.

But in a maneuver so practiced I wouldn't have noticed it if I saw them more regularly, like Drew, my father went instantly deaf. Throughout my childhood I would hear Frank and Nina talking, and if I interrupted them, even to pass through the room trying not to attract their attention, Nina would swivel toward me and Frank would become absorbed in whatever was at hand. Now he concentrated on fanning the fire in the stove, watching the kindling catch and burn. He always seems to assume an aura at these times, a force field around him, impenetrable, electric. I imagine it in the neon blue and white of special effects. Touch that field and you're fried.

I realized no matter how many places I'd lived, no matter how many lovers or jobs, in some deep way I didn't want to acknowledge, I'd never truly left home. As I listened to the rise and fall of their voices I knew the depth of me was still anchored to these people.

Grabbing a broom, one of Nina's more practical purchases, I moved to the far corner of the building, near the fireplace. Cobwebs frosted with soot hung there, as intricate as gingerbread on Victorians, sinister as gargoyles on castles. The morning light catching the strands set off tiny rainbows. I hated to tear them down. If Drew and I lived here I would have been content to leave them festooning the corners, to see the sun come through them every morning, watch the firelight bounce off them in the evenings. But Drew and I didn't live here and only God knew how long Frank and Nina could cut this place. They seemed to have passed the night quite comfortably and were getting on with the endless planning of their day, which seemed to revolve around the gun idea. I listened to their voices as they talked, a disjointed music-like dialogue composed by Phillip Glass. I went to work on the cobwebs.

I've always loved houses, so much so that at one point I wanted to be an architect. I didn't want to own a home; I wanted to build houses. House after house after house. I like to imagine all the different people who will live in them, creating a history for my imaginary houses in the future. To this day when I have trouble sleeping, I design houses, plumbing, wiring, windows. If I still can't sleep I furnish them. The mental blueprints of a house can take weeks to work out all the details, night after night staring at the ceiling like a blank canvas, drawing straight white lines, white—the absence of color, detailing an imaginary place where everything will be wonderful. The water pressure in the shower will be strong. The windows won't leak air. Sun will hit every room. I envied Drew his unfinished house down the road.

Of course, I never learned how to take care of a house. Maintenance has never been my strong suit. I wouldn't think to wash a wall or a baseboard. I mostly just neaten up, organize the obvious. If the windows hadn't been washed when we moved in, why should I wash them? We'd be leaving soon. My father and I were very different in that respect. He always wanted to leave some mark on every place we lived, a new patio, a half bath. Most of these projects, like the dock, were never completed. In that sense I'm more practical than my father. I only wanted our stuff to blend in, to be quickly available when we took off again. On long winter afternoons I would reorganize boxes of books, coats in the closets. My mother always undermined every achievement. If Frank wanted to leave something permanent, and I wanted to be organized for flight, Nina seemed to be determined to undo everything we'd accomplished. BOOKS: HISTORY I'd mark on a box set into a shelf. No sooner had I done this than I would find the box open, history books strewn across the shelves, and a collection of poetry or an essay on mummification lying in the box.

I never minded this. Nina's searches meant there was always something to do.

Frank was going into town to talk to the insurance agent again, then on to his volunteer job at the School for the Hearing Impaired. "How about a ride?" I asked, although I had nothing to do there. I simply didn't like the idea of being trapped in the cabin all day with my mother.

He gave me a 'significant' look, exaggerated as a mime. The look ordered me to stay with my mother. I was in charge. I was to look out for her. "Maybe tomorrow," he said as he limped toward the car.

I followed him. "Why do you have to go in there today?" I knew I was being peevish, but it seemed like he was always ducking out when I needed him. Today I needed him to help look out for my mother. If she'd been drinking all night I didn't want to be responsible for what she would do all day.

"You know the deaf can't whisper," he said. "They place their hands on my Adam's apple," and he placed his own hand to his bruised throat, "and feel the sound vibrate. They're amazed the same sound can be loud or soft. First they have to concentrate on just getting their Adam's apple to move. One kid signed to me he thought his Adam's apple needed oil, like the wheel on his bike."

"Look," I said, "you can help those kids any time. I might need a little help out here. Today. Right now."

"We all have responsibilities," my father said. "Just keep an eye on her. I have to go in and check on my kids at school."

"Why?" I wanted to shake him, wrestle him away from the car, his escape.

He gave a little shrug. "This is the sign for 'I love you.'" He pointed at his heart, then raised his arms and crossed them over his chest. After what looked like giving himself a hug, he pointed to me. "They do that all the time," he said, and slid into the car.

I stood on the dirt track and watched him pull away. Damn him. Why had he left me saddled with my mother for the day? Coward. Escape Artist.

I heard Nina noodling along on the piano. It could have been 'Camptown Races' or 'Jingle Bells.' If she and her sister had played duets, 'Chopsticks' would have been the height of their achievements.

"Don't you think a houseboat would be a fine place to live?" she asked as I came back into the cabin. Her fingers trailed up and down the C scale. Her voice had shifted down an octave. I wondered if this damage would be permanent.

"Be better if you had some water." Did she know about the lake over the hill? I wondered what Kiskejohn and Tree were doing this morning.

"I think we should move to Raleigh Bay or Hilton Head.

Move to one of those islands off the Carolinas. Do you know we've never lived on an island?"

We've lived on islands all our lives. Islands in uncharted waters.

"Do you realize we've never lived anywhere I wanted to live? Not once in all those years, following your father around, have we ever lived anywhere by choice."

"What about here? I thought you and Frank wanted to live here. I mean, not here," I gestured with the broom toward the cabin, "but near Drew."

"Well, that's the point, don't you see. Near Drew. You can count on that boy. What will I do when something happens to your father? Call you? Some help that would be. You're as useful as fog. So we have to live near Drew."

So nice to know how deeply you're appreciated by your family. "You expect Drew to move to the Carolinas with you?"

"Of course not." She tried for a chord, and came up with a squeak, pleasant as chalk on a blackboard. "Unless, of course, when your father dies."

"So what's the point?" I asked. "You buy another house and settle down. Although if you ask me, Frank doesn't look in any danger of tipping over dead."

"Nobody asked you."

I went back to working on the cobwebs. With only one car, and Frank gone, we'd spend the rest of the day sniping at each other. I wished she'd brought a deck of cards, a pack of jacks, a Ouija board. My mother's imagination sparkles when she cheats.

"You know," my mother said, her hands clumping down on another collection of sounds. "I've always admired you, in a way. You've always gone out and done whatever you pleased. Maybe you've done some stupid things, but at least you've done what you wanted. I've never had that chance."

"Oh, the poor victim. Your favorite role. Sometimes I

wish you'd wake up to your life for just five minutes. You'd be amazed what you'd find."

"And people wonder why I drink? Believe me, kid, I've been awake to my life quite a lot. It stinks. And I can't change it. So, I ignore it. Can you give me a better idea?"

"It's hopeless talking to you. You only allow certain questions. You've got all the answers. Frankly, I think you enjoy this little drama. You're the star. The rest of us are just bit players."

"You know," she said deliberately, biting off the words, "I raised all you kids to be your own persons. I suppose the only mistake I made was that I didn't raise myself to accept who you would become."

"And that's your only mistake, huh?" I swung at the ceiling, clubbing the gossamer threads. Killing a gnat with a sledgehammer.

"Just what are you doing here?" she asked, and I could feel her swing toward me, her eyes boring into my back. "I mean, this has nothing whatsoever to do with you. Why don't you go on back home and get on with your own business?"

My mother had nothing new to give me. Visiting with Nina was like listening to a scratch in a record. I would have to talk to Drew about getting back to San Francisco. I wasn't doing him any favors staying here.

I dragged the broom along the ceiling, above the windows. Chunks of dry rotted plaster fell. Dust motes swarmed in the sunlight. "We're all drama queens in this family. Right now this is the best show going."

"You know, your father and I can get on quite well without you." She coughed, that new burnt sound in her voice.

"Yeah, I can see that," I said. "You guys get along fine enough to ride the moon."

She coughed again and cleared her throat. "What's that supposed to mean? Is that drug talk?"

I could see Kiskejohn breaking through the treeline and striding toward the cabin, his legs long and supple as willow limbs. A tall, handsome man. If he weren't dressed as a hippie he could be anyone, a doctor, an engineer. Yet there was a vulnerable air about him, as if some piece of himself had been broken and mended poorly.

If Kiskejohn and Tree were terminally fucked up, my family must be terminally marginal. We were a normal, middle-class family. On the right track in a wrecked car.

"There were drugs in my day too," Nina said. "Your generation didn't invent them. We just didn't glorify them. I think it's funny how your generation worships everything we took for granted. Drugs, money, nature. You act as if you discovered them, Columbus and America style."

"You missed your calling, Nina. You should've been one of those TV commentators, Andy Rooney. You'd set the whole country straight, now wouldn't you." Kiskejohn waved to me as he stepped across the gravel track separating this cabin from the broken-down shed. The wave seemed stiff, a practice test at being cordial.

Nina was trying to find the notes for the 'Dragnet' theme when Kiskejohn came through the door. "Morning, ladies." His voice was formal and dry.

Nina swiveled on the piano stool and with that she stepped into another role as if walking into a different room. Her voice shifted, she straightened her back beneath the fur coat. Passing her hand through her hair, she became her imitation of the perfect hostess. "How nice to see you, Mr. Kiskejohn. Would you like some coffee? I think there must be some coffee around here. Maura, make Mr. Kiskejohn some coffee."

"No thank you. I came to see what you need. There'll be snow before the end of the week." He shuffled uneasily from foot to foot, cutting his eyes toward me. He acted as if we shared a secret.

"Snow?" Nina said, her rusted voice attempting to hit some high, excited note.

"Snow," Kiskejohn said, looking at me again.

"Snow," Nina said. "How would you know? Before the end of the week?" She rose from the piano stool and came over to the window next to me. "That sky's so blue and clear it could be a stage set." The smell of her coat was as subtle as silk.

"Before the end of the week," Kiskejohn said. "If you plan to be here much past that we're going to have to do some winterizing on this cabin."

"But Drew said this was a hunting lodge. As I recall, men go hunting in the winter. You know, tracking panthers through the snow."

"Panthers," Kiskejohn said. "I don't think there are any panthers around here."

Nina waved her hand dismissively. "Well, whatever."

Kiskejohn's eyes surveyed the room. "You'll need more wood." He looked up at the window frames I'd just swept. "Some caulking."

"Yes indeed," Nina said, in charge here as if he were a moving man. She was always very good at ordering strange men around.

Kiskejohn rocked back on his heels. "Of course, if you have other plans."

"Well, of course we have other plans. But these things take time. I think you should start on the wood. There's no heat here, you know. My husband is in poor health." She moved toward the kitchen area, purple tumbler in hand.

"Yes ma'am." Kiskejohn went out the door. I watched the roll of his walk.

"This is ridiculous," I said. "That man has better things to do than chop wood you won't need. You've got to start thinking this through." I watched her mix another drink, although she thought she was hiding this from me, her shoulders hunched forward theatrically, keeping the scotch bottle close to her chest, enveloped by the fur coat.

"And how do you expect me to do that, Maura? Your father, and the phone, is gone. We're stuck here until he returns. That man volunteered to help us. It would be rude to refuse him."

"Rude." I took another swing at the cobwebs. "I wish you'd sober up and look at your situation for a moment."

"A lot you know, Miss High and Mighty. Do you have any idea how long a settlement might take? The insurance people said there might have been a gas leak. We might be involved in a lawsuit against the contracting company. Do you have any idea how long that will take? And, in case you aren't aware of it, your father and I are broke. Completely broke. We had everything tied up in that house."

"And that's how you could afford a fur coat? A piano?" I could hear Kiskejohn's ax ringing against dead wood.

"They were on sale. This coat was 50% off for pre-Christmas clearance. The piano was 30% off. A person needs some luxuries to help them through crises."

"If that's the case we should have done nothing but buy racehorses and yachts. We should have eaten diamonds for breakfast, slept on gold lamé sheets."

"We gave you a very good childhood," my mother said. "If your life is messed up now, it's not because we didn't give you everything we could when you were a child."

I took the broom to the other side of the room and began on the cobwebs again. As I've discovered more about how my childhood has affected me I feel as though I've been told I've contracted adult onset diabetes. You can take insulin to slow the deterioration, but you can't ever be free of it, can never be cured.

The beat of Kiskejohn's ax was rhythmic, soothing. I could visualize the muscles in his shoulders, the tension and pull of his arms.

"I should have gone into town with your father," Nina said. "There's nothing to do out here."

"You could help clean up. If you expect to live here until you get an insurance settlement this place could use a little work." But I could see her point. A place like this would never be clean. Dirt was the only thing holding it together. "Here," I said, handing her the broom. "Try your hand at this."

I walked out to find Kiskejohn, and felt the way my hips rolled in their sockets, the way my shoulder bones lay under my skin. He'd stripped off his shirt and I watched him work, the swing of his body as the ax bit into the wood.

"Snow," I said as I leaned against a tree. "Before the end of the week." Kiskejohn's chest was a rivered map of scars. Purple-blue livid scars snaked around his heart. A rictus of bright white trails exploded across his belly. Scarlet lines sliced his torso into quadrants. Scars don't tan. Scars don't heal. Scars don't. Scars are. His shoulders had been decorated with tattoos, a mountain lion on a rock, golden-scaled fish swimming over his back. A peacock strutting down his arm. Yet each tattoo was marred, spoiled, the design transfigured by the circling scars in their own unique colors. The tattoos looked as natural as fingers on a hand. I wanted to check my own body, see what tattoos I might have, what scars. Ocean liners. Chainsaws. The twists and squiggles of the bright scars seemed foreign, malicious, as if Kiskejohn had decided to destroy his tattoos, the way punkers shag their hair in strange shapes and variegate it.

"Right," Kiskejohn said. "I like snow. When I was in Nam I used to dream about snow all the time."

I sensed him opening up a bit. "What kind of dreams?"

"You know, snow." He steadied a log on the block. His body arced back, the tattoos and scars swimming as he swung forward, absorbed the shock of the blow. The rhythm was as regular as an oil drill, pecking slowly, precisely, up and down into the earth.

"What kind of dreams?" His long gray ponytail followed the movement of his body like an afterimage, fanned around his head catching the light.

He rested the ax against the chopping block. "You should get out of here," he said. "None of this is going to come to any good."

"What kind of dreams?" I wanted to see behind his crystal eyes.

He looked off to the sky, as if searching for a plane, a bird, something sailing toward him, cutting through the air. "We're in the jungle, but it's snowing, a bad blizzard, and we're all in dinner jackets, carrying plates and glasses. I throw the plates like grenades. The glasses hum like radio signals. The gooks don't kill us. The snow does. We start to freeze and begin to rot."

"What do you think it means?"

"I don't." He picked up the ax again. "I read a book on dreams that said we dream to clean information out of our head, like dumping a computer bank. So I don't believe in any of that Freudian bullshit. It's more like my mind is taking a crap." He pulled back, the scars shining in the morning light, and swung with his whole body, biting into the log.

"I sometimes think no one survived that war." I held my breath. All these feelings about that time, yet I never felt my words could describe them, that I had no right to talk about something that touched me deeply, but never actually happened to me. My knowledge of the war came from what I heard on TV, as opposed to what I felt at demonstrations.

"How would you know?" He was taller than Paris, all angles and bones. But he had fine, broad shoulders, strong hands. I couldn't tell if I'd offended him or not. I couldn't read his face any more than I had been able to read Paris'.

I shrugged, spread my hands helplessly. "I don't. It's just that I've never met anyone who didn't come back feeling foreign. Different. I bet you never dreamed about dishes before you went."

"Dishes don't matter," he said as he steadied another piece of wood on the block. "None of it matters. Beaucoup nothing. It's just your brain taking a crap." He gripped the ax again, then looked at me, deeply, into me. "The things you learn in Nam are usually useless once you get back home. Like trying to get water from the moon. But you've learned them, all the same. Danger has a smell, usually a sweet smell like perfume. Your body reacts to it, like the way you feel heat in a bruise."

"So what's going to happen?" My palms began to itch and I tucked my hands behind me, cushioning my ass against the tree.

He shrugged and looked off in the direction of Drew's unfinished house. "It'll snow by the end of the week. You folks aren't prepared for snow."

"It's only October," I said. "Can't snow much in October."

"You're in the mountains. Never trust weather in the mountains."

"How'd you get to be such an expert meteorologist? It doesn't snow in Vietnam. And the snow in your dreams isn't real."

He shrugged again and passed his arm across his brow. "Vietnam isn't the whole world," he said solemnly. "And dreams aren't true." His voice was full, cutting across all the male ranges. " 'Nam only offers up a world of options. A world of shit."

I slid down the trunk of the tree, resting on my haunches, aware of how my knees splayed out toward him. I wished I had ballerina thighs, that's where a woman's power lay. In the folding and unfolding of her legs. I could feel the rise of my nipples against my flannel shirt. "Options aren't always available. Look at the Donner Party. Remember the Donner Party? Snowed in on a mountain pass on their way to California. They ended up eating their dead. I've always wondered about the first death, how many had died before they decided to cook up the most recent casualty."

"You won't have to worry about that," Kiskejohn said. His eyes trailed over my body. Ballerina thighs. "You folks have already eaten each other alive. Stone cold gone." He reached in his pocket and pulled out a joint, lit it, took a long, deep drag. "I might be fucked up," he said slowly, "but do you have any idea how unfurled this whole setup is? About as right as galoshes in the desert. It's that smell. As tart and sweet as plastique."

"Eaten each other alive," I repeated. I didn't want to think about what all that might mean. "You know, some Indians used to ritually eat their enemies. The brain, the heart, the liver. To take strength from their spirits. And there's one of those peaceful tribes in Africa who take the heads of their dead and set them out in the desert to be picked clean. Once it's a completely bleached out skull they use it for a drinking gourd. 'This is grandmother,' they say each time they take a drink."

"So you've been to college," Kiskejohn said. "The Elizabethans used to worry about how many angels could dance on the head of a pin. But what's the real question? How many angels? Or what's the dance? I'm telling you, it's going to snow by the end of the week. You folks are in a world of shit out here."

"And your life is so perfect? Aren't you a beauty. Just what do you think is going to happen to us out here?" I hated the way my hands tingled, my nipples itched, every time Kiskejohn came around. Of course we were in a world of shit. I knew that. But what kind of trouble? Could he tell me that?

"You have no idea how beautiful I used to be," Kiskejohn drawled. "I was gorgeous. I was so pretty I should have been bottled in glass."

"I'll bet you were. Regular movie-star gorgeous." His eyes were clear and sparkled like light in gems, sunlight on water. I wanted him to look at me with the light in his eyes Paris used to have, or the soft focus you see in love scenes in movies. But his look was hard; you could slice glass with that look. The muscles in my thighs quivered. I stood up.

"Let's get one thing straight," he said after taking another hit on the joint. "I'm not responsible for what's going to happen here. Ain't got nothing to do with me. I've already lived through a world of hurt. I'm not looking to have anything else happen."

"So what do you think is going to happen?"

"Something's going to fuck up round here. Bad. Bound to. It's like it's written in the stars. You best save your ass, sweetheart." He took a long look at me, as if X-raying my bones.

"That sounds pretty practiced, fella. Like the way doctors prescribe Valium." I tried to return his hard stare, but could only imagine the softness of his gray hair loosed from the ponytail. He was beautiful, gorgeous. But as incomplete as a picture without a background. Tangled as a clump of cooked spaghetti. The scars on his chest gleamed in the morning light.

"Well, that's the problem, you see. We're only brave about the things we know nothing about. When I was getting drafted I had a friend, we used to play basketball together, who didn't want to go. He got this fine idea the Army wouldn't take him if he was injured. So he had his girlfriend smash his knee with a sledgehammer. They didn't take him, that's for sure. And now he don't even have VA benefits to cover all those operations on his knee. He's spent all his money trying to rebuild that knee. The two of them, him and his girlfriend, were real brave because they didn't know what the fuck they were doing. When I was in Nam, I'd do any damn thing. I didn't know nothing so anything was possible. But you, you know. You can smell it too. I know you, because water seeks its own level. So you best save your ass." He took another long puff on his joint. "What we always forget is that you can only lose your ass once. Even if you survive, once you've lost your ass, you're starting with a different deck. And each time there's fewer cards to play."

He picked up the ax and took another swing at the chunk of wood he'd been reducing to kindling. He attacked another piece. And another. There was nothing more to say. Water seeks its own level. Kiskejohn and I were floating side by side. I walked away, feeling trapped. With all the country-side and woods around us I had nowhere to go. I couldn't keep talking to Kiskejohn, and I couldn't go back in the cabin and face my mother. I couldn't go over the hill to Drew's un-finished house. I couldn't even worry about when Paris would arrive. I longed for that yellow biplane I used to dream of as a child, the buzzing engine sound dropping down out of the air to swoop me up and take me away. Orphan Island, any place real or imagined. My most consistent dream has always been to turn life off, for just a while. Take a break. Fast forward to a better time. Only you never land in a better time. Invariably your biplane touches down in a world of shit. And you have fewer cards to play.

And people wonder why children bang their heads against walls. Why the certifiably insane don't want to be cured. Why some people don't want to get off the rocking horses they've come to love.

We all have to love something, even if it's only our own pain. But the truly odd part is that love isn't something you're born with, like the toes on your feet. Love is an acquired taste, like music, like a preference for certain colors. And you can't be talked out of it once you acquire that taste. Try to tell a jazz buff gospel music is superior. Convince a painter that white, the absence of color, is preferable to a royal blue. Explain to a cook that pepper is better than honey. Just go ahead and try.

I left Kiskejohn chopping wood and decided to walk all the way around the lake, having no idea how big it was, only that a walk would eat up the time. Was that what I was supposed to be doing out here? Bide time until something happened? 'You folks are in a world of shit,' Kiskejohn had said. 'You've got to help me, Maura,' my father had said. Drew depended on me, wanted me to stay as a favor. I had about as much of an idea of what to do as a duck trying to pilot a plane.

But then I heard the rattle and cough of an old truck and watched a ratty blue pickup pull up in front of the cabin. I stood there as Coleman hopped out, followed by a raccoon the size of a basset hound.

"Hi," Coleman said as she juggled a large baking pan covered with foil. "This is Jake." She jerked her head at the raccoon, who looked up at her with the patience of a well-trained dog. She reached across the seat and handed me the iron triangle. "You forgot the dinner bell."

"Another rescued beastie?" I was beginning to envy

175

Coleman, so much easier, and rewarding, to rescue animals than to try to rescue people.

"His mother was hit by the gas meter guy. He felt so bad. He corralled this little fellow, such a baby he had to be bottle-fed, and brought him back to the house. Jake's been with me about four years now." She moved toward the cabin, the raccoon following obediently at her heels.

I watched the swish of his long, ringed tail as it disappeared through the door. Raccoons always make me sad. Before Julia was born, when I was six and Drew was four, my mother's father offered to take us to our first circus. Nina and Frank were going out to dinner, to celebrate something, maybe their anniversary or the fact Nina was pregnant again, since Julia was born at the end of that year. For this very special occasion we'd traveled to Cleveland to stay with our grandparents and on the night our grandfather was to take us to the circus he bought Drew and me Davy Crockett coonskin caps.

We sang "Davy Crockett, King of the Wild Frontier" all the way to town and circled the big striped tents until we found a place to park, in an alley between a dumpster and some dented trash cans.

We were walking away from the car, Drew and I on either side of my grandfather, holding his hands, when he stopped suddenly, gasping, his eyes rolling in their sockets, his lips turning blue. 'Dadda, Dadda,' I said, but he only gripped my hand that much more tightly before pitching forward, face first, onto the concrete, pulling Drew and me down with him. I watched people moving past the mouth of the alley, heading toward the circus. 'Dadda? Dadda, get up.' I didn't want strangers to see my grandfather lying in the dirt. He was always dressed immaculately, in a suit and vest with a watch chain looped across his big belly. The cuffs and collars of his shirts were the whitest white I'd ever seen.

'What's wrong with him? We're going to miss the circus!' Drew wailed. Dadda lay in a broken position, his nose crushed into the pavement.

A man and a woman, about my parents' age, carrying a baby and holding the hand of a boy slightly older than I, noticed us crouched in the alley, shaking my grandfather, who didn't respond.

'What's wrong, little girl?' the woman asked as she ventured into the alley. Never to talk to strangers, my mother had said, and so I continued to wait for Dadda to wake up.

We never got to the circus that night. Policemen showed up, an ambulance. Drew and I were packed into the ambulance right alongside Dadda as it shrieked off into the traffic, to the hospital. Drew and I in our coonskin caps held hands, but I refused to tell the white-coated attendants our names. I refused to say anything, and clamped my hand over Drew's mouth when he tried to ask questions or started to cry, until, what seemed like hours later, we saw our parents and our grandmother rushing down the hospital corridor toward us.

And the rest is a blur. The sharpest memory I have is of the feel of the red velvet curtains at the funeral parlor. I kept rubbing the nap of the velvet between my palms. What should I have done so that Dadda would have gotten up from the alley and taken us to the circus? What could I do to make him rise from the box? He would be a vampire now, since the only thing I knew about death at that time was that vampires lived in coffins, coffins like the one Dadda lay in. We never saw our Dadda again, and a year later our Mamma died too. But for a long time I'd wait at the window at night, looking for my grandfather to sail across the moon.

"Apple cobbler," Coleman was saying as she moved around the cabin. She began tinkering with the wood box in the stove. "I'm Coleman," she said to my mother. "Drew told me about the fire. Just because we're out in the country doesn't mean one isn't neighborly."

"You're very kind," Nina said in her formal, hostess

voice. "It's nice to know Drew has such good friends." She clutched at the collar of her fur coat.

"Ever tend a wood stove before?" Coleman asked in her soft voice as she poured water into an old coffeepot and set it on a burner.

"Of course not." There was a slightly offended tone in my mother's voice. "But my husband was raised on a farm in West Virginia. He knows all about those kinds of things."

I watched as Nina tried to slip the scotch bottle behind a box. I hoped, for Coleman's sake, Nina had replenished her drink when she heard the pickup pull in. Coleman, bent over the wood box still fussing with the stove, kept her back to my mother but I had a feeling she knew what she'd walked in on.

"My husband and I were raised so differently," Nina said airily. "He lived on a farm until his mother died and he was literally an orphan. His father, his brothers, his sister, were all dead by then. But my sister and I," there was an arrogance in her voice, "we had three sets of parents. In the winter we'd stay with my father's sister and her husband in Florida. Summers were spent in the orchard country in upstate New York. The migrant workers lived in cabins like this, but we lived in the big house with my mother's parents. My parents mostly stayed in Cleveland, where my father ran a factory."

"Well, there's not much to running a wood stove," Coleman said, clearly unimpressed with my mother's family history. "You have to be careful not to get the fire too high. A little nest is best. Try to keep the flames the size of your fingers. Think of the fire as your hand." And she waved her fingers through the air to demonstrate.

"Our house burned down," Nina said, as if she just remembered this. Her Eskimo mind skipping across the variegated ice floes.

Coleman turned and gazed at my mother sympathetically. "Why don't you sit down and I'll make you some coffee." She looked at me and rolled her eyes.

"That's very kind of you," my mother said, and moved out of the kitchen area and settled herself on the musty couch, waiting to be served. "Yes," she said, almost to herself. "The workers' cabins were very much like this. There were apple orchards, and some plums and pears. When we stayed with Constance and Leland there was an orange tree in our yard."

Jake was exploring the cabin, picking up odd socks, pieces of paper, in his almost-human hands. His black face mask reminded me of the Lone Ranger, and every flick of his ringed tail brought back the image of my grandfather, lying on the pavement in the alley.

"We should have sugar cubes," my mother said. "There were some tame raccoons living in the orchard and my sister and I would give them sugar cubes. They'd wash them, and wash them, until they dissolved. Then they would be so mad. It was so funny, their chattering little faces, waving their paws, wondering where their sugar cubes had gone."

"How about some coffee and a little apple cobbler?" Coleman said, and her voice reminded me of the way nurses speak in the plural when talking to patients. 'How are we today?'

'We have to look out for her,' my father had said. 'This is upsetting her much more than she's letting on.' 'I'm the baby brother,' Drew had said. 'I depend on you.' Coleman seemed to know what to do, not me.

"Actually," Coleman turned to me. "I was wondering if I could borrow you. We're going to have to start haying soon and we could use another hand."

"Sure," I said. "Why not? Although I don't know a damn thing about haying."

"Don't have to," Coleman said. "We'll put you on the flatbed and all you'll have to do is stack."

179

"My mother always had help," Nina said. "And my grandparents hired the same workers every season. I always looked forward to the day when they'd pull up in their old trucks and wagons. Some of them took great pride in their teams of horses. Bays, chestnuts. There was one family who owned a pair of lovely big-chested roans. Every year I asked my grandfather if I could have a horse, but he always said no."

"My husband raised Arabians," Coleman said as she lifted the warmed apple cobbler out of the oven and poured boiling water over instant coffee crystals. "Here, try this," she said as she handed my mother a piece of the cobbler and a cup of coffee. I wondered if Coleman had once been a nurse.

"How much haying is there?" I asked.

"A couple of fields. Enough to get the horses through the winter. Kiskejohn and Tree and I do it, but if we all pitch together it'll go that much faster."

"So you know Mr. Kiskejohn," Nina said brightly. "He dropped over just a while ago. I believe he's chopping wood." Although that was fairly obvious since we could hear the steady ring of his ax. I envisioned the scarred tattoos.

"We've got to get the hay in before the snow falls."

"Mr. Kiskejohn said it would snow soon. But," Nina waved her empty coffee cup like a baton, "it's only October. You don't get much snow in October."

"We're talking crops here, Mother. Not getting out your winter clothes or putting up storm windows. In California they worry about rain in August and September. Too much rain then will ruin the grape crop."

"Well, this isn't California," my mother said. She turned to Coleman, seated across from her now in the broken rocker as if we three ladies were having tea. "Maura lives in San Francisco. She'll be leaving soon, won't you?"

"In a heart beat," I said. "In a New York second."

"Which is it?" Coleman turned a cold eye on me. "Can I count on you or not?"

"My ticket burned up. I've missed my flight. I'll have to make some new arrangements." Part of me really did want to stay, although I wasn't sure whether I wanted to stay so that I wouldn't have to face making a new life for myself in San Francisco or if I wanted a sense of completion, a sense of closure with my parents. Perhaps I had no reason to stay, or go.

"I'm going to have to talk to Kiskejohn, see what he and Tree are planning with the . . ."

I raised my finger to my lips, and Coleman understood. So far as I could tell, my parents knew nothing about Drew's new house.

"We can go any time next week," Coleman continued.

"That's a man's work," my mother said. Burgundy ice floes. "Women don't do haying. Hay bales look very heavy. You can tilt your pelvis out of whack lifting heavy things."

"Everything to you is man's work," I said. I was embarrassed for my mother. Perhaps I shouldn't have stayed with Drew last night. Maybe if I had been here I could have put her to bed. My bet was she'd been up over twenty-four hours, running on alcohol. Perhaps she'd spent the night waiting for Mrs. White.

My mother looked at me as if she pitied my ignorance. "Well, if there weren't a division of labor there wouldn't be separate sexes. We'd be like paramecia, totally self-contained."

"My husband left me," Coleman said. "He wanted to be a gambler. So I don't have much choice about who does what to keep the place going."

"That's too bad," Nina said. "I'm truly sorry to hear that. A woman is so incomplete without a man."

Coleman smiled, that professional nurse's smile again. "Some of us just have tough luck."

"I was going to be a dancer, you know." She tossed her

hand through her hair, straightened her shoulders underneath the fur coat. "It was a mistake to have children. Maura,
you know that. Joseph Campbell, he's a mythologist, he says
everyone should follow their bliss. That's where I made my
mistake. You know," and she leaned toward Coleman. "All
that excitement, all those hormones rushing around when
you're young, clouds the vision. For a while there, I was
thinking of going into politics. Of course, it would have never
worked, but I wanted to make a law, a law like having to be
twenty-one to vote, stipulating that people couldn't marry
until they were thirty. I'll tell you, that would change the
make-up of the country quite a bit."

"I'm sure it would," I said. Nina in politics. "There must
be a God after all," I said looking to Coleman, "since you
didn't go into politics."

"Ah, well." Nina leaned back into the sofa, pulled the
fur coat closed around her throat. "There's so much I didn't
do. And now it's too late."

I gave Coleman a look, indicating my mother, who was
showing the tell-tale signs of fading out. And then I noticed
Jake, or rather his ringed tail, as he slipped under the Hudson
Bay blanket on what must have been my father's bed last
night. The other two futons were still neatly made up. Imagine my father's surprise if he were to come home and crawl
under the covers and find Jake licking his toes.

"So nice of you to drop by," Nina said, her voice now
sounding like a record on the wrong speed. "My doctor says
I have to rest."

Coleman stood. "Of course. I'm the next farm over if
you need anything."

"I'll walk you to the truck," I said. "But you'll have to collect the raccoon."

"Hey Jake," and then she whistled, and Jake popped out
of the covers like a Jack-in-the-box. He was as well trained as
a dog. I wished you could train people that thoroughly.

She picked up the dinner bell, that iron triangle, and gazed around the yard. A large walnut tree, with a conveniently low hanging branch, stood near the ruined cabin. A tree very much like the one where Paris and I tried to hang our trapeze artist snow woman. Coleman handed me the iron triangle and rummaged in the bed of the truck for some rope. I stood there, obedient and silent as a child, while she hung the dinner bell. She grabbed a tire iron and gave the triangle a good whack. I thought the noise would split my eardrums.

"I'll hear that across the lake," she said.

Coleman paused, her hand on the door of the truck. She looked around at the cabin, the tumbledown shack with the rhododendron and rhubarb growing out of it. "You don't have a car out here?"

"My father's got it. He's in town, working at the School for the Hearing Impaired. He's the world's oldest candy striper."

"You can't stay out here without a car," Coleman said. "I've got a truck you can borrow. The clutch sticks, but it'll get you around."

It wasn't an offer I had to debate. "No," I said. "Thanks anyway. If I had wheels I'd be out of here in a second." We could hear Kiskejohn's ax ringing against the dead wood. "This way I have to stay. That's what I'm here for, isn't it?"

Coleman gave me a quizzical look. "You starting to take this role of keeper seriously?"

I shrugged. "Want to know how I learned to drive?" I took a cigarette out, lit it, and leaned against the cab of the pickup. "I came home from school one day and my mother, dressed up in heels and a sweater and skirt, her makeup smudged, was lying on the couch. Julia, who was seven at the time, was sitting under a chair. 'Oh, Maura,' my mother said. She always calls me Maura. She fished in her purse on the floor beside the couch. 'The car's at Levine's. I've got to get it home before your father gets here.' Then she handed me the keys as if I knew how to drive and promptly passed out."

"Your mother's a humdilly, isn't she?" Coleman picked up Jake and started stroking him like a cat.

"I was thirteen. I took the keys and began to walk across town to Levine's, which must have been about five miles away. I should have gone in the bar and asked someone to drive it home for me. But as I kept walking I kept seeing the way my father's hands held the wheel. I knew the difference between a standard and an automatic, and since our car was an automatic, I couldn't see why I couldn't drive it. Turn the key, touch the gas, steer the car as if it were a boat on the street." I could feel that steering wheel in my hand, the cold plastic from that first time.

"I remember when I was about that age," Coleman said. "I wasn't afraid of anything in the daytime. Just at night. It wasn't until I got older that I began to have fears in the day-light."

I nodded. "It was around five when I got to Levine's. My mother's car was sitting in the lot, slightly away from all the other cars. I watched the people laughing and talking and they all looked so busy. Sitting in the car, my hands on the wheel, my foot just able to reach the gas and the brake, I knew what I was going to do was wrong. But my images of car wrecks at that time came from watching television, where the women always survived with a fetching little bruise on their cheek, nothing bloody or gory. I wanted the power of being able to pilot this machine, and so I turned the key in the ignition."

Coleman laughed. "Watching TV when I was a kid, the world always looked so nice. Lassie always came home. Matt Dillon always got the bad guys. No one was ever seriously hurt. I still can't shake that."

"Yeah, screwed us all up royally. We were brought up to

believe everything would work out in half an hour." I looked off to the ridge, at the fleecy clouds overhead. Millions of kids grew up believing it would all work out.

"So did you get the car home?" Jake looked asleep in Coleman's arms. I could see his eyelashes resting against the black mask.

"Yeah, sort of. The bar was in the middle of the parking lot so you could drive around the building instead of having to back up. I thought I'd just try to take it for a spin around the lot, and then ask someone to drive it home for me. But as soon as I felt the car moving under my hands I knew I'd try to take her all the way. I loved the feeling of being in control. I loved knowing that if I could get the car home, then any time I wanted I would be able to get in the car and go anywhere. So I drove slowly around the parking lot, then eased out onto the street."

Coleman was watching me intently. I couldn't tell what she was thinking.

"I probably held my breath for that whole five miles. I drove so slowly, straight down the middle of the street. Cars were honking, lights flashing at me. But I kept going, imagining driving away forever while my eyes stared out over the immense hood. Levine's was a pretty straight shot from our house and I managed everything until I had to make the turn into the driveway and stop the car.

"I hadn't realized I would have to turn and hit the brake at the same time. I thought I would turn into the driveway, and once the turn was finished then I'd hit the brake. But the car was going too fast, the driveway was too short. I smashed into the garage door at about eight miles per hour."

"Great." Coleman laughed. "Kids are so funny. We thought we could do anything."

We could do anything. It wasn't until Paris married that I'd given up that notion. "When my father came home my mother told him she had wrecked the car. And perhaps she believed she had. There was no mention that I'd driven the car home. Even though the front end was popped up like a poorly opened can, I wanted my father to know *I* had been the one who had gotten the car home. I wanted him to know *I'd* negotiated the parking lot at Levine's, had managed the five miles in between, and only failed at that last moment. But I also knew I stood as much chance of being beaten as being praised, so I said nothing."

Coleman opened the cab door and put Jake on the seat inside. She slid in behind the wheel. "That's more interesting than your basic Driver's Ed. class. That's how I learned to drive. When we'd change drivers we'd pull into shopping malls. I always parked in front of light posts. Pissed the other kids off because that meant they had to back up."

A bluejay squawked and Coleman looked around. "I gotta go," she said. "There's work to do. We're going to have to start the haying in about three or four days."

I watched her pull away down the dirt track, the pickup rattling and coughing the whole way. It didn't sound like it could make it to the first gate.

A breeze lifted the hair on my neck. Nina. I rushed back into the cabin, remembering the fire the other night and picturing my mother falling asleep again with another cigarette burning. I was half right. She was nestled in her fur coat in the corner of the musty couch, but no cigarette was burning.

I took her hand in mine. "Mom. Mom. Wake up." I stroked her fingers, ran my hand over her forehead. "Wake up, Mom. It's time to go to bed."

She blinked her eyes several times. "Maura," she said as if she'd just recognized me from a lineup of various people. "I must have dozed off."

"Up you go." I helped her stand and walked her over to one of the made-up futons. I held the fur coat as she slipped her arms out of it. "You need a little nap," I said. And I watched as she lowered herself to the floor and crawled under the Hudson Bay blanket. "We'll take a trip on a cloud."

I sat in the broken rocker, the fur coat across my lap. "Once there was a little girl who loved her parents very much. But she couldn't make them understand this. They were always so busy, with their own lives, that it seemed to the little girl they had no time for her. She got mad at them and ran away. But they didn't notice. And the little girl grew up. And she found a man, and the two of them played games of running away. And they ran, and they ran, until they got old and had nowhere else to run. They stopped then, and looked around, trying to discover where they were."

She looked so peaceful, the gentle curve of her eyelashes resting on her cheeks. The steady rise and fall of her breathing. She probably had been asleep before her head hit the pillow. She wouldn't have liked my story anyhow, my trip on a cloud.

I put on her new fur coat, felt the richness of the silk lining, the smooth hairs of the fur against my palm.

Wearing her coat felt like playing dress-up. And as I watched her sleep I remembered those nights when we had been closest, when I had been Mrs. White to my mother, when she had explained everything to me.

'You know, Mrs. White, I don't know what I'd do if you didn't drop by like this now and then. Before I met you, Lord, I had some times. I thought having children would solve everything for me. But you know, they're not babies for all that long. Once they start school they get so secretive and leave you as lonely as you were before you had them. I used to phone in to talk shows, just to hear the sound of an adult voice, to talk about something more substantial than whether we could have goldfish or not. I even went to bars, for a while there. I was so desperate to know I wasn't in second grade again. I needed something more than doing the laundry. Frank was no help. His idea of home is a place to sleep. That man would be happy living his whole life in a hotel room. I'd meet all these interesting people in the bars, only nice bars, I never went to dives. I always took Julia with me so no one would think I was available to be picked up. Julia was such a good child. She'd sit right beside me and watch everything. I felt she was my guardian angel. Such a shame children grow up. She was so sweet when she was little. Not at all like the other two.'

The other two. Drew and I. What had we done to cause our mother to be so disappointed and lonely? And now, over thirty years later, was it too late to change it? Maybe Drew was wrong. Maybe I wasn't here to see my father before he died. Maybe I wasn't here to help my brother. Maybe that was only part of it. Maybe I was here to make peace with my mother.

My mother always told me men snore, women purr. I listened to Frank and Nina snoring and purring, the chirp of dying crickets outside, and thought I could hear clouds sliding across the moon. I watched frost on my breath in the moonlight. The embers in the fireplace had died hours ago, improperly banked.

I crawled out of the thick wool blankets and pulled on a pair of thermal socks I'd tucked under the covers. How many nights of my life had I gotten up, gone to the bathroom, gone back to bed? Easy. You don't even think about it. But out here, no light, no heat, no water, you plan every action like a campaign.

All the money the hunting club had put into their deco bathroom was of little use to us. The holding tank was empty due to numerous holes drilled by woodpeckers and the drying effects of sun on the wood. The toilet was still connected to the septic tank, but you had to pump water from the well and pour it down the basin when you flushed. We brushed our teeth with bottled water. We showered at Drew's.

So I pulled jeans over my thermal underwear, grabbed a down jacket and my cigarettes to go out and take a leak. That sounds so masculine, take a leak. One time Victor and our friend Sunny Bill and I had gotten coked up and hopped in Victor's Mercedes for a ride in the country. We had our credit cards and a big stash and found ourselves near Glacier Park a couple of days later. We'd been drinking beer as we crossed the Continental Divide at Marias Pass when Victor and Sunny Bill felt this was an auspicious place to have a pissing contest. We pulled over and climbed out of the car. But no matter whether you're on the Continental Divide or not, a woman in the wilderness always ends up pissing in her boots.

Outside, the moon was egg-shaped, resting on its side. Dead leaves cracked and snapped underfoot. Trees were sugared with frost. The heady scent of wild mint, wintergreen pine. There was hardly any wind but the trees creaked as the sap sank. I walked away from the cabin, over to an outcropping of rock where I could sit and watch the night shadows. Silence is like music, with rhythms and themes of its own. Cirrus clouds dusted across the face of the moon.

Paris and I once lived on an estate in the Blue Ridge Mountains not far from Charlotte, North Carolina, and all we had to do was look after the place. Paris and I were very good at that kind of work. We could supervise the growth of grass on a turf farm, man fire towers in the mountains. We were born to live in lighthouses. One particular night, the moon a full, white headlight, the air was so still we listened to night sounds sliding around us with the flow of a symphony. And then we heard the deliberate cadence of something slow and smooth and rich with resonance. We looked at each other and joined hands as we walked out the door.

The yard was quiet, the chickens gone to roost, the horses nodding in their stalls. We could hear the progress of a solemn procession in the ripening barley field over the crest of the hill. As we mounted the slope a slight breeze flitted across our faces and we sniffed in the musk of deer.

There were about twenty of them. Yearlings, does, bucks not yet ready for battle. The moon was so crisp and bright their shadows seemed etched on the bleached grass, moving in a counterrhythm over the blossoming barley heads tall enough to tickle the bellies of the adults, cover the backs of the young. As Paris and I stood on the crest of the hill we saw the whites of their tails flick in the bright moonlight, watched them lift their ears, stare at us with their great, soft eyes. We were invisible in the night, standing downwind of them.

They moved through the field in harmony, the wind tossing back the barley heads, the deer leaning into them. The white grass sang and sighed as it brushed against them. Their shadows more distinct than their bodies in the night.

And I remember my body moving, even before Paris took me in his arms. We circled the crest of the hill in a slow waltz. Our bodies balancing together, our hips fitted close. Our upper thighs locked in line as we moved from the waist.

We danced while the deer grazed to their own music, moving across the crest of the hill with the slow, timed motion of trees in the wind. We danced to the music of our bodies clasped together, the music of my hair against his cheek, his hand supporting my waist. We danced to the music of our breath blowing across each other's ear. We danced to the rhythm of our hearts. The moon cast our shadows down the slope, toward the browsing deer.

Then an owl hooted from the woods encircling the field. The deer raised their heads, flicked their ears, and with one bound, disappeared. We were alone on the crest of the hill. The music had stopped. We turned to the empty field, back to look into each other's eyes.

'We could watch the sun rise from here,' I remember saying.

'We're always a golden sunrise,' Paris said.

I lit a cigarette, wishing I could hear that owl call again, wishing I could see those deer standing in a field below me. Paris. Some Indian tribes believed deer were the memories of their ancestors and as the deer were driven out the Indians worried their ancestors had nowhere to go. That there would be no home for their souls to inhabit when they died. An Indian's idea of Hell: no home for the soul. A home for the body could be anywhere, any stopping on the prairie, any encampment in the woods. But the soul needed housing in the body of a deer. And the Indian must hunt the deer to keep in contact with his ancestors.

Off to my left a match flared, died. Paris. He would tell me it was going to snow and we would catch the first flakes and build a troop of acrobats, snow people tumbling through the air. They would cartwheel across rocks, swing from branch to branch with the agility of apes. They would leap into the air and spit fire. They would have emeralds for eyes.

A branch snapped. A slow step. My father, young and strong thumbing his way across the country, his family buried in a small rocky plot, his future ahead of him. He is on his way to mine gold in California, to sail across the Pacific. He will climb the Himalayas surrounded by Sherpas, communicate in a language he doesn't yet know.

Another slow step. The crack of another match. The dot of light from the end of a cigarette. My breathing stopped, my lungs suspended between my ribs.

The dry, sweet smell of sawdust or earth. Pungent as grapefruit. Heat lightning filled my hands. Paris always smelled like gardens and horses. Tart as an apple. Solid as sun-dried stone.

The glow of a cigarette in the dark. So close I could reach out and touch it.

"I'm checking the perimeter." The voice belonged to Kiskejohn.

Bats had been let loose near my heart. My breathing wasn't clearing my palate. A buzzing tickled the inside of my nose.

Kiskejohn squatted on his haunches beside me. My shoulder blades felt bouyant, air bubbles coursing through my bones. I could smell the candy odor of his shampoo.

He leaned back against the rock, the top of his head level with my thigh. "We had a guy in Nam who couldn't sleep. Said sleep was vastly overrated and volunteered for guard duty night after night. I never saw him sleep, never saw him with his eyes closed, even as he bought the farm. He said he dreamed in the daytime, a scrim over everything he saw. Colors shifted like on a bad TV. He'd see organs and bones before he'd recognize bodies. Claimed he could hear the tune and pitch of your soul. Guitar player. Said his soul was pitched to E flat."

"What are you doing here?" I asked. "You scared the shit out of me."

"Just doing my job. Checking the perimeter. Your mother's liable to walk into the lake some night. Your dad might fall down fixing his fly."

"What are you? Some kind of bodyguard? Are we prisoners?"

Kiskejohn shifted. "You people are too dumb to live. Got as much logic as Chinese arithmetic." He stretched his long legs, legs I would have gladly gripped in my tiger-thighs. "Actually, I'm waiting for the snow. If you look," and he pointed toward the moon, "you can almost see the cold drawing up into the clouds."

I looked at the feathery clouds tracing around the face of the moon. I felt the cold in my bones. I felt the warmth of his body near mine.

"Little sister," he said. "Get your ass out of here. Take them with you. Do something, for god sakes." I watched the flow of his gray hair as he shook his head.

"Sometimes," I said, "it seems like I've been picking up their pieces all my life. Maybe, just now, I've run out of steam. Maybe all the holding tanks are full."

"Sometimes," Kiskejohn said, "you have to use dynamite. Dynamite is an awesome fucking thing. Totally rearranges your notion of permanent. Grenades. Napalm. Shit happens."

"I've always been more tuned to earthquakes, volcanoes. Tornados, hurricanes."

"Well, then, that's the problem," Kiskejohn said. "You got no control over those babies. We do what we do. Volcanoes got nothing to do with us. My job is to watch you. Your job is to move so I can see. You can spend a lifetime waiting for the eruption of a volcano."

"Maybe I'm also a watcher. Maybe I've realized I've spent all my life trying to push around mountains, trying to bring back the Inland Sea. I'd like to see sharks circling silos in Nebraska, you know? Maybe the universe is flawed because this is a field test. So if it's only a field test, you can fool around with the playing pieces. I might not be able to turn the heartland into a trout farm, but I can watch out for tornados and hurricanes. Volcanoes. You watch me. I watch them." I moved my ass down on the rock, drawing a little closer to Kiskejohn. "But neither of us can predict what we'll see."

Kiskejohn shook his head. "There it is. That's where you're wrong. We've already seen it."

"You're a fine one to talk. A real expert opinion. You've really gone and changed your life. Here you are, twenty years later, still checking the perimeter for someone else. Watching out for people whose actions you can't predict. Having no idea as to the outcome."

"It doesn't even take luck to wake up and realize you're living in your own patch of sunlight. Or shade. You just realize it one day. You just know your world has changed."

"Oh yeah? Vietnam do that to you? Show you some soul beneath those black pajamas?"

"The only thing in black and white is a police car." Kiskejohn's eyes were sharp and clean as the cleavage in crystals. The moonlight seemed to go deep into his eyes, back beyond the retina, back beyond his dreams. "When I was about ten I was taken on a camping trip in Canada. I had my own little pup tent, mosquito netting, sleeping bag. We pitched my tent right next to the big tent, and my father saw to it I was tucked in and rolled up tight. Then he handed me two tin cups. 'If you see a bear,' he said, 'you bang these two cups together.' He rattled the cups in the dark. 'Just like that. It will scare the bear away.' And then he crawled into the big tent and I was left out there in the dark. I heard them moving around, getting in their sleeping bags, and then it was all quiet. But I couldn't sleep. I was propped up on my elbows, those two tin cups in my hands, staring out of the opening in my tent. There was only this thin silk of mosquito netting separating me from the night. I kept staring out into the darkness for a long time. And then I smelled something, sick and nauseous stuff. And I watched the bushes outside the fire ring. I heard branches breaking, shuffling sounds. I kept hanging onto those cups, one on either side of me," and he positioned his hands to frame his cheeks.

"A bear stumbled into our camp. I realize now he was probably a cub, a yearling. About the size of a Great Dane, but I was lying on the ground looking up at him and he looked bigger than God. I could see him very clearly in the moonlight. I still had those cups in my hands, but that's the thing about when your life changes. Sometimes nothing happens. The bear took a few swipes through the fire. He rooted around a bag of stuff and pulled out a tube of toothpaste. Toothpaste. He bit into it and white goo covered his face. I was still holding the cups. He had this amazingly long tongue and licked up most of the toothpaste. Then he took a step or two and he was right outside my pup tent, nothing between us but that silk of mosquito netting. His eyes were as shiny as polished stones. I could see stars reflected in them. I kept holding the cups, knowing if I was ever going to bang them together, now was the time. Then he pushed his nose up to the netting, right against mine. He sniffed me a couple of times, one, two, three. And I looked into his eyes, felt his breath blowing across my face. His eyes were so far apart I couldn't see both of them at once. But I kept looking into his eyes, one to another. Staring at him like looking at fish in a tank. Then he turned around, swallowed off the rest of the toothpaste, and moved back into the woods."

"You looked into the eyes of the bear."

"And you see, that's the beauty of it. Now I can't remember the smell, the fear, the pain. It's only a memory. No pain. No fear."

"No pain," I said. No fear.

"Yep. And that's why we're both sitting out here in the night, waiting for snow."

And maybe that's what we were doing, Kiskejohn and I resting against the rock waiting for snow. The swimming tattoos beneath his flak jacket. Rimbaud said a man who mutilates himself is truly damned. Yet the mountain lion, the golden fish, the strutting peacock, had appeared on his skin as if pieces of his soul had burst out of his heart for all to see. I wished he had a bear etched across his chest, that the tattoos weren't damaged by the spidering scars. It was that darkest hour of night when the only time is the rhythm of your body as it breathes. The moon hung as if it had been pasted on the sky. I could hear Kiskejohn's slow breathing. Kiskejohn, with his tapestry of scarred tattoos. Kiskejohn, who'd looked into the eyes of the bear.

Once Paris and I sat beside the ocean, long after the sun had set. We'd met at the beach to say goodbye, a ritual which had become as precise as a Japanese tea ceremony by then.

They say the sun takes seven minutes from the time it appears to touch the horizon until it sinks beyond the rim. I remember feeling the hollowness in my shoulder bones, where Paris' hands would be when we made love, where wings would grow if I were an angel. Chips of pain circled through my body like drifting blood clots, moving counterclockwise, left shoulder, arm, wrist. Left hip, thigh, knee. I kept wondering if my heart would stop, if the pain slicing through me would eventually grip my heart like a hand and squeeze the life out of it. Seven minutes. We sat. The sun imperceptibly moved lower and lower on the horizon. There was nothing to say, but we sat together as if we were strangers sharing the same seat on a bus. Seven minutes. And, as if I hadn't been watching, suddenly the sun was gone and there was only the afterglow.

And I felt the pain moving away from me, lifting off me, out of my shoulders, at that moment when the sun disappeared and only the afterglow lit the sky. Paris and I sat together as the afterglow died. Sat on the cold sand facing the largest ocean in the world, the deepest ocean, the peaceful ocean. Now I don't remember leaving that beach. We might have sat there all night, past dawn the next day. I don't remember when one or the other of us finally rose, brushed off the sand, and walked away. I only remember sitting next to Paris in the dark, and how easily I breathed once the pain vanished. How peaceful and cool the night felt, how warm Paris seemed sitting next to me.

Kiskejohn and I sat on the rock. Kiskejohn, who looked into the eyes of the bear. Once you've seen the bear, the bear has seen you. There was nothing to say, although I remember now wanting to tell him something. Yet what we had to say had been said. I believed I could predict his favorite colors, select the music he'd most like to hear. I felt he knew everything about me that could be known. We could talk to the stars, hidden behind the glowing echo of the moon. We could sing to each other songs learned from whales.

Mr. Bosson, the arson inspector, wanted to see us,
but before we could meet him we needed all new everything.
Even Frank agreed with this, although as far as I could figure
the only thing he'd bought was the new Buick. When it
comes to furnishing a home, buying for a family, the division
of labor is simple. Anything portable is purchased by the
man. Anything stationary is the woman's province. Over the
years I remember Frank buying cars, a boat, a camping tent
that remained set up in our backyard for two months, tennis
rackets we never used, tools, a couple of fishing rods. Nina
bought new tables or chairs or dressers or bookcases for each
new place. And all the new couches and cabinets were duly
packed up and shipped to the next location and remained
stacked in spare bedrooms or hallways. A piece of furniture
had to survive three or four moves before we ever really used
it.

Right before we moved, Nina, wearing makeup and
high heels, would come down the stairs in the mornings and
spend a few days putting little labels on everything we

owned. Bookcase. Dish. As if no one would recognize these items without those tags. On a Saturday morning she would wake Drew and me before dawn and we would cart everything out to the driveway. If Drew and I couldn't carry it, it couldn't be sold, and that was the only reason we hung on to beds and couches for years. By nine o'clock our mother and Julia would be sitting on chairs in the driveway, all our goods spread before them, waiting for the neighbors to arrive.

The exchanges were always the same. A woman would approach my mother and say, 'Moving so soon? We never really had a chance to get acquainted. I live right across the street and have been meaning to come over, to welcome you to the neighborhood. How much for this radio?'

'Philadelphia,' our mother would say. Or Hackensack. Or Gary. Or wherever we would be moving to. 'What do you think that radio's worth?'

'Well, it doesn't have a price.' Our new neighbor would look guilty, buying used goods from a woman who'd lived right across the street, yet whom she'd never bothered to meet before.

'I paid fifteen dollars for that radio,' my mother would say. 'Philco's a good brand.'

'Well, it is used. The warranty you know. How about ten dollars?' And our mother would part with the radio, pocket the money, and probably never think about that woman again. Her reasoning for not pricing our goods was that she wanted to see what the market would bear. She'd only paid ten dollars for that radio, or that platter had been given to us at Christmas, or there was no reason to think we'd need curtains in our new house. The money she made at these garage sales was hers. I'm not sure she even told my father, who had already left us for his new job and to get things ready for our move. We'd spend the money on the train, or for special treats when we reached the new city. Never to replace the dishes or curtains we'd sold. When we'd arrive in Newton without a dish to our name, or no towels, our mother would claim the movers lost them or broke them and demand the moving company reimburse her for new ones.

This particular morning we drove into town just as the stores opened. Since Frank was always early, and Nina was always late, we practiced 'Hurry Up and Wait' whenever we were scheduled to appear anywhere. In this, Frank and Nina were a compatible couple, adjusting to each other so we were usually approximately on time. The days so far had been filled with Nina and Frank driving into town for doctor's appointments, meetings with insurance people, and occasional walkthroughs of new houses. I'd spent the time walking over to watch the work on Drew's new house. Kiskejohn and Tree were raising walls and they whistled, as clear and sweet as a bird song drifting over the water. No one seemed to have anything to say, as if we all knew we were biding time. 'Something's going to fuck up around here,' Kiskejohn had said. 'Bound to. Bad.'

Or perhaps all this happened on the same day. A profound change had taken place in my notion of time. Living from sunup to sundown skewed the hours. Days seemed markedly shorter from one to the next, but the hours seemed longer. I couldn't tell if we'd been at the hunting lodge three days or three weeks.

There was nothing to keep me, yet I stayed. A moth to my parents' flame.

This morning we stopped at a hardware store since Nina had decided we needed a Swiss Army knife. Her Eskimo mind skipping across ice floes, ocher, burnt sienna, rose. Frank and I sat in the car, shades of so many trips in the past, until Nina returned with a long black industrial flashlight, half the size of a baseball bat, and a blood-red Swiss Army knife with twenty-six tools: blades, saws, screwdrivers, files, even a toothpick. If they were truly going to live in Drew's hunting lodge this would have been a good sign. So much more practical than the piano. "Oh yes," I said. "Just the ticket."

Nina beamed and fluffed at her hair.

The next stop was a department store and the three of us went in and came out with several new pairs of jeans, shirts, sweaters, underwear, socks, jackets. We hadn't thought far enough ahead to worry about laundry, and I wasn't about to bring it up. Nina might decide to buy a washer and dryer. Order the city to pipe out some water. So we quietly stowed our dirty clothes in a box and bought new ones. The popular image of an alcoholic is vastly distorted. They don't all live on skid row. Many are like Nina. Like me. Maybe out of commission for a couple of days, but then, as if that binge had rested them, an incredible focused burst of energy. Buoyed by a few maintenance drinks a day, Nina had been more active since the fire than I'd seen her in all of my childhood. She was short of breath and spoke in a rusty croak, but she organized doctors' appointments and supplies with the efficiency of a field marshal. However, like the dirty clothes accumulating at the cabin, she seemed to have blinders to the full parameters of any given problem. Today was on track because of a Swiss Army knife.

We stopped at Drew's for showers and to dress in our new clothes. Frank and I had chosen new jeans and shirts, practically identical to the outfits we'd stripped off. But Nina came out in a chalk-white business suit, stockings and apple red heels, earrings and bracelets. "You look like you're going for a job interview," I said.

"And you look like you're going to work on a road gang," she replied. "Both of you. Honestly, what's Mr. Bosson going to think?"

Frank shook his head and limped toward the door. The bruises on his face were now in full flower, his limp as pronounced as the day after he jumped into the tree. I imagine his whole body must have felt as if he'd been flensed with a

rusty knife. But in all my life I'd never heard my father com-
plain of pain, not even a headache.

Mr. Bosson, a portly man in his mid-fifties, greeted us
formally and asked us to be seated. A stenographer was positioned in a corner by the window and I had the distinct
feeling this was a formal inquisition, aimed at corroborating
already foregone conclusions.

"I think we can establish that the genesis of the fire was
accidental. The question to resolve now is how the fire came
to spread so quickly. Mrs. Murrow, next door, claims she
smelled gas on several occasions. The problem here is that
Mrs. Murrow isn't consistent about when she smelled gas,
and if she did so, why she didn't call the gas company to
check for a leak." Mr. Bosson sounded as if he'd learned how
to talk from watching *Perry Mason*.

"You know, that's a very interesting point," Nina said
brightly, flashing the kind of smile a woman gives a cop
when he's about to hand her a speeding ticket.

Mr. Bosson nodded and looked at my father.

"I've been an engineer all my life," Frank said. "I can't
say I was overly impressed with the construction of the place.
But then, you know how people are. I wasn't looking to live
in a fortress when we bought it. I assumed it was up to code
and really didn't check it out structurally. There could have
been a leak."

I began to relax, and felt the muscles in my chest
unknot. When Frank said Mr. Bosson wanted me to come to
this interview I was sure he had some suspicion about the
scotch Nina threw on the flames. But as I ran that night,
the sudden flash of the fire, back through my mind, even I
couldn't believe a bottle of scotch could have been enough
to burn down the whole house.

My experience with fires was limited to the accidental
kitchen fires Drew and I had started as children. When we
lived in Illinois Frank devised a plan to right our lives. I was

twelve at the time, old enough, in Frank's opinion, to assume some responsibility. He hired a Czech woman, Mrs. Jaro, to come on Saturdays and teach us housekeeping. Frank saw his children as workers on an assembly line. Mrs. Jaro, who spoke almost no English and talked with a heavy accent, would go through the motions of running the house, Julia, Drew, and I trailing at her heels. She showed us how to load the washer, which clothes went into the dryer, how to run the mangle. We watched as she dusted and vacuumed, made our beds, washed windows, cooked our dinners. Much of this seemed quite useless to me. Dishes would dry in the rack without my help. We would make the beds only to crawl back into them a few hours later. Drew and I got a big kick out of trying to run the mangle. We looked 'mangle' up because it was one of his spelling words. But in the dictionary mangle means to cut, bruise, or hack with repeated blows. To spoil or injure. And that's exactly what we did to the sheets before we tried to wrap them around the mattresses. From Saturday to Saturday Mrs. Jaro seemed more and more disappointed with our progress.

At that point our father, with his efficient engineer mind, called us his 'little workers.' Julia, since she was the baby, was to empty the wastebaskets, take out the garbage every day, and feed Ajax. Chores she didn't perform even once during Frank's campaign. Drew and I weren't sure Julia spoke or understood English. We would hear our mother talking to her, but we never heard Julia respond. I remember only the high-pitched wail of her screams. But our father had assigned her these chores and Drew and I did them. Our father would never know as long as the garbage was outside when he got home. Drew and I were to alternate cleaning and cooking. One day I would do the cleaning when I came home from school, while Drew prepared dinner. The next day Drew would clean and I would cook. Each week, under the tutelage of Mrs. Jaro, we were to become more and more sophisticated at these chores. Our father had solved the problems of housekeeping.

But since our father was at work all day and didn't come home until late in the evening, and our mother spent her afternoons in the big double bed upstairs with Julia, Drew and I were left to our own devices. We simplified things. Mrs. Jaro might mangle the sheets and make the beds on Saturdays, but since our mother and Julia were in bed every afternoon and our father never checked our beds, Drew and I abandoned bedmaking. We still don't bother, thirty years later.

But we couldn't get out of the cooking requirement as part of our father's team of 'little workers.' Our first kitchen fire, which I started while trying to cook bacon, taught us that kitchens are fairly safe places for fires. Mostly metal, about the worst that could happen would be the loss of some dishtowels and maybe some charred places on the walls, a little blistered paint on the cabinets. There were worse disasters, like the time Drew tried to make a Chef Boyardee pizza from a box mix and the yeast exploded, splattering globs of dough onto the ceiling. We weren't tall enough, even with the help of a chair, to scrape the glutinous mess off the ceiling and could only hope our father wouldn't notice. We quickly switched to scrambled eggs, a disaster standby, and felt pretty safe until our father, wandering into the kitchen for his nightly bottle of booze, was hit by a glob of dough peeled off from the ceiling. How do you explain dough all over the ceiling?

Mr. Bosson went on at some length in a dry, bored voice, and I still had no idea why he had called me into this conference. Even if he asked me about Nina and the scotch that night, I would lie, protect her. One of the indelible lessons of my childhood.

We decided to stop by the house on the way back to Drew's cabin. Because of the investigation the charred remains of my parents' condo sat in the baking autumn sun. This was the first time I'd seen the place since Drew and I stopped by the morning after the fire and I expected the lot to be bulldozed clean. A spare, empty space that had once been their home. Approaching the cul-de-sac the whole community looked like the gap-toothed smile of a first grader. Every little condo sitting neatly in its row, and then the blackened hole of the missing home. The burned refuse in the courtyard had been dumped into the skeletal cube rising out of the foundation, cordoned off by the yellow plastic police streamers. The black bricks of the chimney stood as if giving the finger to God, the fire screen protecting the grate. Above us, the lattice of the roof beams quilted the bright blue and white patches of sky. The kitchen was the most recogniz-able. Although covered with soot and debris the sink, stove, counters, and refrigerator, the hot water tank and washer and dryer were still in place. The bathroom on the second floor hung like a trapeze. Much of the second floor had rained down into the first floor. Iron bedframes were tossed onto counters, hangers and clothes poles, chests of drawers and nightstands, littered where the dining room and living room had been. A silver sheen, tiny as tiles, lit the charred beams.

Nina, in her chalk-white suit and red heels, stepped into the house. She walked through the detritus, soot clinging to her clothes as if drawn to them like electricity swarming through wires. Frank stood on the dirtied lawn, gazing at the ruins like a tourist. An orange cat slipped through a hole chopped into the wall near where the couch had been.

"Look at this," Nina said, holding up a metal cookie tin that had been decorated with cameos. She pried open the lid, black dust rising all around her. "See? All the buttons are still here."

A can of loose buttons saved from the flames. Nina would probably take it back to the cabin with us.

I walked over to the refrigerator and opened the door.

The metal shelving hung in suspended ropes. Husks of food, singed cardboard takeout boxes canted against each other. I tried to open a drawer, which crumbled to dust when I touched it, exposing the shining steel of the knives inside. The coffee pot still held coffee, the same color as the charred walls.

I tried to decide what had effected the most damage: the actual fire, or the forced blast of the hoses trying to put the fire out.

What did I miss in all this? Of course, my suitcase for this visit, which I found sitting on the back of an armchair, dropped from the floor above. Opening it I discovered all the plastic vials melted, the clothing crisped to a papery lacy beige. But I kept looking around for familiar items. The trunks and wardrobes, suitcases, crates and boxes, that had held everything we owned and had followed us across the country. These containers were my only past, connecting me to those always elusive times that flicked like shadows in my mind. My grasp on the past was as ephemeral as sky writing.

A footlocker near the dryer held laundry soap and singed books. A steamer trunk, the size of a desk, sat in the dining room, where other people would have put a buffet. In Sandusky, when we lived in a tiny two-bedroom house, I'd appropriated that trunk, flipped it on its side near my bed and slept in it with my china animals. At one time those china animals were my clearest image of perfection. So vulnerable, yet exquisite in the delicacy of their design. I kept a bottle of Elmer's Glue so I could fix them, repair any damage so no one could see.

The three of us picked through the ruins like children, doubly surprised at anything we found, anything that could survive fires and looters. We cataloged the losses. Ginger jars Great Aunt Constance brought back from the Orient, now blue and white shards scattered across the rooms. Melted spools of home movies. Nina's calendar collection, saved each year since she married my father. An oak student desk. A giant starfish.

But there are some things even fire and water can't destroy. Ajax's leash chains. My mother's red clay pots. Frank's mineral collection: sodalite squares, fluorite crystals. Seashells.

My father unearthed the greatest treasure: my mother's mirrored jewelry box. The mirrors were shattered, slivers of silvered glass like fossilized tears. Although the faux pearls and plastic bangles had melted into a glue-like substance, embedded in the hardened muck were emeralds, diamonds, sapphires, rubies. Nina went back to the car for the new Swiss Army knife and she and Frank leaned against the stove and tried to cut the gems away with the knife. At the discovery of the jewelry box I realized how automatically we'd walked away from everything we'd held dear. My mother wanted to save the insurance papers, nothing else. She'd asked for my father. Then we'd abandoned the house and everything in it without a thought of rescuing anything from the past, as if we were liberated from a concentration camp.

I watched them, standing back by what had been the entrance to the dining room. 'Becoming an expert isn't a result of age,' Frank had said. 'It's the result of what you know. There's only one thing I'm truly an expert on. Your mother.'

I saw them fifty years ago, sharing an ice cream or a root beer while dreaming up their future. Nina in a white summer dress, flared skirt, conscious of the way Frank's eyes flicked toward her breasts. Frank, dreaming of all the things he would do for this woman, this girl. The places they would discover together, the gifts he would give her. Nina envisioning candlelit dinners. Frank imagining bullfights in Spain.

Perhaps all we can ever really save from the past are our dreams.

I watched them, the tender light in their eyes as they

pored over the ruined jewelry box. Perhaps we can only love those who are vastly different from ourselves, a strangeness we can appreciate but never truly understand. Love isn't the kindness and kisses you bestow on a cat. In all my years as a child I'd never seen my parents as in love as I felt them to be at this moment. Prying those gems from the burnt history of their life together, the way other people pore over scrapbooks.

We salvaged spatulas, the buttons, the jewelry box. A tool chest, the seashells and rocks, and loaded them into the new Buick. The orange cat followed us as we crossed the ruined rooms. Almost every expression of my mother, her fantasies, needs, extravagances, had gone up in the flames. What remained were my father's tools. Hammers, saws, nails.

Frank, in his jeans and work shirt, looked untouched by his tour of the ruins, while Nina, in her white suit, looked as though her clothes had been savagely beaten. Although the remains of the house were a solid mass of black, her white suit had picked up yellows, greens, reds, splotted across the fabric like expressionist painting. A bumper of black crossed her ass from leaning against the stove to paw through the jewelry box. A lipstick red streaked her new jacket over her heart.

Back at Drew's cabin we discovered someone had been there. Gobs of chrome white spackling daubed the chinks near the windows. A mayonnaise jar full of wildflowers sat on the new piano.

I was trying to keep the fire going in the wood stove, a project that took all morning since I just didn't have the knack Coleman and my father possessed. I'd get the fire going and close the door. Ten minutes later, smoke rising through the burners, it would be dead and I'd start all over again. My parents had gone to town, Kiskejohn and Tree were over at Drew's new house, attempting to raise some kind of roof, some protection from the snow Kiskejohn said would be here soon. Drew was at the bank, and Coleman was probably feeding the pelicans with their bills chopped off. I heard a car pull up and stop outside the cabin.

It wasn't the Buick, I knew that, or one of Coleman's ratty pickups. I opened the door just as Paris stepped out of a rented Chevrolet. We stared at each other. There was nothing to say. The sun could have fallen from the sky. We wouldn't have noticed.

Finally Paris came over and took me in his arms, lifted me off my feet. The smell of his new leather jacket, his shampoo, made me drunk. "I've brought you a present," he said.

"What the fuck are you doing here?" I felt the hair rise all over my body. Electricity surged down my spine. Paris. My lovely, lovely Paris.

He set me down and took my hand as we went back into the cabin. He looked around, noticing the smoke coming out of the burners on the wood stove. I watched him go over to the stove, the shine of his silky hair, the new leather jacket, how his 501's cupped his ass, fashionable butterscotch boots. Paris the clothes horse, so proud of his beautiful body. He opened the stove door and began tinkering with the fire box. "I got in last night," he said.

"What the fuck are you doing here?" I wanted to run my hands all over him. I wanted him to jump in the Chevrolet and drive away.

"Victor told me where your brother works. So I went to the bank this morning. Drew is not a very pleasant fellow. Stubborn little fucker."

"I told him I'd shoot him in the elbows and knees if he let you come out here," I said. His wedding ring was a filigreed gold band.

"Yeah," Paris said. "He told me that. He's very protective of you. But I finally convinced him. There." He stood back, looking satisfied. Smoke was no longer rising through the burners. "That ought to hold it for a while. You had the damper closed."

I wanted a drink. I lit a cigarette. "What do you want?" I wished my parents would come back and chase Paris off. When my father first met Paris, back in the sixties, Paris' dark, silky hair hung below his shoulders. He had a huge cross dangling from his left ear. Frank said: 'If you show up with a dress on and a flower behind your ear you're never taking my daughter out again.' Paris and I left on his Harley, and I didn't return home until the service for Julia many years later.

"I brought you a present," Paris said again, and went out of the cabin, back to the car. He rummaged around in some packages strewn across the back seat. I watched his shoulders, his ass, his long legs. My belly tightened.

"Here," he said when he turned around. I watched the light in his eyes as he took the three or four strides from the car to the doorway. "So you won't forget where you belong."

He handed me several packets of seeds. Pampas grass, Chinese Houses, California Poppy. "Paris," I said, and looked at him in exasperation, "I'm not staying here forever. These are California flowers. It snows here. They'll never come up."

"They're a reminder," he said. "You are one crazy woman. Crazy as a poisoned coon. Always have been. Maybe that's part of my attraction to you. Each place you move you act like you're going to stay there forever. And I'll lose you. So," he looked around the cabin, "if this is another one of your little dramas, when these babies come up you'll remember where you really belong." And then he took me in his arms again. Twenty years fell away from us. I felt young, passionate. I felt he was mine. My partner in life.

I looked over his face, re-memorizing it. At his slightly imperfect teeth, the long, pointed nose, the deep, blue eyes that shine with a light only Paris possesses. "Don't do this to me," I said. "We're in a world of shit out here. You're just making things more difficult." His arms were so strong, his hands roaming gently across my back where wings would grow if I were an angel.

"You're too precious by half," he said. "Talk about a world of shit. On the plane I was reading an article about arctic garbage. Mammoth tusks from thousands of years ago. There's an island off Siberia where they're stashed. Tinned beef left as caches for the lost Franklin expedition, and we're talking 1847 here. But the one I loved was Salomon Andrée. In 1897 he decided to take a balloon over the North Pole. He crashed only two hundred miles from land, walked over the ice to an island, but the bodies weren't found for thirty-three years. In 1930."

I pulled away from him. "Paris, you're a walking ency-
clopedia of useless, esoteric knowledge. Please get out of
here. Leave me alone." Paris and my father would get along
famously, trading recondite topics.

"You don't mean that, Emery. We both know that."

I straightened my shoulders, pulled myself up to my full
height, trying to look determined, uninterested. "So what do
you want?"

"Victor's in the hospital," he said. "Pneumocystis. He'll
make it this time. But he was critical for a couple of days."

"Christ," I said. A world without maps. Victor was dearer
to me than anyone. He didn't think of me as someone else,
Mrs. White, or as portable tables and chairs. "What am I
going to do?"

"Want to come to New York with me?" There was the
light of a smile in his eyes. He settled himself back on the
musty couch, hooked an ankle over his knee, his hands
locked behind his head.

"Paris! My best friend is in the hospital in San Francisco,
my parents have been burned out in a fire, I suspect my
brother's gone nuts letting you come out here, and you want
me to go to New York."

"Yeah," he said, naturally, slowly. "I want to book into a
hotel with you, fuck your brains out, feel your body next to
mine, all night long. I want to spend the days checking out
the museums, I want to eat New York food and see plays.
With you. You never seem to understand that. You never
seem to believe I still love you."

"Right. You love me so much you married someone
else. And that was years ago, Paris. You've been happily married for how long now?"

"Five," he said, with his eyes trained on his butterscotch
boots. "But I'm not sure I'd call it unqualifiedly happy."

"Why isn't your wife going to New York with you? What
the hell is Jackie going to do without you? What are you

going to New York for anyhow?" I eyed a bottle of my mother's scotch. My head was so light I thought I'd faint away dead on the floor.

"Just some business. And Jackie doesn't like New York. She's convinced she'll be mugged. She's very proud of the fact she's never been east of the Mississippi. Come on, Emery. What can you possibly do out here? Your parents are old enough to take care of themselves. They've had a lifetime's worth of practice. Leave it alone. Come with me."

I was pacing around the room, describing small figure 8's through the futons. "Haying," I said. "I promised I'd help with the haying."

"Haying," Paris repeated. "Come on. I don't have much time. Just grab your stuff and we'll go. You don't know anything about haying."

"Oh for Christ sake, Paris. What stuff? We've been burned out in a fire." I looked down at my flannel shirt, my jeans, logger boots. I had three practically identical outfits. No suitcase. "I can't go to New York like this."

Paris shrugged. "So while I'm tied up in the negotiations you can clean out Bloomingdale's. Then we'll hit the town. *Phantom of the Opera*. There's a Picasso retrospective at the Modern. We'll eat chestnuts on the street."

"If I go anywhere I should go back to San Francisco. See what I can do for Victor." This was the second time he'd been hospitalized this year. I could see the plastic oxygen noose threaded through his nose.

"There's nothing you can do for Victor. He's going to be all right, for a while." He stood again and walked over to the piano. "And I don't see what you can do out here." He trailed his fingers along the keys. "You tried to learn how to play piano once, remember? You were pretty terrible at it."

"My mother bought that. And a fur coat. Her idea of the necessities of camping out in the woods. What I call her

Eskimo logic." Chartreuse ice floes. Cadmium red. Orange. There's no word in English that rhymes with orange.

"So where are dear old Mom and Dad?"

"I dunno. In town. Consumer therapy. Or maybe insurance. Yesterday we talked to the arson inspector. Maybe there was a gas leak. They're all worked up about a lawsuit. The odd thing is, my dad seems to really like it out here. I think it reminds him of when he was a kid. He grew up on a farm in West Virginia." And it was true. Frank and Nina didn't seem at all anxious to find a new house in the city. Each little improvement, the wood Kiskejohn chopped, the caulking, the rediscovery of his tools in the burned-out shell of their house, delighted them.

"Well then, you're free to come to New York. We can be on a plane this afternoon. I'll buy you dinner at the Waldorf tonight." He smiled, that smile I could never resist. The smile I see mostly in my dreams.

They say love was invented in the eleventh century by the troubadours. Prior to that people had sex based on convenience or lust. Love wasn't an excuse or an option. But after all these years I don't know if I love Paris, or lust for him, or simply need him. Need the fantasy of Paris' love to keep me feeling I am a worthwhile woman. Everyone needs to feel loved, and somehow, as my other lovers have vanished, so has my belief in their love. But I knew exactly what would happen with Paris: I'd open my heart to him again, we'd take New York by storm, and when we returned to San Francisco he'd go home to Jackie. Leaving me. The love that is never returned is the love that lasts the longest. I wouldn't still be susceptible to Paris' charms if I'd ever felt he really loved me.

"What is love, Paris? What is it to you?" I searched his eyes. Watched his face tighten.

"Love?" He shrugged his shoulders. "Is that supposed to be an issue? Teenagers worry about love. You should outgrow it, like pimples."

"Come on. Tell me what we're still doing together, out here for God sakes, after all these years."

"It's not love that's important. It's who you are, or become, when you're with someone. You've always held a part of me hostage, Emery. A part I can't get access to with Jackie. So maybe you're a need. You're like a fix for me. I have to get a dose of you at fairly regular intervals, like I'm addicted to you." He shook his head slowly. "I guess I never needed you every day. But I can't live without knowing I'll see you, talk to you, make love to you."

"You told me at Christmas you didn't need me anymore."

"I lied." He took me by the shoulders. "Emery, I'm on my way to New York. There's no reason, except you, for me to stop through here. I had to boogey up my schedule to make this work out. If you want, you can come back here after New York."

I shook free of him. "I can't go to New York with you."

He went over and tinkered with the wood stove again. "I saw a piece of graffiti at the airport. 'Camouflage conceals, costumes reveal. Choose your weapon.' You're just trying to hurt me. Your notion of loving someone is to see how much you can make them suffer. I call your house, I drop by. No one home."

"I'm not on call for you, Paris."

"I was worried. I called Victor and when I finally get a hold of him, through his boyfriend, he says you're here, something about your father dying. But he's not, according to your brother. Camouflage. And then I find you in some goddamned cabin in the woods. Look, Emery. I'm offering you a chance to go to the Big Apple, buy a bunch of costumes so you'll look like a New York lady. Because you are a New York lady, a city girl. You don't know anything about haying. You can't even get the goddamn stove to work. Choose your weapon."

217

Sometimes I think of my emotions as belonging to other people. "You're just trying to manipulate me, Paris. You were always very good at that."

"You know, Emery, when you're unhappy you become a predator. A vampire. You make everyone around you unhappy too." He took a tumbler from the cabinet and helped himself to a splash of my mother's scotch.

"No one asked you to come out here, Paris. And you aren't the best person to pass judgment as to whether I'm unhappy or not." I wanted a drink of that scotch. I wanted it to burn my throat, sear my soul. But I knew if I started drinking I'd end up in New York.

New York. We'd crayon pictures on the butcher paper on the table while we waited for our meal at *Un, Deux, Trois*. Our palms would sting as we clapped and shouted *Bravo!* after *Phantom*. We'd hail taxis and listen to guttural Brooklyn accents as the drivers talked about baseball and football on the way back to our hotel. Room service would bring us jeroboams of champagne. And our bodies would wind together as if we were still twenty years old. Time would stop and our history would be as steady as a sunbeam. A history only the two of us shared.

"Emery, no one asks to fall in love. And what you've never understood is that there are all kinds of love. There are more kinds of love than there are types of weather. I love you in a different way than I love Jackie. I need you in a different way. Please stop being so obtuse. We're both too old for it."

He stood behind me, wrapped his arms around my waist, nuzzled my neck, nipped at my earlobes. I felt I had the specific gravity of a cloud. Spots of color filled my field of vision. "Come on," I said, as I pulled away from him. "I want to show you something."

My plan was to take him to Drew's new house, have Kiskejohn and Tree take our minds off each other. Besides, it wouldn't do for my parents to return to the cabin and find

Paris and me together. They've never understood why our relationship wasn't about marriage. I grabbed his hand and led him out to the car.

"Remember when we lived in North Carolina?" Paris asked, as I directed him over the rocky ridge toward Drew's unfinished house. "This country kind of reminds me of that place. We used to race those Thoroughbreds. You know," and he cut his eyes toward me, "I let you win. You always looked so happy, so pleased with yourself. It was worth it, just to see that look on your face. Maybe we should have stayed there. We were happy."

"Only for a while. With us, happiness only lasts a moment. Our salvation was always flight." His strong, fine chin. The way his long fingers hooked over the steering wheel. The power of his thighs. Dancing in the moonlight, watching the deer browsing in the barley.

"The brighter the candle the quicker the flame. And we burned very, very brightly. We were an inferno."

I laughed. "Yeah. We set the world on fire. A couple of times." I watched the countryside sliding by, the stately trees, maybe hundreds of years old. "You know when I'd really like to see you again, Paris? When we're old. We can compare our lives, how things worked out."

His hands tightened on the wheel. "I don't want to wait that long."

We parked between the unfinished house and the lake, the only car. I looked around, but there was no pickup truck, no sign of Kiskejohn or Tree. I whistled. "Hey guys!" But no one appeared. I felt my belly tighten again as Paris and I walked toward the unfinished house.

They'd made progress: the struts were boxed in. Great vacant spaces for the windows fronting the lake. The first floor was now roofed over with thin sheets of plywood. I led Paris up the ladders, explaining Drew's fantasy, the hot tub, the solarium, but by the look in his eyes I could tell he wasn't listening. His eyes scouted the area, spotting Kiskejohn and Tree's camp. There were sleeping bags, a fire ring filled with ashes. A coffee pot, a sack of empty beer bottles, a large cooler, locked and chained. Kiskejohn, who looked into the eyes of the bear.

I started to chatter, one of my more disgusting nervous habits. "The second meaning for architect is one who plans and achieves a difficult goal. So in that sense, even though Drew didn't really design this place, he's an architect, by the second meaning. He might just see this through. He likes things to be permanent. He's always said I was like the spoor on a milkweed, but he was more like a rock." I would talk him to death, bore him so he'd leave. And then I would mourn.

Paris wasn't listening. He's always been aware of all my nasty habits, knows them better than I do. His eyes drifted over the lake as I explained the spiral staircase, thermal panes on the roof. I kept going on, and on. "You should see the blueprints. They're huge. Big as a sail."

"Come here." He took my hand and led me to the middle of the floor. The smell of sawdust stung my nose. He began unbuttoning my flannel shirt.

"Oh no, Paris." Yet I wanted him more than anything at that moment. My nipples itched and my thighs burned.

We lay on the plywood flooring, shucking our clothes, tossing them away as if we'd never need them again. The cold air raised the hair on our bodies. I ran my hands over the bristly black hairs of his chest, pinched his nipples. Our tongues attacked each other's teeth. My legs scissored his waist, our bodies tied in knots. I kept my eyes open, staring at the bones in his face, the flecks of black in his deep, blue eyes. Defy him.

The rustling leaves of the trees. I felt that sound inside my body, the hissing consonants of the wind. The little lapping waves of the lake kept time to the rhythms of my heart.

And then Paris was inside me and I felt neon surging up and down my spine. He moved against me slowly, gently, gaining momentum. The rough boards pressed into my back as I rocked into him. Our bodies slipped against each other as if we were soaped. Ballerina thighs, snapping turtle cunt. I breathed in the air of his mouth, scotch and peppermint.

"Only you," he murmured, "always only you."

We rocked together, spasms shooting through me. I grabbed his hair, his silky hair. My elbows rubbed across his muscles. My instep circled his heel. We crawled under each other's skin. I wanted to hold his heart in my hand, feel it beating against my fingers.

"Shark," I said. And then all the colors came together, vanished, a total absence of light, free from color. Black and white at the same moment.

His sigh echoed against the empty room. A cry. I floated, free fall, fell. Returning to this unfinished house as slowly as raindrops sliding down a windowpane.

There was no way to discover how long we lay there, the cooling breeze drying the thin film of sweat on our bodies. The air pricked my skin. Paris' breath was ragged, labored. His chest pushing heavily into my breasts.

He rolled off me. "Shark," he said. "This all began with a goddamn shark."

I laughed. "It's perfect for us, Paris. I wouldn't have it any other way. We've eaten each other alive."

He ran his finger along my jaw, circled my lips. "Yeah," he said. "Shark."

We lay still, our cold bodies cuddled up to each other for warmth, our fingers entwined. "It wouldn't have worked if we married," Paris said.

"I know," I said. "Remember when you told me you were getting married?"

"I don't really remember telling you. I guess I thought you always knew." His fingers traced my rib cage. "But I remember being real nervous, afraid, of what you would do."

"We were lying in bed. You said you were getting married. And then you said your marriage wouldn't change anything between us."

"God, I said that?" Color rose in his cheeks.

I stroked my fingers through his blue-black hair. "You know what? You were right. When I think about all my other lovers there's only one of them I have any affection for at all. And that's because he was married and I was never tempted to look at the future with him. I guess we always blew it when we started looking at the future. But you were right. Even though you're married, nothing's changed." I held his stare, wondering if he could see the lie in my eyes. Or if he had no more clue into my soul than I had when I looked in his eyes.

They say when you drown your whole life flashes before you. And at that moment every image, memory, thought of Paris seemed to be present. It was as if I could hold all of our history, a quarter of a century, together and apart, hold the full circumference of our lives in the palm of my hand. Paris and I. Finite. Silver Jubilee. Paris and I, drowning in each other.

"Maybe I will marry you some day," Paris said, his deep blue eyes searching my face. "So we'll really be together when we're old."

"Not a good idea. I suppose it's best this way." I gave a bitter little laugh. "I don't know exactly why, but it just seems best like this. You're almost like a dream in my life. A dream that surprises me by becoming reality on occasion."

He stood and began pulling on his jeans. "So you'll come to New York with me." It was a statement, not a question.

I reached for my flannel shirt, thrust my arms through the sleeves. New York. Once, when I was living in Wisconsin, without Paris, I became color blind from depression. Everything turned gray, cans on the shelves in stores, leaves on the trees. I felt I was living inside an airplane hangar. I went to New York for a weekend, and experienced a riot of color. The dresses on the women, yellow taxicabs, the green of vegetables in the markets, palettes of color on billboards.

I watched as Paris dressed himself, looked at the wooden struts for Drew's new house, the plywood ceiling and floor. I couldn't go to New York. I might not be able to do much for my parents, my brother, but I couldn't let Paris smash my heart one more time. Not now. I felt that wrecking ball moving through my chest again. "No," I said. "I can't go to New York with you."

"Emery," he said, and his voice was broken, sad. "Don't do this to me. Don't do this to yourself." He picked up the leather jacket, put it on absently, still looking at me. "We've got to snatch our moments when we can. Don't waste this."

"I've got a job here, Paris." I pulled on my jeans. "My brother needs my help. My parents are living in fantasyland and someone has to look out for them. Sure, I'd love to go to New York with you. But we've run this movie before. And it always has the same ending." I began stuffing my feet into my socks, reached for my boots. "You can't trust those two out here, alone. I've shirked my responsibility to them all my life. It's time to pick up the sticks. That's what being a grown-up is all about, I guess. Picking up the sticks. Tidying up the wreckage." I would take my mother on trips on a cloud. I would learn sign language and talk to my father.

Paris began to pace, his boots banging on the flooring. "Well this is certainly an abrupt change of heart."

"Yeah." This was as rehearsed as a play. "You know so much about abrupt. When was the last time I saw you? Christmas? Ten goddamn months ago."

"This is the lady who was always asserting her friends were her family. This is the lady who would hang up on calls for help in the night. The lady who wouldn't go home when she was told her father was dying. You were holding the goddamned telegram, telling me you weren't going home, even for the funeral!"

Stay calm, stay calm, I told myself. "We're middle-aged, Paris. We're no longer young, and bright, and full of promise. Half our lives are over. We've got a lot of debts to pay."

"You damn betcha," Paris said, anger clouding his face. "What about us? What about the debts you owe me? The debts I owe you? We haven't been part of each other's lives for this long for no reason."

I stood, halfway across the room from him. "The account between us is square. We've paid each other off. In smashed hopes. In pain. We don't owe each other anything. But there are other debts on the books. That's what I'm trying to straighten out. That's why I'm not going to New York with you." My voice sounded as if it belonged to someone else. Even the words I spoke didn't seem to belong to me. I felt like looking around to see who else was there, to see who was saying all this.

Paris turned away from me, walked to the opening for the door and looked out over the lake. "You break my heart," he said. "And I let you do it. Time after time after time." He stuffed his hands in his hip pockets. "Come on," he said, and his voice was sad and low. The air seemed to go out of him. "I've got a plane to catch."

And then he turned and faced me again. "But remember this, Emery. You're wrong. There's nothing square between us. Maybe the debts have been paid. We've certainly hurt each other enough. But we haven't worked off the interest. We're in hock past our asses. We're in hock to each other for our whole lives."

I wanted him to go, at least I thought I did. But as we descended the ladder to the ground Kiskejohn and Tree's green GMC pickup pulled up to the camp and stopped with a spray of gravel, tires screeching.

Tree hopped out first, and looked at us with the cautious curiosity of a trapped animal. Kiskejohn took his time getting out of the cab, flicking a roach over the hood of the truck. "I'm Kiskejohn," he said to Paris. "This is Tree."

Paris held out his hand. "Paris," he said. "I'm going to marry Emery."

"That's bullshit," I said.

Kiskejohn looked at me. Tree scrutinized Paris as if he were sizing up an obstacle to breach. Paris stared at Kiskejohn. "He's leaving," I said. "He's got a plane to catch."

"Too bad." Kiskejohn gestured to the back of the pickup, loaded with rolls of tar paper and boards. "We could use another hand to finish this up."

"I've done some construction in my day," Paris said, sidling over to inspect the back of the pickup.

"Everyone's done some construction," Kiskejohn said, still looking at me. I felt my whole body blush. I thought my hair would stand on end.

Tree hefted a roll of tar paper and Paris grabbed the other end. They walked it over to the unfinished house and worked it up to the first deck. Kiskejohn and I watched them. Paris in his fancy city clothes, Tree in old combat fatigues. "He's got a plane to catch," I said again.

Kiskejohn fished another joint out of his pocket, twirled it through his fingers, but didn't light it. "Doesn't look like he's going anywhere." Then he looked at me, those X-ray eyes. "At least it doesn't look like he's going anywhere without you."

"New York," I said. "He's going to New York. I have to go back to San Francisco." My crotch was sticky, I smelled like dead fish. I moved downwind from Kiskejohn. Tree and Paris came back for another roll of tar paper, working wordlessly. The sun caught the waves on the lake in little silver circles. The scent of pine was on the air. Wind feathered the leaves of the trees, making the shadows tremble.

The more complicated your life becomes the more you find yourself caught in the web of other people's emotions and interpretations. I could practically see what Kiskejohn was thinking, see what Paris was feeling. And none of it was true, yet even if I told them, they wouldn't believe me.

We watched them take the next roll up the ladder in the same fashion, Paris underneath it, Tree on top, pulling it after him. "People like you," Kiskejohn said, "always going somewhere. What's the point? You just step in the same shit wherever you are."

"I thought you wanted me to get out of here. That smell you were talking about. Remember?" We were both watching Paris, the smoothness of his movements as he worked with Tree. I began to shiver, as if the temperature had dropped sixty degrees. I wanted it all, Paris, Kiskejohn. I wanted nothing, to be left alone, to vanish into the air. I compared their shoulders, their legs. I wondered if Paris' blue-black hair would turn as gray as Kiskejohn's some day.

We stood there, watching Paris and Tree work the third roll of tar paper onto the deck. Next they unloaded the lumber and stacked it on the ground near the truck. Kiskejohn lit his joint, but didn't offer it to me. He didn't offer to help them. Neither Paris or Tree said a word and I wanted to hear some high, frightening sound. A whistle blast, a siren shriek. I realized I was grinding my teeth, holding my breath, shuffling from foot to foot to hide the fact my whole body was trembling.

'Life is all process,' Drew had said, 'only you never completely finish.' Paris and I would never finish the business between us. Kiskejohn and Tree would never really return from Vietnam. Drew's house would never be completed, I was certain of that. And not even death would finally separate me from my parents. I hated the randomness of it all. Random: without definite aim, direction, rule or method. No point in doing anything. No point in not doing anything.

Maybe I should go to New York with Paris. It would be easy. All I had to do was walk over, get in the Chevrolet, and by evening I'd be in New York. But I didn't even want to look at Paris' rented car. I didn't want to look at Kiskejohn as he watched Paris and Tree at work. Out of the corner of my eye I could see the sun beginning to slip behind the hills. Seven minutes and we would all be in the shadow of the mountains.

Paris dusted his hands on the back of his jeans when the last of the lumber was unloaded from the truck. Tree gave him a nod, reached in the pickup and handed him a beer. They both came around to where Kiskejohn and I had remained standing. Tree squatted down on the running board, Paris leaned against the tire well.

"New York," Kiskejohn said and there was a tone of dismissal in his voice.

"Business," Paris said. "I just stopped by to say hello to Emery. You know," and he glanced at Tree as if he were an accomplice, "this lady's the great love of my life. Always has been, no matter who she's fucking."

"Paris is married." I looked Paris square in the eye. "His wife's afraid she'll get mugged in New York. A provincial type. She's very proud of the fact she's never been east of the Mississippi."

"Well," Kiskejohn drawled, "some ladies are built to travel the world. And some are made to stay home. Damn few can do both."

"Emery missed her calling," Paris said to Tree. "She should have been an astronaut. This lady could colonize Mars, Venus. She'll flit through your life the way she flits through everything. She couldn't stand still if she was nailed to the ground." He took a long swallow of the beer and focused on Kiskejohn, eyeing him up and down. "She'll leave you too. That's what she does."

"No news there," Kiskejohn said. "The only permanent thing in the world is a farewell. The first Buddhist saying is: All life is sorrowful. I think you best take her to New York with you. Everything arises out of emptiness. Be mighty lonely without the great love of your life."

"Both of you," I said, "shut the fuck up. What I do doesn't have a damn thing to do with either of you."

"That's where you're wrong," Kiskejohn said. "That's the whole point, you see. What you're going to do."

I zipped my jacket. "I'm going to go see if my parents are all right." I looked Paris hard in the eye. "Maybe I'll see you in San Francisco."

He crushed the beer can in his fist. "In your dreams," he said. "I'm the lord and master of your dreams."

I turned and started walking up the dirt road toward my

brother's hunting lodge. And I knew Paris would follow, catch up to me in the car somewhere down the road. I walked, long hard strides that felt like my heels were echoing across the lake. I kept walking, marching, concentrating on the yellows and reds of the maples, the dry brown weeds, my ears trained for the sound of the Chevrolet.

About a third of the way to the cabin I heard an engine pulling up behind me. I stepped to the side of the dirt track as Paris coasted beside me, his elbow jutting out the window. I stopped. He cut the engine. "You're making a mistake," he said.

"I've got a new philosophy, Paris. I try to only make the same mistakes four or five times." His deep, icy eyes that caught sunlight like flames. The way he always smelled of gardens or horses.

He laughed, his lovely, melodious laugh. "What are you saying? That lets me out so you can break those two in? You hot for the top dog in a kennel of curs?"

"It has nothing to do with them," I lied. "And everything to do with you." That part was the truth, the whole truth, and nothing but the truth.

He shook his head. "Emery, there's no point changing the rules now. Come on, get in the car. You'll see. It'll be fun."

"I can already see. I know exactly what's going to happen. Don't you realize that after a certain point things just don't heal like they used to? You've smashed my heart to where there's nothing left." Again, a part of me felt as if someone else was saying this, standing in the dappled autumn sunshine by the side of the dirt track, talking to a stranger.

"Bullshit. If there was nothing left we wouldn't be debating this. Get in the fucking car. The Big Apple's calling." But I could see the hope had gone out of him. He would be more surprised than I if I were to jump in the car with him. Yet years ago he would have manhandled me, kidnapped me, to take me off to fulfill his dreams. And years ago, I would have let him, played the game out the way we both wanted, willingly.

"Shark," he said. "As in loan shark. You're never free from a loan shark. You know that as well as I do."

"Goodbye, Paris. Maybe I'll see you back in the city." He was right: I would never be free of him. He would always be tied to some part of me. The way I held a part of him hostage. I started up the road again, every muscle tensed to hear the click of the ignition, the engine turn over, the tires beginning to roll. And then Paris drove by me as if I were just a tree on the side of the road. He never looked back. I slowed a bit as I watched the Chevrolet vanish around a curve. But the sound of the engine hung in the air as I walked all the way back to the cabin.

Paris was right. I didn't know anything about haying. The only physical labor I'd ever done was clean my apartment. But I got up in the predawn darkness when I heard Coleman's pickup outside and went with them.

I enjoyed being out in the fields as the sun rose over the mountains. The prickly, itchy feeling of the green straw, baling wire cutting through my gloves as I arranged the bales on the flatbed. Coleman driving, Kiskejohn and Tree following to throw the bales up onto the truck. I watched the swing of their bodies as they moved through the work. Maybe I'd never go back to San Francisco, stay here and buck hay bales, feed horses and birds. Made more sense than developing ad campaigns for toilet paper.

And I tried to push Paris out of my mind, tried not to see myself selecting silky nightgowns with him at Bloomingdale's. It was easy. The smell of the fresh cut hay, the wind whipping my hair, sweat rolling down my spine. The rhythmic sput of the diesel engine. New York, with its loud cabs and bustling people, could have been on another planet. I bucked hay bales. I thought a lot about my father. What did Drew and I know about our father? There's no one to verify his past, not even my mother. He talks about his childhood the way people summarize plots to movies you haven't seen. I wonder how he connects those West Virginia years to other aspects of his life. I suspect he doesn't. As if it happened to someone else.

He was born at home, on a hill farm outside Nitro, West Virginia, not far from the Kanawha River. He never knew his father, a coal miner who died in the influenza epidemic of 1918. His two older brothers went into the mines to support his mother and older sister. They had a guernsey, Polish China pigs, a flock of hens, a truck garden, and seven acres of flat land they planted in cash crop rye and winter wheat. As a child he shot squirrels, wild turkeys, and deer for meat, butchered hogs the first Sunday after Thanksgiving, and spent June afternoons picking tiny wild strawberries. His mother, whose hero was Abraham Lincoln, wanted him to study to be a lawyer and as long as the older boys worked in the mines she allowed Frank the luxury of reading and helping run the farm.

Meg, his older sister, died when she ran off with a Bible salesman who wanted to become a figure skater. Their car pitched into the Greenbrier River near White Sulphur Springs when they failed to negotiate a curve and a loaded coal truck rounding a bend in the Allegheny Mountains. They were on their way to Washington D.C. and some said they'd been drinking, white lightning most likely since Prohibition was on. But my father has never really believed that since bootleg whiskey always sat right next to the pitcher of milk on the kitchen table. His mother ran the still after his father's death and his first memories of being in the woods are of riding on his mother's hip as she went to tend it. He learned to cook liquor before he could read. Drinking was as natural as yawning or sleeping. It had its own time and place, was part of any day's cycle.

My father is a self-made man and I marvel at how alike we are in certain ways. Throughout my life I've emulated a man who terrified me. I never considered being a wife or a mother, always fearful I would end up like Nina. That was one of many reasons Paris and I never married. I wanted a job, a career, no matter what the price. The goal was to leave my childhood behind as completely as my father had peeled away his West Virginia past.

Perhaps growing up on a hillbilly farm skewed my father's ideas about childhood. Perhaps the word 'childhood' doesn't even exist in his interior vocabulary. He would some-times tell us about milking cows, plucking sucker shoots off tomatoes, killing chickens. To him, the difference between being a child and an adult is that a child doesn't have to think about the work. It seems the only value he picked up from those years was a belief in education. Education could change your life, the way it had changed his. I believe cir-cumstances changed his life, rather than the rudiments of a West Virginia education. History was against him, sabotaging the life he was born to along with any of his dreams and plans the way it does all of us. In 1935, at the height of the Great Depression, both his brothers were killed in a labor dispute. The following winter his mother died of pneumonia. Seventeen years old, with twenty-five acres of hill farm to his name, my father dismantled the still and sold the farm and went west. He got as far as Cleveland before he found steady work in a tool and die factory. He went to night school, where he met Nina.

Work. Paris was right. I didn't know anything about hay-ing.

When Paris and I managed an estate in North Carolina I spent some time shooting a .22 rifle and the kick of the gun butt rocking through my shoulder was the same feeling I had

233

in my upper back and arms after a day of haying with Coleman and crew. I wondered if firing a gun constantly, or haying on a regular basis, would make your arm ache the way a pitcher's arm aches in the middle of the season. But I felt pleased. I'd done a good, solid, day's work. Designing ad campaigns for Harold at the agency seemed a bit dishonest now. Spending eight hours a day, five days a week, rain or shine, creating hype. Is anything really 'new and improved'? How many microwaves does one household need?

As Kiskejohn and Tree threw the green bales up on the flatbed I struggled to stack them. The first row was easy. I just kicked them in place. The second row was harder since straw doesn't slide well on straw. The third row was impossible. But we'd finished an entire field and a half.

Tree knew Julia in Vietnam. Tiny Tree, who walks with a limp and still wears camouflage fatigues. A quick look at Tree and you would think this person was completely self-contained. But a deeper look reveals the thousand-yard stare, as if Tree could see other worlds occupying the atmosphere. He's not a man you'd want to play poker with. He keeps his cards too close to his chest.

"Do my parents know you knew Julia?" I asked him as we sat in Coleman's kitchen as dusk began to fall. She was cooking us dinner, my parents had been invited, while Kiskejohn and Tree and I sat at the table drinking shooters and beers.

"Drew told us not to tell them," Kiskejohn said. "Especially your mother."

"Does he do all your talking for you?" I asked Tree.

Tree nodded and took another swig of his long-necked beer. He toyed absently with his shot glass.

"Did you know Julia?" I asked Kiskejohn.

"Nope. I'd been flown out to the hospital. That was the last time. Lost my lung. Tree stayed in country, and that's when they found the kids. About ten of them living in a cave.

He was detailed to take them to the orphanage in Da Nang. That's where he met your sister."

"That was over a decade ago and half a world away. How did all this come out?"

"Lannier's not a common name. When Drew first came out here and offered us work, Tree mentioned he'd known a nurse named Lannier. Turns out, she was your sister."

"So he can talk." I looked pointedly at Tree.

"Sure he can talk. He just doesn't feel like it sometimes. Sometimes there's just not much to say."

"Talking upsets him," Coleman said, turning from the stove to us. "Listening doesn't seem to bother him, or maybe it's like he's got some private Walkman plugged in his ears and he doesn't hear anything but his own music. But he can get real upset when he starts to talk."

"So I do the talking for him," Kiskejohn said. "Doesn't bother me. He doesn't know anything I don't."

"You didn't know my sister."

"According to Drew, neither did you."

"So what? I still have a right to be curious, don't I? She was my sister. Doesn't Drew want to find out what happened to her? I mean, it's possible she's even still alive."

"That's up to Drew. Your whole family's shell shocked. Gone to the zoo. But it's unlikely she's alive. Not after all this time. Drew just doesn't want to get your mother upset. My money's on Drew for this one. He's been to all the agencies. Probably she was in the orphanage when it was hit. You just don't always find people, maybe only a hand or some toes."

With all the traveling I've done, I've never been out of the country. Yet I believe I would know where I was if I were blindfolded and whisked off half way around the world. I would know I was in Hiroshima if they took off the blindfold and I saw the shadows on the stones, images of people who'd been sitting on park benches when the atom bomb was dropped, August 6, 1945. That's the way I thought about

Julia. In March, 1975, maybe it was a Tuesday or a Wednesday, the Communist troops blew Da Nang to hell, and the orphanage where Julia worked as a medical volunteer. If she'd been attached to the regular Army, perhaps there'd be more paperwork to confirm that she'd died. But it's impossible to imagine Julia standing up to the Army's basic training. Medical volunteers came from the private sector, just folks lending a helping hand. So I imagine Julia leaving behind her image as a shadow on a stone somewhere in Da Nang. That image of her shadow consoles me. I didn't want to think of her, the child with the large eyes, buried alive in an avalanche of rubble.

"My father disappeared in World War II," Coleman said. "Officially you're supposed to wait seven years to declare someone legally dead. But my mother could never bring herself to do that. So when she died, my father was still officially alive. After I buried my mother I had to go around and get my father, whom I'd only seen pictures of, declared dead too. Since my mother had been so faithful to my father all those years, I thought she might like it if I had him legally buried next to her. It was a very odd time."

"After a death there's only the paperwork," Kiskejohn said.

Drew came through the door, brandishing a large package wrapped in butcher paper. "This looks like a happy crowd. Hell of a party. Put you guys to work and you look like you're about dead."

"Want to talk about death?" Coleman asked him. "Or you could fire up the grill. I understand your father only eats steak."

"Claims he went around the world three times and had steak and potatoes every night in every country," Drew said. "Imagine what they served him in India."

"Dog," Kiskejohn said. "I've seen places where they tried to pass off dog as filet mignon. Since they don't eat beef

236

they figure if you curry the hell out of it, no one will notice."

"Ugh!" Coleman said. "Curried dog steak."

"Hasn't anything happened to you since Vietnam?" Drew said, with what I thought was an unnecessary edge to his voice. I don't believe I'm psychic, but I'm always amazed when I feel threads pulling together from different spools. Did Drew know we'd been talking about Julia?

"Not much," Kiskejohn said. "I try to keep it that way. I've already had more than enough happen for one lifetime. I'm going to spend the rest of my days trying to figure it out."

"Good luck," Coleman said. "None of the rest of us would want that kind of work. You know, I once tried to figure out how many moves it would take to start a war. Nothing I figured out panned out. Like the Falklands. If there was ever a place to test out the concept of a limited nuclear war, the Falklands was it. You can't give a kid a new toy and tell him not to use it. So, whether it was accidental or on purpose, I figured someone would blow the Falklands off the map, just to see how a limited nuclear war would go. What would be lost? Some piss-poor islands and the fallout would land in South Africa. No major loss there. I read the papers. I listened to Ted Koppel. Nothing. You're going to waste your whole life away, Kiskejohn, with that kind of thinking."

Drew was setting the steaks out on the counter. "Dangerous business," he said. "Very dangerous business. I hope you're prepared for any answer you might find."

"Well, there it is," Kiskejohn said. "It's only a way of passing the time. I really don't have to go any further than that if I don't want to." He took a swig on his beer and began peeling the label with his thumbnail. In the last few days he'd loosened up some, but there was still the feeling that social situations were as comfortable for him as a too-tight tuxedo. "But you see, you got to keep busy. It's like I've got this parrot on my shoulder who'll chatter all kinds of nonsense into my head if I don't keep it filled with something. So like when you're marching or on watch, you got to keep your head full or that damn fucking parrot will start asking the Big Questions. Anything will do to keep that parrot quiet. I used to debate noise and silence." He leaned back in the kitchen chair and I stared at the long bones in his thighs. "It's not even a question of which is worse. Noise meant action, death. Silence was torture, waiting for the noise. You know how you toss a coin, heads or tails? I'd do that with noise and silence, to pass the time while marching or on watch. You do not want to engage that parrot with the Big Questions at times like that. I'd flip noise and silence like a coin. Noise was red, silence was silver. I'd watch it spinning through the air. The odds are the same, no matter which side you bet on. Statistically, that is."

Drew trimmed fat off the steaks, sure and skillful. "I tell you Kiskejohn, a mind like yours belongs in a cage."

I looked at Kiskejohn's long legs flared out, the heels of his boots dug into the floor. Pieces of chaff in his long gray hair caught the evening light. Paris smells of horses or gardens. Kiskejohn smelled crisp as sawdust. Although I could feel my back tensing up from bucking hay bales all day, I discovered I was enjoying all this. Their company, their work.

The new Buick pulled up outside and I watched as Nina and Frank got out of the car. I watched my parents move closer to the house as if they were underwater and felt all the contentment drain out of me like water in a cracked glass. A slow seeping, almost imperceptible, except for the fact you can see the water level slipping down the inside of the glass. Frank and Nina.

"Heads up," Drew said. "Flotsam and Jetsam have arrived."

My mother wasn't wearing her new fur coat. She had on the chalk-white suit, newly dry-cleaned, and the apple-red high heels. "I hope we're not late," Nina said brightly, in her burnt voice. She sounded as if she'd walked into a formal dinner party, not a slow autumn evening designed solely to keep her entertained. Keep the two of them busy, out of trouble. At what point do our parents become our children? Drew acted as ringmaster, I was the assistant, and we wanted to keep these two as engaged as kids at a circus.

"Your mother," my father said, "probably won't be on time for her own funeral."

Silently, Tree moved into action. He fetched chairs for Frank and Nina, handed out beers from the refrigerator, brought glasses, and went out to fire up the grill. Tree operates like an animal, purely on instinct. He would not be able to sit through the predinner chatter, so for his own peace of mind he performed all the right, correct moves, then banished himself to the yard.

Imagine any country dinner, the women in the kitchen working with the food, the men sharing a drink and a smoke before supper. But Nina could never fit into a scenario like that. Tearing lettuce for a salad was beyond her, although I once saw her folding napkins into intricate shapes while the other women stirred beans, warmed bread. I was tired from haying all day and Coleman had made it clear she was in charge of her own kitchen. I watched Coleman and Drew put together the dinner as practiced as if they were a married couple.

"My sister and I used to spend summers on a farm in upstate New York," Nina said. "Of course, it wasn't anything like this. Acres and acres of orchards. Apples. Late in the summer the workers would start coming through, to harvest the apples. I found it all very romantic and remember at one point I wanted to grow up and become a migrant worker. So I could travel all over the country, harvesting apples, peaches, plums. I thought you could specialize and I only wanted to harvest fruit. Now, those workers lived in shacks, I mean, Drew's cabin is a palace compared to the shacks those families lived in. But they were so different from us, so free. I'd

239

wait every summer for one old woman. Her skin was as wrinkled as an elephant's hide. She had gold hoops in her ears from here," she touched the top of her ear, "to here," and she traced the shell down to the earlobe. "She had a ruby in her tooth and diamonds in her nose. She told fortunes by reading palms and tea leaves. Each summer I'd wait to have my palm read. 'There is only one cloud on your horizon,' she told me once. 'You must learn to see your blessings,' was another message. I kept her predictions in my secret diary and at the end of each summer I'd make a list, string all her predictions together and see if I could read her vision of my future."

We all watched as she poured herself a shot of rye. Downed it straight. She gave her head a little shake as the rye worked through her. "And then one summer she didn't arrive. I asked the workers and they said she died in Georgia. I was distraught, unconsolable. She seemed to be the only one who knew what was going to happen to me. But one of the other old women said to me, she said: 'All women are fortune tellers. When you are a woman you will be able to see your own path.' But you know, she was wrong." Nina toyed with her glass for a moment. "Don't you think it's funny that only men can be magicians and only women can be fortune tellers. I wouldn't trust a man fortune-teller, would you?"

Kiskejohn looked at her gently. "Sometimes we do see our futures. The trick is in learning to believe what you see."

"I don't know," my father said. He seemed to be looking at something far away, out the window and over the horizon. "My mother used to say life is like a Crackerjack box, a surprise in every package. Those Crackerjack boxes were real special to me when I was a kid. Kids now, you can have anything you want. But when I was a kid, a Coke was a special treat. I'd get maybe one, two boxes of Crackerjacks a year. Talk about surprise, hell. I was raised on a farm. I never thought I'd end up living on one." Frank, my father who spoke only to give orders, was in a warm, expansive mood this evening.

"You know," he said to Kiskejohn, "that farm was sort of like this. Much hillier, ground had more rocks than a beach has sand. When I left that place I was determined I'd never come any closer to a farm than a country club. But you know, things haven't been half bad." The bruises on his face shone as brightly as Kiskejohn's tattoos.

"We almost retired to a country club, didn't we Frank?" Nina's flushed face held a false brightness.

I could feel my mother slipping away from us. Watching her made me feel slightly dizzy, because I knew where she was going.

My father didn't seem to notice. He laughed. "We went down to Florida when I retired. Hell, everyone moves to Florida when they retire. There was this one place, Kings Port, and they had a little jingle. 'The city of Cadillacs and cataracts, newlyweds and nearly deads, where fun is a full-time job.' I didn't feel I was ready for that." He shook his head in wonder and took a sip of the beer Tree had set before him.

"I got spoiled in country," Kiskejohn said. "Cities make me nervous."

"I tell you," Nina said, "I never heard anyone singing their swan song so loudly. And do you know what they do? They have screened-in garages. Yes indeed. They probably have parties while they change the oil."

"And alligators on the golf course. They don't penalize you any strokes if your ball lands near an alligator." My father smiled, pleased as if this was a joke.

"There were alligators near us when my sister and I stayed with Aunt Constance and Uncle Leland. They claimed one had eaten the neighbor's dog. A poodle. We had orange trees and grapefruit trees in the back yard." My mother reached for the bottle of rye and poured herself another shot.

Frank gave her a look, but Nina didn't notice. My hopes for this evening sank, scattered about like sand in the wind.

"I had a family," Frank said, trying to steer the conversation away from Florida. Nina might get on a roll, tell us everything she knew about Florida when she was a kid. "Farming's awfully risky when you're trying to raise a family. And as an engineer, sometimes I felt like a migrant worker, always going where the work was. Now Drew's got the right idea. A banker. A steady way of life. That's the way to raise a family."

From behind us, at the counter, Drew snorted. Drew with his vasectomy.

My father spoke to Kiskejohn as if he were the only one in the room. My mother looked on intently, as if her husband were saying new, wonderful things, stories she'd never heard before, ideas that had never crossed her mind. Perhaps she was practicing for the new husband she envisioned once Frank died. Or maybe she was truly hearing his history for the first time.

"But when I think about it," Frank was saying, "especially now that we've got things a bit settled at the cabin, this is a pretty damn good way of life. It's got a natural rhythm to it that makes more sense than punching a clock. I remember a labor dispute I worked on. We had to get the negotiations going before a walkout, set for midnight. Now a banker, he gets up in the morning, goes to work, does his job, and at five o'clock he can go home. But there we are, six, seven, eight o'clock all going by. And even if we do have some kind of package by midnight, it doesn't stop there. Industry has no concept of the natural rhythms of the body. And the mind can be a deceptive yardstick."

Kiskejohn was watching my father steadily, his head cocked just a bit so that he caught Frank with the corners of his eyes. They were hooded, wary. "War's like that," Kiskejohn said. "No concept of the natural rhythms of the body. But it's real easy sometimes. Everything is very clear over there. A soldier only has his own ass to look out for. There was only one thing to do. Stay alive."

My father didn't seem to be listening. "Well, but just figure," he said. "Say you could get up every morning and do exactly what you wanted. When I was a kid I had a week or so like that. My mother had some hens, and believe me, in West Virginia if you've got anything at all it's precious stuff. Now there was this fox that started in on the hens, picking off a couple each night. We couldn't afford that. It was in the fall, about this time of year, this kind of weather. And my mother told me she'd do all my chores if I could get that fox for her."

He leaned back in the chair, the braced leg stuck out at an odd angle, as if it were broken. My father, slender as an apostrophe, unbruised cheek hollowed to a question mark. The deep, sculpted Vs hanging under his eyes. Yet I saw the young, swimmer's body, the coil of the muscles of his shoulders as he mortered bricks for a new patio, dumped boulders into the dock crib. Photos of my father as a young man show a brooding boy, no laughter or mirth. But the man sitting across from Kiskejohn wore a mild smile and a far-away light in his eyes.

"It was fall, all those dead leaves snapping under the soles of your shoes. I had my brother's .22 and took some blankets out to the henhouse. He generally struck an hour or two before dawn. The first night I waited until he had a chicken, Rhode Island red, before I fired. Missed completely. I thought I might do better with the shotgun, but then this odd idea came over me. I wanted to get him with one clean shot. No reason for it, really. I didn't just want to blast him to hell. I wanted one nice, clean shot. He took off over a ridge and I spent that day tracking him through the brush, looking for his hole."

"It was a red fox, wasn't it Frank?" my mother said. Her eyes were focused past the kitchen, on a hill farm in West Virginia that she'd never seen.

"Yeah. Big fellow. Been around a long time. When I think about it, it's surprising he hadn't hit our chickens before. So I figured he must have come some distance for them. The next night I didn't take a shot at him, but followed the chicken feathers as far as I could into the woods. I must have been a mile or so from the house. Up on the ridge, right at the crest. Next night I sat in a tree, waiting for him. I listened for every noise. Foxes aren't as clever as they make out in stories. He followed the same path every night, up over the ridge, down to our henhouse. I was waiting for the moon, for that nice, clean shot."

"You know," my mother said to Kiskejohn, "this was the Depression. We didn't waste anything in the Depression. They really couldn't afford to lose those extra chickens. When my sister and I stayed with Constance and Leland sometimes we wouldn't have dinner if we hadn't caught any fish that day."

Kiskejohn looked at her, annoyed. He wanted to hear the story, hear it the way my father was telling it. In that look he gave my mother I could understand why he didn't seem to have a woman. Kiskejohn had passed into an exclusively male realm. My father's story didn't need my mother's interpretation.

"Finally, one night the moon was high and full. Fat. I'm sitting in the tree, freezing my tail off. But I knew this was the night. I got a real tingly feeling, knowing I was going to get him that night. And I waited all night for him. He didn't show, as if he knew what was on my mind. He didn't come anywhere near the place. We didn't lose any chickens that night, that perfect night to kill the fox. But I was there the next night, overcast, drizzling rain. Miserable night. Three nights went by, raining almost all night every night. It started to clear finally. And there he was, right under the tree. 'Hey,' I said to him, God knows why. No point in giving fair warning to a fox. But I said 'Hey' to him and he looked up into the tree like a dog looks up at his master. And I shot him. That one clean shot. I sort of felt like he knew it was going to happen. He dropped like a rock. I dragged him home, and I thought he was beautiful. This big, tough red fox. One shot right across here," and my father passed his index finger across his forehead.

"I tanned that hide, and really, he was a scabby old thing. But he was still beautiful to me. I kept his hide on the wall of my room. When I sold the place years later, after my mother died, I thought of taking it along. But just like the idea of that one, clean shot, I knew he belonged with the farm. So when I left I buried his hide, all ratty and patchy. But I made a little ceremony out of it anyhow."

"Ceremony," Kiskejohn said. "Ceremonies are important. Keeps you in touch with the real spirit of things. There was a guy in our squad who refused to bury uniformed slopes. Not that we found many. I guess it's just universal that you go in and haul out your dead. He didn't mind burying the old men, women, children. He'd bury civilians. He was very solemn about that. Couldn't get over the fact that going to war meant burying women and children. But he refused to bury any body in uniform. I never minded. I had this fantasy that they knew no more about what they were doing out there than we did. So why the hell not bury the guy? He died confused, as I guess we all do. I liked to believe that if you buried them the confusion left them. That the earth kind of soaked up the confusion and the body could rest in peace."

"Rest in peace," my father said. "Hell of a shame you've got to die before that happens."

"There it is," Kiskejohn said. "Rest in peace is the big beaucoup nothing. All that time in country turned some of us into action addicts. A lot of guys became smoke jumpers. One guy I know tests parachutes for the Air Force in Silver City."

"My daughter died in Vietnam," my mother said, in a

proud, patriotic voice. This surprised me. I couldn't imagine Nina being proud of Julia's death. "She vanished, like a cloud on a breezy day."

My father looked at her, his brow notched with concern.

Nina toyed with her empty glass. "Yes," she said, as if answering some question only she could hear. "She never came back."

Kiskejohn got up to get himself another beer. "Like I said, it was a fantasy. Maybe the earth doesn't soak up the confusion. But hell, you got to believe in something. Don't matter if it's candy bar wrappers or God. Rest in peace. Gives you a reason for going on."

"There will only be one cloud on your horizon," Nina said, and I could tell she was drunk, flipped over into her fantasies as quickly and quietly as a breeze skips over the surface of a stream. "You must learn to see your blessings."

My father looked at her sorrowfully, as if he were watching her go away and there was nothing he could do to stop her. As if he could see her sailing off a cliff and he couldn't catch her. He gave a great sigh. "Maybe I'll go out and see how Tree's coming with the grill."

He rose slowly, stiffly. Kiskejohn followed him out the door. Drew and Coleman and I exchanged looks. Nina sat up regally in her chair. "Like a cloud on a breezy day. Like a shooting star," she said.

You could feel snow on the air when we left Coleman's that night, the raw slicing feeling of snow that burns your nose. There were no clouds and I stared at the sky imagining vapors solidifying. A hush had fallen over the countryside, as if all sound had been vacuumed up into the atmosphere. Drew had gone back to his apartment in the city, my parents weren't fighting. I felt as though I'd gotten away with something, and if I kept quiet, went to bed like a good girl, we would have mastered this day in a passable fashion. Disasterless.

It would have been nice to build a big fire, curl up and watch the flames lick through the wood. Dream away the night. Paris, in his hotel room in New York. Kiskejohn. It would have been nice to have Victor there, talking all the nonsense we talk. Lalique crystal. The mystery of swallows at Capistrano. Russian lacquer boxes. Basque heroes. Instead, my father and I built up the fire, banked the coals, and crawled onto the futons under the Hudson Bay blankets.

Nina donned her new fur coat and sat on the musty couch, a bottle of scotch nearby.

I dreamed I was discovering a large house, room by room. The house was flying, a sailship, soaring steadily, safely, over deep water. As each room unfolded to reveal another room my wake was filled with oak tables, Tiffany lamps, chaise longues. Pastel colored trim. A summer house before the wars. I took a lamp from room to room, the light revealing only what I wanted to find. It was a beautiful house and at some point Drew stood beside me and said: See? It can be done.

Perhaps it was the beer, but I awoke, surprised Drew wasn't there to show me this new, wonderful house. I could see my mother in the glow of the dying fire, lost in her own dreams. I pulled on my jeans and boots to go out and take a leak. She didn't seem to notice me as I walked past.

The ground was brittle with frost. My breath blew great clouds toward the sky. Paris and I making a trapeze artist snow woman on a winter picnic. Kiskejohn looking into the eyes of the bear. The sky was indigo, lacy clouds, stars as bright as new pins. The sting of Scorpio approaching Orion's heel.

Rest in peace. I couldn't imagine anything more peaceful than this cold, the enveloping darkness. Not even the night birds called. Deer grazing in the barley, Paris and I dancing on the hill. Time stopped and the pain was far away, belonging to someone else. I thought of sailors at sea, living on their memories as the fathoms slide by. Pioneers pushing westward, living on their plans for the future as they slept under the stars. These hours of the night used to terrify me and I would walk, and walk, trying to work the fear out of my muscles, out of my bones. My dog Ajax and I walking through the night. Paris and I.

But it was cold, bitterly cold. Nina hadn't noticed me when I'd come out into the night. Perhaps she'd dozed off and wouldn't notice when I went back into the cabin to crawl under the blankets. I didn't want to talk, I wanted only to keep this peaceful feeling, as if everything in the universe were in its proper place.

"Julia," she said when I walked through the door to the cabin, her eyes shining as if she'd been crying.

"It's Emery, Mom. Maura. I'm going back to bed." I felt my heart sink slowly down my spine, as slow and liquid as mercury.

"Here. Come have a drink. You know, we had the loveliest evening. I wish you could have been there." She rose and moved to the kitchen area for another glass. My father snored melodically across the room. "You know," she said. "I wasn't expecting you tonight."

"It's Maura, Mom. Maura. Maybe it's time for you to go to bed."

She returned to the couch and poured a drink for me. "Really, a very lovely time." She handed it across to me, and I took it, set it down beside the broken rocker. "There's this woman named Coleman. I think she's a widow. Has a farm not far from here. I was hoping to see some spark between them, Drew and Coleman. What a name for a woman. I don't know what's to become of Drew. I haven't really seen him with a woman friend since Ginny. He needs to get married. He's going to end up just like Maura if he doesn't."

"Drew's fine," I said. "Marriage doesn't solve everything." My body tensed, a spring being wound too tightly. A live thing prowling through my soul. Poised for fight or flight.

She wasn't listening, as she never listened to me when I was Mrs. White. Perhaps just another body, sharing her scotch, made her feel less lonely. I tried to think of one friend my mother made during all the years of my childhood. I couldn't. I couldn't see her talking on the phone, sharing a cup of coffee with another woman. It seemed my only memories of my mother were of nights like this, late, the bottle of scotch, my mother talking to imaginary people. My mother holding Julia.

"We're going to have to come to some arrangement," she said. "You're just not as dependable as you used to be. Now, I know we've talked about this before. But, honey, you just can't go gallivanting around like this. I mean, look at Maura. No roots whatsoever. That's bound to make for a very confusing life. You don't want to end up like Maura, do you?"

Her sadness was a low note coming off her tongue, the throbbing wail in the alto of a violin. A slow mournful song.

"And you never think of me." She lit a cigarette, used it as a baton to punctuate her rant. "There are nights when I need to talk to you. Don't you see? I need to talk to someone. Yet you just float through here whenever you damn feel like it. Not necessarily when I need you. Now, that's not fair, Julia. I gave you everything I could, and I gave it freely. But I think it's only common courtesy for you to be here when I need you. Not just whenever you decide to flit through."

"Mom, it's Maura." I felt so sorry for her, and pity is a terrible thing.

"You know, I've been thinking." The firelight flickered in her eyes as she stared past me. Julia was Nina's baby, a child she conceived, bore, cuddled, confided in. I couldn't imagine the pain of missing anyone more than I missed Paris. But my mother had suffered a deeper loss, lived with a larger pain. It was impossible to imagine how much she must hurt, how that loss cut into her heart, her mind.

"This isn't such a bad place, you know," she said, and bundled herself deeper into the fur coat. "And Frank loves it. Now, that was a surprise. We looked at a house the other day, and you know how Frank loves to look at houses. He wasn't interested in the slightest. Not the least little bit." She shook her head. "I think he's really happy here. Maybe it reminds him of when he was a boy. But you know Julia, I always thought Frank hated his childhood. Hated that hill farm his family had. Yet tonight he was talking as if it had been the most wonderful place on earth. I'll never understand that man. Never."

"It's okay to like it out here," I said. "But it will probably snow tonight. Things might get more difficult once winter really sets in." I picked up the scotch. It burned my throat. But it wasn't the alcohol. My whole body was on fire. My nerves singed.

"Well now, you see that's the problem. Frank's talking as if we'll be here forever. As if we could possibly stay out here. There's no heat, I mean, a fire," and she cast a glance at the fieldstone fireplace, the dying embers, "a fire is nice to look at, but you can feel how cold it is. And there's no water. You know he's not well. And did I tell you, do you know what Frank did the night of the fire? He jumped into a tree. That's right. He just jumped into a tree. You know, his leg really isn't healing up the way it should. I think we need to go to Florida, where it's warm. The cold is going to set into his bones. You're a nurse, what would you do?"

I felt the sadness sweeping over me the way you feel a chill invade your body. The way a light wind dies in a sail. "I think you should probably get some rest," I said. "Tomorrow's going to be completely different, with the snow. Tomorrow would be a good time to make a decision like that."

"What do you know? Sometimes you can be as bull-headed as the other two. Look at what you did? Nursing. Vietnam, for god sakes. And then you got yourself killed, do you realize that? Killed. Or maybe you're just disappeared. Disappeared. MIA. Missing in action. We couldn't even bury you. Gone. Just a letter saying you died and they buried you in the church cemetery. Buried you in Vietnam. Don't you know how much that hurts? All the hopes and dreams? At least if you'd joined the Army they'd be required to send your body back. The Army's not allowed to bury Americans on foreign soil. Why, any day now you could walk right in the house, as if you've come back from a long trip and simply forgot to send postcards. I watch the door. I'm always waiting. The years go by. I'm not getting any younger. You left me," and she shook her finger vehemently. "You left me. You didn't have to do that. Maura was bad enough. Then Drew plants himself like a weed." She shook her head sadly, took another sip of her drink. "You left me. I'll never understand that."

"Don't worry," I said. "I'm right here. In a couple of hours the sun will be up. Things will look different. Maybe we'll see the first snow. I've always loved the first snow. It makes everything so clean and white. As if we could start all over, the past erased." Why not play Julia for my mother? Perhaps it would give her some peace. But it hurt me. I could feel my bones breaking.

"You don't erase the past. If I wanted to, right this minute, I could put myself back where I was when I was your age. We used to go to my uncle's farm in the summer. A fortune teller once told me there would only be one cloud on my horizon. Well, she was right. You're that cloud. The one cloud on my horizon. A shooting star. That's what you were, a shooting star. You make wishes on shooting stars. You were my wish. But you didn't come true. You didn't have to do it. No way. You did it to spite me, now didn't you?"

Her look was harsh, hostile. Yet beneath the look I saw the softer woman of my childhood, dreaming of Rio and a life she'd left behind before she even had a chance to explore it. How can you miss something you never had? My mother was composed of loss upon loss. If her life were a stone to be polished and loss had a color she would turn deeper and deeper as the stone became smoother and smoother.

"It doesn't matter now," she said, and poured herself more scotch. "What's done is done. The only trick now is how to live with it. How do you live with it, Julia? How in the world do you live with the fact you went off and got yourself killed?"

This was too painful. We always need our mothers to know us, understand us. No matter how much we try to run away from that need. "Mom," I said. "It's Maura. Remember me? Julia's gone. We're out in the woods. It's late at night. It's going to snow. You better get some rest."

"And Maura! God. I feel sorry for that girl. Talk about messing up your life. You know, she lost her job. She's got nothing. No one to love her. Now no job. It's as if she deliberately went out to sabotage everything that could possibly happen to her. All the good things she could have had in her life. But no. That girl seems to only understand how to live when things are a mess. Any time something good happens she destroys it. She had a boyfriend. For years, did I tell you that? And for all those years all she could ever do was run away from him. Run away. Drew told me. Those two are as thick as thieves. She's going to be a very lonely old woman. Anybody can see that. She can't depend on Drew forever. He's resourceful. He'll find his own way. He's just a little bit slow sometimes."

"I don't think that's going to happen to Maura." But my hands and feet were numb. There was a buzzing in my ear. My breathing fluttered shallowly at the top of my lungs.

"Sometimes I wonder whether you just ran away too." She looked puzzled, confused. "Why would you do that? Why do children run away, like trying to cross the street against traffic. You didn't have to go to Vietnam. There were plenty of good causes right here in America. But off you go, half way around the world. Why?"

Why indeed. Why do any of us do what we feel we have to do? Why is it necessary to cause so much pain?

"Isn't it strange how one mistake can change the direction of so many lives. I should have been a dancer. I was going to marry an actor. I should have done that, not gotten sidetracked with Frank." She gave me an odd, warm smile. "Of course, I still would have had you. Maybe not the other two, but I would have had you. And then maybe things would have turned out differently."

"The other two," I said. I could feel myself going blind, my vision narrowing to a pinpont of light, in the center of which sat my mother. I swallowed more of her scotch, to dull the pain, so that I could pretend this wasn't happening.

"You know, there are two types of babies. I didn't know this until I had you. One type of baby, you cuddle them to your breast and all they want to do is get away." She threw her arms out like doing a breaststroke. "They want to get out and experience the world. They push away from you. Maura and Drew were like that. Always wanting to get away. So I thought all babies were like that, always wanting to get away and out into the world, even if they couldn't handle it. They simply want to get away and experience it. But you, now you were such a surprise. Such a delight. I'd hold you and it was like you wanted to curl back into me. Your little arms would circle my neck. Me and you, kid." She gazed into the fire. "I'd hold you and rock you. It was almost as if you could purr."

Was that it? Was that what I'd done wrong, what had separated me from my mother's love? Wanting, even as a baby, to get out and see the world? My eyes began to burn and my hand, holding the drink, trembled. And what do you say? I'm sorry? My blood stopped flowing in my veins. Collecting in great pools. Coagulating.

"You know, just in the way children love one parent more than the other, so parents love their children. You can't love a child who doesn't love you. Maura was the worst. She didn't need me as soon as she could walk. If she'd been taller she would have walked out of the house and out of our lives. I mean, look what she ended up doing with her life? She just kept right on going. Didn't stop to look back for a moment. Poor Maura. Life to her is like a race, full tilt to the end. No time to smell the roses. She's going to steam right off the planet. There's nothing I can do to stop her."

"Maura's not like that," I said. "So she's a little confused sometimes. Everyone gets confused sometimes. But she's trying to fashion a life for herself. And she loves you." Why was I speaking of myself in the third person? Only criminals and schizophrenics think of themself in the third person.

"What would you know? I tried to keep you as far away from Maura and Drew as I could. They weren't good for you, I knew that. There are just some people you have to write off as a loss. A total loss."

A total loss. My mother thought of me as a total loss. I stood, carefully putting the drink down, sure I would spill it all over the room, sheets of scotch flying around the cabin. My blood had started moving again, but slowly, in clumps like squeezing toothpaste from a tube that is nearly empty. "No," I said, but could not think of anything more to say. "No," I said again.

The keys to the Buick were on the counter. I walked across the room, feeling all the bones in my feet as I separately set each one down. I had to look and make sure the keys were in my hand, clench my fist tight and feel the edges of the keys biting into my palm. "No," I said as I walked out the door.

I accidentally hit the horn as I climbed into the car. And then I was driving, fishtailing out of the gravel in front of the cabin, gunning the engine as I wove down the dirt road to the first gate.

Pickets splinter against the grill. Pickets splatter over the windshield. Pickets clatter on the roof of the Buick.

The sound of the broken fence hums like electric wires caught in the wind.

Slow motion as I floor my foot on the brakes.

The car skids down the dirt road sideways, comes to rest at a right angle to the barbed-wire fences.

The smell of burnt rubber hangs in the air.

I couldn't see. I couldn't breathe. My hands and feet were numb. And then, mercifully, I couldn't think, my mind resting against all those scars. All the memories and scars from my childhood, a block, a wall, a dam, holding back any thought.

I pounded on Drew's door a long time before he opened it, rubbing sleep from his eyes and adjusting a pair of jockey shorts.

"Who's dead?" he asked as he walked me into the living room and poured me a drink.

"I am." I drank the vodka thirstily, like a marathon runner at the end of a long race. Electricity shot through me. I thought I could hear the sound of laughter around the corner. "She thought I was Julia," I finally said. And I began to cry.

"Whoa," Drew said. "Tears are for attention. You're wasting them on me." He gently touched the corners of my eyes. "Come on, you haven't cried since you were twelve. Save them for when it counts. She's the one who should see you cry. I know how you feel." He sat down and pulled me into the wing of his arm. "She sometimes thinks I'm Frank. She even came on to me once. Said we should do it for old times sake. 'Like we did in Cuba,' she said."

"A total loss," I said. "She thinks we're both a total loss." I couldn't breathe. I felt I was choking.

"Calm down. Take it easy," Drew said. "She's a sick woman. You can't take it all that personally."

"God." I shook my head, my vision swimming. "Looney Tunes." I sniffed and blew my nose and accepted another drink. I felt calmer now with my second drink. I could hold it steady in my hand. Only the Eskimos, in the history of all cultures, had been able to live without mind-altering substances. Before they were civilized the Eskimo were said to live on dreams.

My breathing was returning, but in short, quick bursts

like gunfire. I turned, to face my brother squarely. "How *do* you miss something you never had? That's your question, that hole in your soul. It's not like a phantom pain in a missing limb. We never had that limb. We were built without it as surely as we weren't given three arms. Three eyes. So why do you miss something you never had? How can you hurt and ache over a loss that's not yours? Over something that never belonged to you. Something you don't even know anything about."

He stroked my hair, his face nuzzled down the side of my neck. "Maybe we did have it," he whispered in my ear. "Maybe we were just too young to know what we had. We have it. You and I. We have each other. What hurts is that only the two of us can share it. It doesn't go beyond us. There's just you and me."

I felt I was facing an invisible barrier. As if I were walking across the Pacific. A question with no answer is an evil gift of the imagination, a trick done with mirrors.

My mind emptied like the flight of a magician's dove released from his hands, felt as clean as leaves of a tree after a spring rain.

A liquid light like snowmelt filled me. As if parts of my mind were becoming unmoored and drifting down a fast-flowing river, to empty into the sea. I wanted to wash it all away, have every memory and feeling dissolve into an ocean I couldn't fathom or chart.

"There was you," Drew said, and pulled me deeper into his arms. "There was always you."

And we rocked together, slowly in each other's arms, the way I've seen mothers rock babies to sleep. The way exhausted people hold on to each other for strength. The way we comfort one another in times of grief.

Snow covered everything when we awoke in the morning. Clean and bright and white, as if the world had been erased. As if we could start all over again. Thick snow, clinging to the leaves on the trees. Untracked across the ground. Pure snow, giving the air around it a luminance. As bright and ephemeral as the light from a firefly. Drew and I looked out the window, across the city to the whitened wheat fields. "Snow," I said.

"Snow," Drew repeated. "Kiskejohn said it would snow."

I looked deeply into his eyes, one to the other. Now there was snow.

"There's always only been you and I," Drew said. "We've never gotten close to anyone else."

"I don't know, Drew. You had Ginny. I had Paris." A laugh stuck in my throat.

He put his arms around me and held me close. "It's even in the Bible," he said. "Something about the child becoming the father to the man."

We dressed, Drew to go off to his job at the bank, while

I would return to the cabin and see how Frank and Nina were dealing with the snow. It had come so silently, no snowstorm with high winds and hail. Quietly, the snow had covered the city, the countryside. When I stepped out to get in the new Buick I estimated there was about three inches on the ground, a soft mist of snow still falling. I thought of stopping to buy gloves. None of us had gloves. If we had gloves we could make a snowperson, a jogger snowman, a trapeze artist snowwoman. I imagined my mother and father and I in the snow building snowpeople. Paris and his snow picnic. I tried to remember building snowmen as a child, but all that came to mind was a snow angel I'd made on the ground for the first snow when I was in the third grade.

I looked at the dent in the grill, splinters of wood from the demolished gate still trapped in the metal. The new Buick was covered with long, mean scratches. There was a crack in the windshield on the passenger's side. The rearview mirror was sheared off. Frank would have my ass for this.

I tried to put that out of my mind, a trick I was adept at. A family trait. I once had asked Drew if he remembered any friends from those years and all those moves when we were children. He couldn't. Neither could I. We couldn't remember playing, except for our excursions to unfinished houses, our buried shoe boxes. I could remember the look of my bike, but not riding it, not the feel of the thing between my legs. I could see a swing set in our yard in Clifton but I couldn't remember the wind passing over my body as I swung through the air. I could see my china animals as they sat on the shelf and I could remember the endless bottles of Elmer's Glue I used to repair them. But I couldn't remember how they'd become broken. Perhaps they were broken during the moving.

My earliest memory, of a time before Drew, was of screaming, screaming to the point my chest ached. I'd suck on the bars of my crib, feel the flakes of varnish in my mouth.

'She'd have walked out the door if she'd been taller,' my mother had said.

Drew had been my only home. We'd formed a shell around us. What must happen when two people live in the same shell?

Littermates. Siblings. Lovers. Male cheetahs hold their litter intact, to help them survive other predators. Female elephants remain together their entire lives. Dinosaurs staying in the same herd generation after generation. Doves mating for life; if one dies the other perishes. Herds, prides, schools, flocks, gaggles, gangs. Swarms, bevys, coveys, broods, droves. Clans, tribes, breeds, kin. Pair, mate, twin. Brothers, sisters. Families. Drew and I.

Even through the mist of snow the sky was a lapis lazuli, bright breaks between the gray, bruised-looking clouds. The blue disturbed me. I wanted it to snow all day, no sun to melt off this new, clean world. I wanted snow to pile up around the cabin, lodge in the corners of the windowpanes the way you see it drawn on Christmas cards. By the time I opened the second gate I was envisioning a Thanksgiving dinner. Kiskejohn, Tree, Coleman. Drew and I basting a turkey brown. My father telling the story of the fox again. My mother looking on as if glimpsing a new world.

I stopped, left the engine idling roughly, while I inspected the smashed gate. Splintered bits of wood strewn about like tossing a handful of toothpicks into the wind. There were tracks in the new snow. The cloven hooves of cattle, and what looked like the paw prints of a large dog. A fox? A wolf? Birds cried in the trees, hidden from sight behind the branches covered with new snow.

When I pulled up in front of the cabin there was a set of footprints crossing the gravel track, partially filled with snow. No smoke rose from the chimney. The cabin looked deserted and as I got out of the car I felt the small hairs on the back of my neck rise. And I knew, the way an animal senses danger, that something was wrong. There would be no Thanksgiving dinner. My breathing was confined to short, quick puffs, rapidly skirting the bridge of my nose. I stood by the car, snow falling all around me, and listened to the heavy silence coming from the cabin. I wished with all my heart there would be no one home, that all of these last few days, the weeks while I visited my parents, had been a bad dream. I wanted it to be over, to wake up in my own bed in San Francisco, my cat curled around my feet.

But this was no dream. Whatever was inside would be with me for the rest of my life.

The Boy Scout motto is Be Prepared. Yet the Swiss Army knife, the industrial flashlight, the snakebite kit, nothing we had purchased for the cabin would prepare me for what was on the other side of the door. Not the piano or the fur coat or the china cabinet. I thought of my father's Crackerjack boxes and listened for sounds coming from the cabin until my ears ached. A spider of fear moved down my spine. I crossed the gravel track and opened the door.

Kiskejohn lay on the floor in a pool of blood, not far from the doorway. Tree sat beside him, Kiskejohn's head in his lap, stroking the gray hair fine as cornsilk. Across the room, on the musty couch, my mother, in her new fur coat, huddled inside my father's arms. She didn't look at me. Tree didn't look at me. But my father raised his eyes when I walked through the door. His sadness and pain were physical, captured in his eyes like birds in a cage.

My mind turned to ice. I was snow-blind, the room frozen in a tableau. I looked down at Kiskejohn, a red-black stain covering his chest, spilling out across the wooden floor. Tree stroked his hair, running his hands through that long, soft hair like handling a rosary. Kiskejohn's eyes were closed, as if he were sleeping. I couldn't see pain anywhere in his face. His hands were loose at his sides, one leg tucked under him like the Hanged Man in the Tarot deck.

"I didn't know she had a gun," my father said, and my mother stirred in the protection of his arms. She straightened and looked at me, her eyes dry and hollow.

She swallowed several times, tightened her eyes to gain control of herself. "I thought he was a prowler," she said.

A prowler. Twenty-five miles from town. My mother with a gun, it was lying on the table next to the couch with the scotch bottle. I'm not familiar with handguns. Maybe the blue-black snub-nosed thing lying on the table was what they call a Saturday-Night Special. Maybe it was a fancy German Luger. It sat on the table next to the scotch bottle, as innocuous as a pack of cigarettes.

"We heard the car leave," Tree said, still staring into Kiskejohn's dead face. "We thought the horn was a signal. He came over to see what was going on. Later, I heard the shot."

I could imagine it as easily as if I were watching it happen. Kiskejohn and Tree, our bodyguards sleeping near Drew's unfinished house. Kiskejohn checking the perimeter, rising in the darkness to see why the new Buick would go tearing away in the middle of the night. Kiskejohn slipping through the underbrush, scouting the old hunting lodge. Nina sitting on the couch, facing the door, when Kiskejohn silently opens it, steps through. And who was it Nina thought she was shooting at? In that moment, where had her mind gone, who was she seeing, when she picked up the gun, fired at such close range.

"It was my mother's," Nina said, her eyes still drawn tight to the corners. "I kept it in the button box. Just a souvenir. But when I found it, that day we were at the house, I decided to buy bullets. I've never fired a gun before in my life. But I felt I had to protect us." She looked at my father. "Protect you."

That gun had been there the whole time she'd talked to me, to Julia, last night before I left for Drew's. My mother had killed a man. Kiskejohn, who'd survived Vietnam to be killed by a housewife in a fur coat twenty-five miles from town.

I took a deep breath and felt the tears rolling down my cheeks. No sobs, just clear tears welling out of my dry eyes as I looked at Kiskejohn sprawled across the floor near the door, his head in Tree's lap.

"You had the car," my father said. "The phone."

"Yes," I said. And a horrible feeling washed through me, pain like tiny needles drilling every pore in my body. The car. The phone. Would Kiskejohn be alive if they'd been able to get him to a hospital? Phone for an ambulance? Would my mother have shot him if I'd stayed with her last night?

The tears in my eyes froze. I looked at Tree, fear glazing my face. Was I responsible? Could I have saved Kiskejohn?

He shook his head. And I knew what he meant. Kiskejohn was dead by the time Tree arrived. Tree, jumping up at the sound of a shot in the night. Tree loping through the woods to find Kiskejohn, dead on the floor in front of the door, my mother holding the gun. My mother's one lucky shot, straight through the heart.

But I was still responsible. If I hadn't gotten in the car, hit the horn, smashed through the gate, Kiskejohn would have slept through the night, dreaming of glasses and plates humming like radio signals. Dreams of freezing and beginning to rot.

Be Prepared. How does one prepare for something like this? I missed Kiskejohn, deeply, painfully. I gave a little laugh. He would know what to do. He would go to the car, get on the phone. He would know who to call, what to do with the body. It was my mind skipping from ice floe to ice floe. Magenta, amber, teal. Tree sat looking into Kiskejohn's face, stroking the long gray hair. My father held my mother's hand while she looked past the room, out the window at the snow.

Water seeks its own level. These last few days Kiskejohn

and I had floated side by side. Kiskejohn, who looked into the eyes of the bear. Kiskejohn, who had lost a great and large part of himself in Vietnam. Kiskejohn, who was going to spend the rest of his days trying to figure out what had happened over there. Kiskejohn, who said danger smelled sweet like perfume. Kiskejohn, shot by a housewife in a fur coat while checking the perimeter twenty-five miles from town.

I walked out the door and over to the iron triangle Coleman had hung from the branch of the walnut tree. Coleman's dinner bell. 'I'll hear it across the lake.' I kicked around in the snow until I found the tire iron. The snow burned my ungloved hands. Slowly, the bell sounding mournful, I beat a tattoo on that triangle. Long pauses, listening to the echo dying away across the water.

I moved over to the new Buick. I tried to remember all the numbers and codes Frank had showed me, how to use the car phone. Be Prepared. How can you be prepared for life? For death?

No one would really know what to do. But I called Drew. I called Coleman. "Mother killed Kiskejohn," I told Drew. "Kiskejohn's dead," I said to Coleman. Neither phrase sounded real. *Mother killed Kiskejohn. Kiskejohn's dead.* This couldn't be true. As I spoke into the car phone, the cold air turning my words to frost, I wanted to go back in the cabin and check. Make sure that Kiskejohn hadn't gotten up off the floor, patted off the bloodstains. That my father wasn't washing the blood from the floor, silent Tree wasn't watching the snow instead of stroking through Kiskejohn's long hair. My mother should be noodling along on the new piano, no matter that she couldn't make music, only noise.

'You only lose your ass once,' Kiskejohn had said. 'And each time you have fewer cards to play.'

When I went back into the cabin I sat down on the floor next to Tree, to wait. I took Kiskejohn's hand, held it in mine, and felt the callouses on his palm.

Paris picked me up at the airport, armed with a bouquet of Persian lilies and two bottles of Charbaut champagne. During the entire flight I kept wondering why I had called him, Paris, as dependable as a freak spring snowstorm. But I phoned when I decided to return to San Francisco, and watched in wonder as he separated himself from the crowd, his arms loaded with flowers, and skipped up the ramp to meet me.

We walked in silence to his car. He gestured toward the grocery sacks in the backseat of his bubbletop Porsche, one of the few things Paris has managed to hang onto over the years. "You never have any food," he said, "so I'm going to cook you dinner."

"I don't want to eat, Paris. I want to go see Victor."

"Too late," he said as he pulled onto the freeway. "Visiting hours are over for today. I'll take you down there in the morning."

'I'll take you down there in the morning.' And so it was

settled, Paris would spend the night with me. "What about Jackie?" I asked.

"New York was terrific, Emery. You should have come."

I really didn't care what lie he'd told his wife. One thing about Paris: Sometimes when you really need him, he comes through. Like gangbusters.

And that was his plan for this evening. The delicious pale-pink Charbaut, broiled shrimp in an herb sauce over rice pilaf. "I don't like to see you alone like this," he said, his back to me as he worked at the stove.

I sipped the champagne. "What do you want me to do? Hire a boyfriend?" It seemed so natural to see him standing by my stove, reaching into my refrigerator, rifling my shelves.

"While you're visiting Victor tomorrow I'll make a copy of your key. At least that way I'll be able to do your shopping. You don't have enough to eat here to keep a fly alive."

It seemed so logical, so destined. And yet so totally impossible. Paris and I would never live together again. Our relationship was an imaginary place. An ideal island in uncharted waters. A place that only exists on the map of the heart. "Paris, you could talk someone into buying a three-legged pony."

"That's me." He turned and flashed me a warm smile. "A one-winged Pegasus. A Pegi. It would only be able to fly in circles. There's an advantage in that, you know. It will never be able to fly away. Like me, it will always be hovering around you."

And so we spent the evening, eating shrimp, sipping champagne. Wrapped around each other in my bed. The power of his body as he entered mine, as he once again asserted his possession of me. As I once again controlled him. Power fucking.

We lay in the dark as the moon rose, smoking cigarettes, tipping down the last of the champagne. "So what about your buddy, Kiskejohn?" he asked as he tucked his hand into the curve of my thigh.

My skin crawled. My eyes burned. And I began.

"He's dead." Although that seemed as unreal as anything else. As the ambulance, the police, the DA, the inquest, the funeral. Kiskejohn seemed to be sitting in the corner by the dresser, paring his nails with a Swiss Army knife. 'It doesn't look like he's going anywhere without you,' Kiskejohn had said.

"That so?" Paris furrowed his brow. "Christ." He blew a lock of hair off his forehead.

"My mother shot him. She thought he was a prowler. She shot him with her mother's gun." I kept my eyes open but I could still see the cabin, Kiskejohn lying on the floor in the pool of his blood, Tree's hand stroking through the long gray hair. I saw the sheriff shaking his head, trouble and sadness in his eyes. I didn't even know they still had sheriffs.

"I'll tell you one thing, Emery. If I ever do marry you, you will never see those people again. One shouldn't have a mother who shoots people."

"That's what she does, Paris. That's the only thing my family is really expert at. We shoot people. Ambush them. Things die. One way or the other."

The next morning Paris dropped me at the hospital. There was no talk of copying my key. "I'll be seeing you, Emery."

"In your dreams," I said.

"Always," he said. "I'm the lord and master of your dreams."

Victor was sitting up in bed, gazing out the window, when I entered his room. Pneumocystis. This was his second hospitalization this year. The IV bottle swung gently between us. Oxygen came to him in a noose across his nose. A friend of mine in Boston, a masseuse, volunteered to give massages to AIDS patients. No one touches AIDS patients, as if the virus lived in contact with the skin. Her boyfriend left her when he found out. He wouldn't date a woman who spent her days touching AIDS patients. Victor's hand was as cold as Kiskejohn's. No callouses. A soft, cold hand.

I didn't want to say anything to upset him, which was pointless unless I decided not to talk at all. He talked about his visitors, his treatment. He was angry I was out of town when he'd been taken to the hospital. He didn't trust Gregory, his new boyfriend, to take proper care of his cat.

"I'll check on Lilith," I said. "Cats are very self-sufficient. She's probably okay." Sometimes my feelings seem as substantial as my wardrobe, that I can try on different feelings over and over again. Sitting beside Victor I had the same feeling I'd had when I'd talked to Kiskejohn about Vietnam. The swing of Kiskejohn's body, his ax biting into the wood. What right did I have to talk to men who had gone to war? To talk to men who were dying because of a lust they felt in their loins eight or ten years ago? Yet it all felt so familiar, though none of it had happened to me.

"This time I've made a will," Victor said. His color was the same as the bleached sheet. "A bitch to do. Ultimately, we have to leave it all behind. The one with the most toys doesn't win. He simply has the most toys. I'd like you to take Lilith."

"Sure," I said. "But not right now. You'll be out in a few days."

Victor made a small grimace.

Nothing I could say would make anything right. Nothing I could do would make anything right. When Drew and Coleman arrived we'd talked about simply burying Kiskejohn on the isthmus across from Drew's unfinished house. Tree didn't know of any relatives to notify. My father didn't want to call the police. But basically, we were all good citizens, decent Americans. No matter how twisted our lives had become it was too much to keep Kiskejohn, his death, our secret. No matter how much practice we'd had, some secrets are too large, too heavy, to hold in your heart forever. By midafternoon, the snow much deeper by then, the sheriff and an ambulance arrived.

But the odd part was that once Kiskejohn's body was whisked off in the ambulance, no siren, my mother became the star once again. The sheriff tucked her into his police car while Drew and my father and I followed down the snowy road in the BMW. Tree and Coleman disappeared. They held my mother for almost forty-eight hours, while we hired a lawyer, a friend of Drew's, to represent her at the inquest. But the burden of proof was on the District Attorney and he didn't feel he had enough to go forward with the case. An elderly woman who'd lived her whole life in cities. A dark night in a cabin in the woods. Kiskejohn was a man she knew, liked. There was no case for murder, premeditated malice, and barely one for manslaughter.

"It snowed while I was home," I said. "I've always loved the first snow."

Victor looked at me steadily. "Seems like a lot more than snow happened. I told you, you should stay away from those people. Seeing them is a suicide mission. On your best days you're merely on the brink of sanity, looking over the lip of the volcano. There are some things you have to turn your back on."

I nodded, and stood, felt the confusion flooding me, swirling images. My mother in her new fur coat. Kiskejohn swinging the ax. Paris in his butterscotch boots. "I better go," I said. I wanted to tell Victory everything, yet I had no notion where to begin.

"Don't," Victor said. He looked at the flowers decorating his room. Roses, gloxinias, mums. "Don't leave yet. I'm feeling better today. I'd like to see if I can push my social life up to forty-five minutes."

I sat back down, took his hand again, and stroked my

271

fingers across his palm. I looked at his lifeline, broken in many places as it neared the heel. Victor would die and I would inherit his cat, Lilith. I knew there were other things Victor had probably left me in his will. Lalique crystal, amethysts, books. Kiskejohn had left next to nothing. When we went to his room in Coleman's house there were some old photos from Vietnam, buddies Tree identified, most of them dead. A collection of knives and machetes. Old faded jeans and flannel shirts. Work boots. Books, no two of them on the same subject. All his possessions filled only a dozen milk crates. 'He always traveled light,' Tree had said. 'He believed everything he needed was in his head.'

"You better tell me," Victor said softly. "That's the mistake folks make when they visit people like me. They don't want to upset us." He gave a little laugh. "They don't realize how ridiculous that is." His eyes took on a far-away look, past the cut flowers and plants. "A kind gesture, but really unnecessary."

"My mother killed a man while I was home." I saw the tattooed mountain lion on the rock, the swimming fish, the peacock strutting down his arm. The spidering scars. Kiskejohn stood in the corner, beneath the TV, and smiled at me.

"That's something I've never done, exactly. I mean, maybe I have, but I wasn't aware of it. Isn't that a bitch? To be unaware of the fact someone has died because of you?" Victor closed his eyes wearily. "I wonder if killing someone, or giving birth to someone, aren't necessary events for us to understand why we're alive. The women have the babies and the men go to war."

"Then we're both wasted," I said. "Lost. We missed the boat. But I'm not sure about your theory. Look at my mother. She's covered all the bases now, birth and death, but I don't think she understands any more than we do."

"Sometimes it doesn't all come clear," Victor said. "A

world of things can happen that you'll never understand. Have you told Paris?"

I scratched my head. "Yeah, I told Paris. He's part of my past. He came to see me when I was there. *You* told him where I was. He picked me up at the airport. But you can't count on him. He's not the future. He'll just touch down like he always does, then disappear like steam."

"So you tell me. Wake up, kid. I'm not going to be part of the future either."

"Don't be maudlin, Victor. You're here. You're part of the present. So I told you. I need to tell someone. I wanted you to know."

Kiskejohn gave me a wink.

"Did you see it? How did she kill him?"

"She shot him. I didn't even know she had a gun. I was with Drew when it happened. I didn't see her shoot him, only after he was dead. But the strangest part was all the things you have to do, whether someone is dead or not. You start with the real simple stuff. You have to keep breathing. After that it's all details. You call the police. There was an inquest, but the judge decided there was lack of intent and ruled self-defense. Then you arrange a funeral. Not many people came. Some guys he drank with in the bars. He wasn't a real social type. Just talking made him nervous, like it was something he wasn't used to doing. Like it was a brand-new experience every time."

"Talking's not essential," Victor said, his voice getting softer, tired. "That's why we keep cats, birds, dogs, fish. Sometimes it's just enough to have another breathing body there."

My mother and Mrs. White. Tree's silence while Kiskejohn spoke for him. The silence of sex. The more different we are the more we cherish the things we share. I took Victor's hand in both of mine, pressed it close for warmth.

Raised it to my lips and kissed his fingertips. "It all gets real circumstantial sometimes," I said.

"Some things have to be said. Some things don't." His voice was sinking to a whisper.

"I'd like to know where her life became so tangled and confused," I said. With everything I knew about my mother, the years of my childhood, her talks to Mrs. White, I'd never been able to identify the moment when she let go absolutely and wandered off into the shadows of her own mind. In my mother's world the sun shines only when she thinks about it. It could be three in the morning, in the middle of an after-noon rain. The life in her mind was much more real than the ticking of an ordinary clock. Ocher ice floes. Black. Cobalt blue.

It wasn't just Julia's death. Before Julia was born, when I was about three or four, I remember a snowy afternoon in New Jersey. My mother solemnly dressed me in my snowsuit and walked me to the door. She opened it, the snow whirling outside, and gave me a faint, far-away smile. I stepped out-side, probably thinking we were going to play, although my mother was still in her bathrobe. She closed the door and I heard the bolt slide in place. I stood on the stoop, watching the snow, knowing my mother and brother were warm and safe inside. I was still huddled on the stoop when my father came home, long after dark.

Victor squeezed my hand.

"She thought I was my sister who died in Vietnam. She thought the guy she shot was a prowler, twenty-five miles from town. A guy we saw every day. Vietnam vet. He was tak-ing care of us."

"Some of those guys," Victor said with an effort, "some of them never really came back. Some act as if they were cheated out of death by Nam."

"Nice," I said. "Real nice." He was right, as far as Kiskejohn and Tree were concerned. But I hated that idea, the notion, like Drew had said, that some experiences are indelible ink. Tattoos on our brains. Colorful scars. At that moment, as I was holding Victor's hand, my mother was in a rehab center in Pennsylvania. The court had suggested it and my father readily agreed. My father was now living with Drew. There was talk of them moving to San Francisco when Nina was released. Indelible ink. Tattoos. Scars. I doubted the rehab center would straighten out my mother. How could six weeks in a rehab center fix what she'd taken a lifetime to acquire?

"I don't know." Victor shook his head, dismissing his idea. "You know, when you can't do anything but lie here, you come up with a lot of weird ideas. You've got to think all the time. You try to find something that makes sense, not just for yourself, but for everyone else. For everyone you know who you know is in trouble."

"Maybe," I said. "Ain't none of us gets out of this world alive."

"I'm sorry for the guy your mother shot. So quick. No time to think it over."

"I wish I believed more firmly in the spirit," I said, although I realized my belief in spirits was gaining ground moment by moment. "Here I am in San Francisco and I see Kiskejohn everywhere. I hear his voice. It's not like a memory. He's caught up in every action throughout the day. He's with us in this room right now."

"The dead do that," Victor said. "That's how I know I'm going to die. I can feel my soul filling up with all my friends, my family, who have gone before me. There's a whole crowd of people in this room, if you want to know the truth."

I could see Kiskejohn, the light in his dead, crystal eyes, staring out the window facing the park. "Yeah. I know. The dead keep giving us orders. The dead are never gone for good." I understood now my mother's madness. Julia still ruled her soul.

"I wasn't there when she pulled the trigger," I said. "I'd run away again, away from my mother. And so I'm responsible. That's the ultimate consequence of all my running away, the literal death of a sweet and gentle man. If I had stayed that night, he would still be alive. I'll spend the rest of my life atoning for that."

"Is that what he would have wanted?"

"He was a watcher. He was looking out, taking care. The dead keep giving us orders. It wasn't his responsibility to check on my parents. It was mine."

"You only do what you can," Victor said. "We're all flawed. You can't love perfection. Because we don't know what that is."

"But we can change," I said. "Maybe only a little bit. We can fine-tune it. Life is all process. It's just that the process is never completed."

Victor sighed. "When I get out, I've a favor to ask you." He looked at me shyly. Victor was never one to ask favors. Victor, always in charge. Victor could get you high. Victor could take you to the Continental Divide. And Victor would take you to the dry-out farm if you strayed too far over the line.

"Sure," I said. "What do you want, Sport?"

"I want to go for a drive. I want to follow the coast, watch the ocean. I want to have that in my mind, my last image."

Being witness to the dying, to the death, of someone you love is a privilege. It is the most important moment you will ever have with that person. I squeezed his hand, brushed the hair off his forehead. And I felt my heart beating like a frightened animal in my chest. "Sure. We'll go down to Davenport, that big rock like an elephant bathing in the ocean. We'll go up to Mendocino and cruise the widows' walks looking for ships at sea." Victor would go to Shangri-La, where he would never age. To Xanadu, where he would listen to the lovers wail for their demon mates.

"Yeah." Victor closed his eyes, gave my hand a gentle pat and moved his hand over his heart, fisted across his breast.

I left him, promising to return the next day, promising to check on Lilith his cat, promising to drive him to the ends of the earth, Tierra del Fuego if that's where he wanted to go. We would look for cerulean ice floes off Geometer's Island where the people draw figures in the sterile sand.

My father had said becoming an expert was the result of what you know. I wonder. Perhaps the important part is the willingness to act on what you know, to act when something happens. Perhaps it's a two-stroke motion like the Japanese koan: when the student is ready, the teacher appears.

Just like the cavemen who never saw the animals they painted on the stone walls, you have to believe. You have to believe in the magic that connects us to each other, believe your actions count, that we are responsible for each other.

I walked away, like a movie star Victor would say. But I didn't feel like a movie star. I felt shell-shocked. I felt a sadness sink in my bones that I knew would be a part of me as long as I lived, an extra weight attached to my heart. Victor would die. Kiskejohn was dead and there was nothing I could do for him. But I could watch him, listen to his voice as he directed me from the shadowy corners of rooms. Kiskejohn wanted me to help my brother, who elected to stay with them and try. Drew was different than I, composed of more courage and compassion than I thought I was capable of. Even though he was my brother, our scars weren't identical. We all grow up differently, learn different lessons. Tattoos. Scars. Scars don't tan. Scars don't heal. Scars don't. Scars are.

I realize now I've spent my life with my emotions bound as tightly as the Chinese used to bind women's feet. After a certain point the feet stop growing, my emotions had stopped growing. The Chinese women were left with little, dainty feet. I had been left with those two pages in Drew's address book, all the places I'd run to to escape. You can't escape your life. We are all responsible for each other, family, friends. Constants, shifting slightly, daily, in the fabric of your life.

I would look for houses for my parents, for when Nina was released, shadows and reflections of what Drew had done when he ended up buying the hunting club property.

And I could help Victor. I could look out for his cat. I could drive him down the coast. I could kiss the tips of his fingers in a way that I couldn't kiss my mother goodbye.

And I would keep a part of Paris hostage, the way he held the key to a part of me.

You don't talk to the merry-go-round horse. You don't ask questions of the wind. Like in the fairy tale, the Big Bad Wolf comes and huffs and puffs and blows your house down. You build another house, a better house. Plumbing. Wiring. Windows. Walk away from the wreckage. Walk toward a possible future, rather than retreat from an impossible past.